Playing Wolf

Catapult New York

Playing Wolf

A Novel

Zuzana Říhová

Translated from the Czech by
Alex Zucker

Playing Wolf

This is a work of fiction. All of the characters, organizations, and events portrayed in this novel are either products of the author's imagination or are used fictitiously.

Copyright © 2021 by Zuzana Říhová
Translation copyright © 2025 by Alex Zucker

All rights reserved under domestic and international copyright. Outside of fair use (such as quoting within a book review), no part of this publication may be reproduced, stored in a retrieval system, or transmitted in any form or by any means, electronic, mechanical, photocopying, recording, or otherwise, without the written permission of the publisher. Additionally, no part of this book may be used or reproduced in any manner for the purpose of training artificial intelligence technologies or systems. For permissions, please contact the publisher.

First Catapult edition: 2025

Angela Carter, excerpts from "The Werewolf" and "The Company of Wolves" from *The Bloody Chamber and Other Stories*. Copyright © 1979 by Angela Carter. Reprinted with the permission of the estate of the author c/o Rodgers, Coleridge & White, 20 Powis Mews, London W11 1JN.

See page 273 for credits.

ISBN: 978-1-64622-227-8

Library of Congress Control Number: 2025934361

Jacket design by Nicole Caputo
Jacket image of hand © iStock / MedicalArtInc;
paw texture © iStock / Vadim Ezhov
Book design by Laura Berry

Catapult
New York, NY
books.catapult.co

Printed in the United States of America

1 3 5 7 9 10 8 6 4 2

the night is bitter
I know why
it's when the wolf
rubs himself against the stone

—TRISTAN TZARA

Part One

She stood shuffling her feet in the manure. Her enormous belly, riddled with pulsating veins, tensed and relaxed in spasms. A sharp-edged hoof peeked from underneath her tail, with a thin dribble of mucus running off the edge. The gray-white trickle stretched unbroken, quivering in the summer breeze, then plopped into the litter.

He swallowed dryly, furrowed his brow in disgust. Watching as Pepa prepared everything at the rear end of the cow. A large metal bucket of lukewarm water, a small cup, some old towels. Pepa pulled on his long rubber gloves, can't call him a pig. Šimečka from Dolní Planá pulls calves without gloves all the time, sticking his arm in up to his elbow like it's no big deal. But that's just nasty.

He started working his arm into the cow, fishing around to the left a bit, then back to the right. The cow shuddered, her belly contracted sharply twice, and the whole hoof emerged. Pepa deftly withdrew his arm and expertly slipped the hoof into the loop of hemp rope he had ready and waiting. Pulled tight. The cow mooed uneasily. She didn't have a clue what was happening at her behind. Her head was trapped in the bars of the metal fence, a space just barely big enough for feeding.

"Whoa, old girl, now hold on there." Pepa delivered a cheerful slap to her behind and glanced over at Bohumil, who faintly smiled back. Why do they always have to call them old girl, he says to himself.

He watched as the hoof slowly inched its way out of the cow. He did his best to look perfectly normal, nonchalantly indifferent, but he badly wanted to get the hell out, run home and pour himself a drink. Then maybe watch a video of a calving on YouTube, in case he wanted to see a birth, which he did not. The scene in front of him was covered in blood and slime, he felt grimy even though he was standing several meters away on a concrete-paved walkway. Still, he took a step or two back, he might get splattered and he'd bought this jacket only a couple of weeks ago.

Pepa ruffled his feathers. I'll show that snoot how things work around here. Harsh village, harsh people. He snorted. City slicker, in his beige jacket and beige loafers, walkin in here like he's steppin out on the town. Starin at that calf like he's never seen veal in his life. No doubt a vegetarian. No doubt a moron. A step closer and he would have caught the delicate scent of perfume. But he stood at the cow's rear end, tugging out the calf. The cow lashed out with her right hind leg and Pepa replied with a proper kick. Glanced over at Bohouš. Guy introduced himself as Bohumil, but only a lamebrain'd call himself that. I mean, my name's Josef, but you'd never catch me sayin that. Pepa scratched at his crotch. He was getting hot.

"I'm sweatin my balls off." Peered at the newcomer

again. Ha, look at him all horrified, no pussyfootin around your precious little feelings here. He gave the cow another kick, she flinched in pain.

"Now whoa, whoooa there, old girl, you know the drill."

Pepa worked his hand back up the rope till he was deep in the vagina. Rotated his arm, groping around the dense darkness of the vulva. He enjoyed calving.

Bohumil couldn't tear his eyes away. He gaped in disbelief as Pepa's arm disappeared first up to the wrist, then up to the elbow. Good lord, how far in is he going to stick it? His stomach pitched. His mouth was agape in astonishment, but he had no idea. Oh my God, look at him fishing around in there, rooting around like that! A thin stream of blood flowed down past Pepa's elbow. He's got it, aah, there she is. He wound the rope around the second hoof, smiled imperceptibly, that oughta do it. He tugged but nothing happened. He tugged again, red-faced with effort. He dug in his heels, pulled as hard as he could, let a fart, definitely let a fart, but the calf wouldn't come out.

"Hey, young one, c'mere and hold this for me, I gotta fetch some tools," said Pepa, holding out the rope. Bohumil peered around the empty cowshed. Oh no, he's talking to me. Uh-oh.

He stepped forward and unthinkingly took hold of the straps. He chastely averted his gaze, looking down at the round balls of cow dung in the hay. He was embarrassed by the spread-eagled vagina, the sharp hooves jutting out of it. A trickle of sweat ran down his back. Flies buzzed loudly around his face, one flew in his ear. But he didn't take a swing at them, didn't want to startle the cow. He was afraid of her. She was enormous. He stood at her rear end, examining the amniotic fluid–spattered hay, the whitish goo on his right shoe, letting the flies gnaw at him.

This is exactly what I deserve, he thinks. Standing in a cowshed, shoes splattered with vaginal slime, holding a calf on a leash. If only I didn't feel like crying all the time.

He raised his eyes to the level of the limply protruding hooves. He felt so sorry for the cow, for a moment even more sorry for her than for himself.

Pepa returned carrying a huge metal instrument.

"Shit, you're gonna rip that calf right out for me, aren't cha?" He nudged Bohumil in the ribs. "Hand me that, would you?" He began mounting the structure onto the cow's rear end.

Bohumil swallowed. If he sticks that in there, I'm going to puke.

He handed over the gnarly leash and stepped back onto the concrete walkway. In a single motion Pepa fitted the cow's rear into the metal frame and attached the ropes encircling the hooves to the lever. He started to pump and the calf slowly came sliding out. The whole thing seemed to take forever. Pepa, face flushed, shook the hooves back and forth, apparently the calf was stuck. He pumped away like a madman, yanked a couple more times, and a head emerged into the light amid a huge wave of slime, eyes wide with astonishment. Bohumil stared in fascination. The animal's eyes had a knowing look. As if it had a prophecy to bring to the world. He knew that was the kind of change he needed, the kind of change he'd been waiting and watching for, dammit, change like that is the reason I came here, isn't it? The calf's head was entirely black, except for a small white patch on its forehead, actually no, he wrinkled his nose, more like a star, it kind of looked like the sacred calf, he had to grin at that. He couldn't wait to see what the calf would preach. What odds would it give him and his family, he wondered. He himself put them at pretty low.

The calf still couldn't perceive anything. It was practically blind and only halfway out, forelegs dangling like an old lady's ponytail. Pepa gave one more tug. It plopped out softly onto the hay, so quiet Bohumil was afraid. Is this normal? It seemed to be alive, chomping its teeth. No screaming or moaning. Bohumil nodded like it was what he had expected. The gift of silence, heaven-sent. Stillness and silence. I am alone, I am evil, and my wish is that no one ever be happy again. He went on talking quietly to himself, watching them bring the calf to life, rubbing it with hay, poking it in the chest, massaging its heart. He wished someone would do the opposite to him. Deliver him from life. Deliver him from this evil person, enveloped in the silence of his loved ones, who didn't love him.

"Are you meditating or what, shit. That's it, show's over." Pepa sploshed him with some of the water he'd used to rinse off the calf. That'd put him on his feet. Bohumil thought he was pushing both the cow and the calf a little too much. Why not leave it alone for a second? Give it a moment or two to breathe. They had left the boy with them for nearly half an hour before they took him away to wash off the blood and goo.

The cow strained toward the calf, but the metal bars kept her from moving. She could sense the new life, still wet and fragile. Unable to turn and look, she shuffled her feet, lowing in exhaustion. Finally some sound, he was starting to feel like he was acting in a silent film: jerky movements, pratfalls and pranks, with a heavy, faded blanket of sadness over everything. Pepa cleaned off the calf and gave it a shake. Not so rough, Bohumil felt like repeating, but they only would have mocked him. They were almost all here now, the village big men. Sláva, the game warden, lived by the field. He was almost two meters tall, thick gray hair, talked slow and not much. Milan had probably come straight from the pub. He commuted to work on the assembly line in Hradec. Had a chipped right incisor and a soft, slight lisp. Seemed like a nice guy. Those two over there, sauntering toward the cowshed, Bohumil hadn't met yet.

Pepa, registering his glance toward the road, stopped rubbing the calf with straw and turned to look.

"The pansies." He grinned. "Buddies from Prague. Best buddies, if you get my drift." He gave Bohumil a meaningful wink.

Bohumil's knees began shaking again. Ever since he had moved here, he hadn't had a good night's sleep. Sure, everyone in the city complains about cars and night trams. But a rooster? It was one thing not being able to sleep because of how fucked-up his life had become over the past few weeks. But sleeping here was impossible, especially after 5:00 a.m. He wasn't sure where exactly the crowing was coming from. But he was going to wait for the fucker and slash his neck. He wanted to so badly. He wanted so badly to cut its throat. He felt like the time was ripe for violence, he couldn't go on suppressing the rage. Yet even just the thought of a knife made him queasy. Then he had to think of trains. That helped. Almost every time. *Diddum diddum, diddum diddum.*

The pair of men reached the cowshed. One bent down to get a closer look at the calf. "Oh my gosh, it's gorgeous, so soft and fluffy."

Pepa lowered his eyes, kicking gently at the metal gate.

"Jesus, I'm sorry, I didn't even introduce myself. Seriously, that calf there is divine." He stood up and shook Bohumil's hand.

"Josef Broumský."

Pepa, observing the introductions, began to kick the

gate faster, then turned his eyes the other way and slightly twitched his head. Josef, Josef, oh boy. He kicked the gate one more time, so hard it rattled.

"Bohumil Novotný."

The other man shook Bohumil's hand. "Michael Horna. Pleased to meet you."

Pepa stared into the ground. Right, Michael, obviously.

"We heard about you. How long have you been here?" asked Josef, still turned partway toward the calf.

"Two weeks now, two." But it had already been four. Four weeks in Podlesí, an entire month at the peak of summer heat in this shithole.

"Just a hot minute. So this is all still brand-new to you, huh?"

Bohumil nodded indistinctly.

"Are you all here permanently, or is this like just a breather from the city, for the summer?"

"Yeah, I guess so. Permanently, for now."

Pepa smirked, poking the calf with his foot. "Where else'll you find fresh veal like this?"

At the farmers' market on Náměstí Míru, Bohumil felt like saying, but he kept it to himself. He felt like this was his new profession. Standing around the cowshed, or the summer pen outside the cowshed, nodding, staring, and never saying another word again. Submitting to silence, lying down in it like a bed of sea-foam. Saltwater filling his mouth. Sinking deeper and deeper into the quiet and metallic dark, kilometers and kilometers down to the bottom, where creatures that no one has ever set eyes on dwell. Until him, Bohumil Novotný. But no one else. Quietly watching. Peering into their oval mouths. Waiting to see whether there will be love in Podlesí, or not-love. Nothing in between.

He agreed to Pepa's suggestion of meeting up in the

pub. We'll get hammered, he said. A few beers washed down with some shots of zelená, figured Bohumil. Did people here still drink that stuff? He looked around. Yep. Definitely, and with milk. Once again, that need to be mean. To tell them he knew they would all end up puking from it in the morning, then hop into their coveralls without a shower and hop over to Bubble's place for a couple of pick-me-ups and a plate of potato salad with sausage. I need to calm down, he thought. Smile. No, that's too much. There, that's better. Just slightly raise the corners. I don't need to look like a little twit.

I'm going to live in Podlesí. Not because I want to, but because I have to.

"So, you up for a drink?" Pepa asked again.

Bohumil watched as they carried the calf into the hutch. No, pen, a hutch is for rabbits. Still, somehow that didn't sound right. All that commie farm coop terminology must have been invented by a maniac, Bohumil thought, a nice warm place for every animal.

"Sorry, fraid not."

"Us either, we've got a rabbit in the oven," said Michael, even though no one had asked him.

For the first time Bohumil smiled like he meant it. He imagined one of those puny little stuffed white bunnies, the kind parents buy for their kids when they bring home a perfect report card, wiggling its little pink snout around the corner of the oven. Then, picking up on the men's astonished looks, he quickly retracted his sneer into an acceptably neutral smile. One of his canines got caught on a bit of his lower lip, his lips swerving left as his eyes continued to smile. He looked insane.

"But seriously, thanks a lot for today, it was great." He had no idea what the best way was to acknowledge a successful birth.

"My pleasure," said Pepa. "Stop by tomorrow, I might hear of something. In summer, though, it's all stuff in the field, or farmwork of course."

"Thanks. I'll stop by," said Bohumil. "And thanks." He thanked him again because he needed to be thankful.

He walked down the road from the cowshed together with Josef and Michael. But he badly wanted to be alone. Go off and sob in the bushes somewhere, or he was going to suffocate.

"How long have you all had your cottage here?" he asked, steering the focus away from himself. Everyone wants to talk about themselves after all, it's the number one topic.

"This is our second summer now. It's great here, seriously beautiful. Especially on bikes. Little by little we've been out here more and more, sometimes we don't even go into Prague anymore."

Was he imagining things? Was that a sigh?

"So you, like, seriously live here? You're from Prague too, right?" Michael asked, and immediately Josef sadly repeated: "It's beautiful here."

Like actors. Like in an ad. Seriously beautiful, seriously, and cheap, and the second pack is free.

Just give it a rest now, stop.

"Yeah, I'm from Prague. Holešovice. Yeah, I'm living here, I live here now. In Podlesí." He hoped by repeating it he could convince himself. His voice wavered with the anxiety of a middle-aged man who's had to choose something he didn't want and can't stand, crushing his eyes into their sockets, carving him up into slices, until soon there will be nothing left of him. Like Bubble shaving salami in the slicer at the convenience store, one piece flopping onto the next, till the last bit, the hard butt end with the string hanging out, is all that's left. No one is going to put that on a piece of bread anyway, so usually Bubble just scarfs it down right on the spot, when no one is watching. What does he do when no one's watching and his eyes are fogged over white? He is ashamed. He squats down on the ground and cries. What else can he do? Nothing, there's nothing else to do but cry.

"I live over there." He raised an arm heavy with insomnia. His fingers trembled violently. Michael gave Josef a meaningful look. Bohumil awkwardly lowered his arm to his side. Now, boys, you can talk this all out at home, strange guy, probably drinks if his hands shake that bad, you'll probably chalk it up to debt, what else would make a Praguer move to an old cottage in the borderlands. But the moment you get a look at how beat-up my wife is and see the scars on her hands, you'll start greeting me with respect, though granted, from a distance, and when I take a swing at a horsefly, those ones that come flyin up here from the pond and bite you on the thigh, you'll flinch a little bit. You might feel stupid afterward, but you'll shrink back, out of the way, and hide your head in your shoulders. Like I said, you can talk this all out at home, over a drink. My eyes won't be turning white today, they'll be bloodshot from your wine. Now, come on, boys, seriously, wait till home, I can't stand those meaningful looks.

"Oh yeah, we know, over there," said Michael, nodding toward the ravine where Bohumil's cottage was. "Seriously cute. Bit of a fixer-upper, right? Still, like we said, the countryside around here is seriously beautiful."

Fuck your countryside.

"Beautiful." He nodded.

Never did he curse, ever, couldn't stand it. But curse

words were all that occurred to him now, like he needed to try them all out at once. Shout something really rude. Refresh himself with obscenity, smear his gums with the nastiness bubbling up from inside him. Sláva is a lizard-fucker!

It was evil, truly evil. I gotta get out of here or I'm going to scream.

"Hey, we're taking off, but we'll definitely see you again, yeh?"

"Yeh, absolutely yeh."

"You should totally stop in if you're passing by. Just bang on the gate, whichever one. We're usually home for dinner." Michael nodded.

"And we brew some seriously good coffee," Josef added.

"Totally. Thanks." I could use a shot right now. He turned sharply downhill along the forest path. I'm having a shot. No ifs, ands, or buts. He walked past the Praguers' log cabins. Lawn meticulously mowed, smoothed, vacuumed. Flower garden neatly mulched. Just like inside their heads. Water daily, trim the hedge, park the lounge chairs away for the night inside the shed. Occasional trips to Baumax and OBI and the flower shows. And Makro, shop in bulk. Currant bush in the corner, dotted red every summer like a little kid's hiney. Covered with earwigs and wasps, but you can't just get rid of it. And the cookouts! Nothing but the best smoked meats, oh, and the fish! And a pool, if they can save. The final seal of approval. It's a beautiful garden. Our garden, a thing of beauty. So, what do you think? You like? Isn't it beautiful?

He stopped and took a deep breath. His head was churning and hissing like a bottle of spoiled burčák. I'll never survive here with this attitude, I know that much. Today I'll pour myself a drink and crawl off to lick my wounds, but tomorrow I need to start doing something about it. So I can like it here. Nature, peace and quiet, clean air and friendly people. Yeah, friendly people, right, did you see those guys? He practically laughed out loud. This isn't going to work. We let it all run through our fingers, and you, my dear, let it run right between your legs.

He left behind the cluster of cottages and the last level surface still drivable in a car. Dusk was falling. He had witnessed it now several times. The sun transformed into a blood orange. And then it was dark. A dense, liquid dark. Even now, in summer, an icy breath drifted toward the cottages from the woods. Sitting in front of the house it was still warm, but as soon as you walked a bit farther, you could feel the chill on your chest and it got harder to breathe. Even now. He could feel his heart cooling down, feel the beating slow. Like the way he imagined death must feel. The dark, cold forest beyond the cottage frightened him. In the daytime it was totally quiet. Maybe a few mushroom hunters. But as soon as it began to get dark, the forest filled with snaps and pops, pine needles squealing under the hooves of God knows what. A strange whinnying and braying woke him at night. Stags barked, supposedly, but no way was this a stag. It sounded like a mouflon, but he would have been laughed out of town if he'd claimed there were mouflons howling outside the cottage. Not howl, dammit, what noise did they make? He never would have thought he'd be at a loss for words here. Here of all places, where the average village inhabitant had a vocabulary of two thousand words, give or take. Passive. He slowed his pace. It can't go on like this, good lord. Here he was again, moaning and groaning, grumbling, griping. Maybe the people here were great. Yeah right, have you ever spoken to them? A shot, I need a shot.

He dipped sharply downhill, the last cottage on the ridge was now far behind as he barreled down into the heart of the ravine. As the blood orange faded, he instinctively stepped up his pace. It probably wasn't a mouflon, but there was something alive in those woods. And it didn't sound friendly. He'd noticed that no one set foot outside the pub or the cottages after dusk. And why bother, when the bewitching eye of the TV was there to keep them occupied? But maybe they were afraid. He could sense the fear in them. He could sense something in the people of Podlesí. He shivered with cold. But enough already. I'll never survive here like this. And the whole reason I'm here is so I can survive. We came so we could survive. He was walking so fast he was out of breath. But the cottage was all the way at the bottom of the ravine. The cottage was the ravine. The place where no one could live anymore. That was where Bohumil and Bohumila lived. Them and the boy.

He tripped, unable to see the toes of his shoes. Uh-oh. He looked skyward with concern as the darkness hungrily swallowed the orange, sucking it up in its velvety maw. The sweet juice came squirting down onto his shoulders. Sticky. He sped up his pace. Something dark enfolded him in its embrace, night sneezed in his face. Uh-oh.

Forgive me, young man. I'm just stretching myself out here, sprawling this way and unfurling that way and breathing a chill of fear and anxiety into you. Young man! You must find that flattering, no? Wrinkles forking from your hands to your back, forehead crinkled. Hairline shiny with sweat. Our hair's not getting any thicker now, is it, oh no, not one bit. Breasts sagging like dog ears. But maybe the best is yet to come, what do I know? So don't worry. No one ever died of anxiety. It chokes the arteries, oh yes, clogs the heart, but no one has darkness, anxiety, loneliness written down on that last final form, let alone night. Because the anxiety I blow over the farms and cottages after dark is soft and tender as silk. I realize when you add in to that the growling and barking coming out of the woods and up onto your doorstep it doesn't add joy to anyone's day, but one mustn't take everything so seriously, my little shaveling. Come, sit with me awhile, have a seat for a spell, we'll just poke a few little fingers in and be on our way again. And where will we poke them? Well, right where it hurts and bleeds, not where it tickles, oh no. You can save all that for morning, all that tickling and running your nose along the ribs to make the children laugh. I'm about to delve into your suffering. Hungrily taking those trembling fingers of yours into my mouth, feeding on your fear, sipping it from your tight-clenched lips. Give me a drink, you scoundrel, you belong to me now, I'll hold you so close you'll be gasping for breath, all the better for me to drink in your perpetual but sweet regret.

Night gives him a poke in the ribs, but he can't go any faster. He's already running as is! Dashing home through the abyss. Home? Finally catching sight of the doorstep, he stretches his arms out in front of him, for the sprinkle of light from the cracked lamp to protect him from the badgering night. As the glow above the gate enfolds him in its sweet embrace, night retracts its bony claws and spits, You know what awaits you here and it will be almost like death, that's right, a dark, forest death.

Bohumil burst in the door, sweat-soaked shirt glued to his back.

"What is the matter with you?" She walked past, kicking a basket of laundry in front of her. Her hand was still in pain.

"Nothing." He didn't turn to look back at the woods,

trying to calm his breathing. "A calf was born," he said confusingly.

"Well, that's good to know." She nudged the laundry out in front of the drying rack, tripping over something along the way. She cursed and began to hang the clothes.

"Want help?"

"Better heat up his supper, he's ready for bed."

"Okay, let me just quick take a shower, all right?"

"I approve."

He drew his shoulders together. She had a knack for that. Telling him he smelled. But without actually telling him. She was good.

He locked himself in the bathroom, slipped out of his T-shirt and pants. He was so skinny. When was the last time he ate a proper meal? He sat down on the edge of the tub and studied his hairy insteps. My little hobbit, she used to tease him. Were they ever going to kid around again? He tapped a loose piece of tile with his thumb. The grout around the edge of the tub had crumbled off, leaving gaps big enough for a hornets' nest. Probably not. They were probably never going to kid around again. He climbed into the tub before turning on the water. A spider sat perched by the drain. Bohumil studied it closely, the spider didn't move. Not even a tad. Every one of you animals can seriously go to hell. Just crawl off behind a cupboard somewhere, you little shit. What're you staring at? The spider edged away from the drain but didn't leave the tub.

I'm sitting in a bathtub with a spider, thought Bohumil, blowing his nose in his fingers. He peered around. Bathroom covered with mold, water heater on the fritz, rusty water from the faucet. And with walls this thick, the sun's warmth can't penetrate, it's always kind of chilly in here.

He fished around in the tools under the sink and found

a small knife. He couldn't get his mind off that tile in the corner, he'd been wanting to take a look at what was behind it for ages. He went back to the bathroom and poked the knife around the tile, trying to wedge it in underneath. He noticed a tension. Was it his imagination, or was someone holding on to the knife from the other side? And tugging on it. But he had to be imagining it. He had a growing sense there was someone else living in the house. The spider nodded: Yes, you're right, in the cottage and around it. And so many flies! I try but I can't catch them all, and the ones I miss are the ones that bother you at night. Crawling all over your face, into your ears and mouth. Gross. I won't even talk about the mosquitoes. You're almost out of anti-itch cream, the tube'll be empty soon. The whole place is crawling with mold, ready to come pouring out on you in your sleep. Not to mention, while you're asleep, restlessly tossing and turning in bed, there's something walking around the yard. Pacing quietly, rubbing its back against the wall, raising its heavy paw and urinating. In the morning you find the corner of the cottage still damp. I know you know. I saw your eyes this morning after being up all night listening to it yap. Glassy like the fox cub on the shelf down at the pub. Like beads, shiny glass beads, the spider went on cracking wise. It glanced at the rusty trickle of lukewarm water, then scurried up to the faucet. Do you dream about the sea?

Bohumil turned on the shower. The stream of water almost washed the spider down the drain, but the creature clambered up and out of the tub. What does it matter anyway, bring on the spiders, Bohumil thought, a thicket of them, for all I care. He shifted the spray from his right shoulder to his left, then back again. Thinking about the sea.

"Almost done?" she called from outside the door.

He nodded.

"I said, almost done?"

"Yep. Just a minute. I'll be there in just a minute."

"I'm not going to warm it up for him."

"All right. I'm getting out." He turned off the water and looked around. Towel, dammit, where's the towel? He didn't have the strength to ask her a favor. No more, no more begging. He climbed out of the tub. Guess I'll just shake myself dry. He bent his knees and gave it a shot. For the second time this evening he smiled. For the first time he almost laughed out loud. He shook his legs and naked butt, giggling at himself. Put back on the same clothes he had been wearing before and exited the bathroom. A puddle was left behind on the floor, she was going to be angry.

"It's on the stove, just turn it on, I need to sit down and get this done. It was supposed to go out this afternoon." She slammed the bedroom door behind her.

He struck a match and burned himself. They had never had gas at home, just a glass ceramic cooktop. He lit a new match, turned on the gas, and the flame whooshed to life. The room filled with the stench of burned skin.

"Where were you?" The boy sized Bohumil up with a probing look. He sat on the couch in front of the blank TV. It wasn't hooked up yet, so he could only use it to watch videos.

"In the village."

"How was it?"

"Great. A calf was born." With him at least it was a selling point.

"Ooo, what kinda calf?"

"Black with a little white map in the middle of its forehead."

"What's a map?"

"Like a picture of the world, cities and villages and stuff."

"But why would the calf have that on its head?"

Bohumil will have to go back. Back to the point in the conversation before he mentioned the map. Beginner's mistake. You can tell the boy's in his own world. Talking like that to him won't get you anywhere. Biologically he may be twelve, but mentally he's six, maybe seven. The last healer, really great guy, said seven. That made them happy. They went for a sundae to celebrate.

"Sorry, my mistake. It wasn't a map, just a white spot."

"Who got him dirty?"

Bohumil turned to the pot on the stove and stirred the contents furiously. Mr. Question, that's what they called him at the special school in Prague. How are you? How're you doing? No one knows what's wrong with him. He's got every "dys" child psychology can come up with. And the IQ of a pumpkin. But what does that have to do with it? He loves his son. He's a good boy. It's just hard to live with him. Everyone has a hard time living for some reason nowadays.

"Coming right up, go sit at the table. Did you wash your hands?"

"Yes."

"Go ahead and put something on," he said, handing the boy the remote and sinking down into the armchair by the window. The music from *Lord of the Rings* resounded through the room. Like every week, like almost every evening. He normally didn't even notice it anymore, but today the goblin's tom-toms hammered at his head. With Bohu working in the bedroom next door, he can actually be almost alone. He is alone. He looked around him. Closed his eyes. He was alone.

The boy sat at the table, eating and watching the elves

in suspense. Bohumil got up, went to the cupboard next to the fridge, and took out the bottle of Jack. There was barely enough for two shots. And the evening was just getting started. Not good. Not good at all. You couldn't just pop out to the convenience store here. Maybe to the field.

He sat in the chair, drinking and watching as Frodo disappeared and reappeared and disappeared again.

The boy finished his meal. He watched the movie, engrossed. Bohumil cleared his plate from the table and washed it in the sink. There isn't a dishwasher, naturally, since who would need one here? Why would you want to save time? If anyone in the village ceased from their eternal work, the nothingness of their existence would swallow them up, pants and all. He washed off the stove. That's why everything is hand-cleaned to a sparkling shine. And once they're done with the inside, they start in on the garden, an endless paradise of meaningless work. Flower beds and roses and herbs, a greenhouse and cactuses and succulents and watering and watering, and you know that septic tank isn't going to empty itself. And if everything goes well and gets done and there's nothing on TV, then it's time to get started on putting up preserves. Phew, and that's that. It will be beautiful and the world will perish of littleness. Not even the slightest remainder of time to just sit around and talk about how it's all for shit. If labor itself is contingent on the futile endeavor to break free from the ephemeral, then here in Podlesí the endeavor is not futile. Here in Podlesí life is not ephemeral, because the market for locally and regionally produced foods is coming here tomorrow. And the rabbit show. He poured himself the last shot. Turned the empty bottle, holding it up to the window. The sun never shone in here, the bottle reflected no light, cast nothing into the gloom in the window, not even a glimmer.

"Did you eat it all?" Bohumila came in from the bedroom, notebook in hand, glasses on her nose. She only wore them for work, but without them she squinted like a five-day-old kitten. Bohumil found her shortsighted helplessness attractive, he himself had a diopter of 5.

"Yep, the whole thing," nodded the boy.

She took out the cream, pulled down the shoulders of his shirt. The boy hissed in pain. How in God's name did he get so burned?

Catching sight of the washed plate, she nodded her head. She reminded the boy it was time to go to bed, but he went right on sitting.

"Bed!" Her tone lifted him to his feet. He slid the chair back to the table. Scratched at his hair.

"Teeth," she emphasized. He vanished into the bathroom.

"It's all wet in here!" the boy shouted.

She looked over at Bohumil. He held her gaze.

"You eat?"

"Yeah."

"What'd you have?"

"Soup."

"You're full of shit."

"I'm full of shit."

Did it matter? What difference did it make? Whether he stuffed himself with beef and dumplings, corn puffs, or nothing at all?

She set a glass in front of him, he apologized to her and lied: There was barely enough for one. He attempted a smile. She looked at him, unsmiling.

"Fairy tale?" The boy peeked his head in from the bathroom.

"Not tonight," they said almost in unison.

"All right, night night."

"G'night, don't worry, we'll be in soon, okay?"

"Hm," he said disappointedly, and vanished into the room next door, designated as the bedroom.

She got up and went to the old cupboard that stood next to the stove. She bent down, took out two metal mugs, a stack of dish towels, felt around and triumphantly pulled out a bottle of Jack. A whole liter! Bohumil took in the sight of his wife. He loved her. At that moment he deeply loved her.

"But then you buy and I'll hide it again," she said matter-of-factly.

Hide it, my love, he thought, gazing at her. Or don't. This dark libation is the only thing that topples me into bed at night and lets me get some sleep. This dark libation is the only thing that stops me from walking off into that ravine and never stopping. Until all that's left of me is a small dot on the horizon, then a little pop, maybe a hiss, and other than that, nothing. Nothing, my love, nothing else would be left. Without drinking I would have walked off into the dark forest ages ago, in a T-shirt and boxers, just like that, to save the animal the work of tearing off my clothes. Because the animal is alive out there, those sounds in the night, that howling, that isn't human.

He watched as she opened the bottle and poured them both a double. They raised their glasses in a well-rehearsed routine. To what? To health? He lowered his hand, she remained holding hers at the level of his chest.

"To us then," she whispered.

He looked at her, startled. Us, is there even still such a thing? After all that's happened? He was no longer sure of himself, let alone the status of his marriage, family, clan, community. She kept holding her glass raised to him, while he kneaded his in his hand. Looking at her. Maybe today I should give you a kiss.

She sensed his hesitation. She tapped her glass against his and took a deep drink.

"Thanks," he said simply.

"Don't mention it," she replied.

I sure as hell won't, Jesus Christ, what was he thanking her for anyway? I was the one who dealt with it all, the diagnoses, the psychologists, the healers. The homeopaths! A few pellets under the tongue, a few minutes till the miracle happens. Me, not her. You, my dear Bohumila, you were knocked flat on your back by it all.

My dear Bohumila. My dear Bohumil.

She had a twitch in her hand. At night the wound would come to life, hacking up blood. The stitches itched unbearably. She sat out in front of the cottage, considering taking the bandage off and scratching the wound till it bled. She couldn't tear the stitches out, it would have left scars on her hand. But the itching was here and now, the scars were the distant future. She looked down at her hand, the wounds were deep, it was going to be scarred anyway. She sat on the doorstep, right fist propped in her left hand, trying to think of anything else but scratching it. But the moment she said the word in her mind, she couldn't think of anything else. She imagined sliding a pine needle under the bandage, grating it back and forth, the intense moments of bliss followed by a heightened desire to scratch even more. And more. She rested her right hand in her lap, observing it like a foreign object. If it hadn't been hers, she would have gone at it like nobody's business! With total abandon, showing no mercy.

If it had been only part of a puppet, stuffed with foam and covered in skin-colored cloth, she would have set it down on the table, cool, calm, and collected. Poured herself a little wine. Then taken a pad of steel wool and, carefully but persistently, rubbed it back and forth. Steady now, gently, now faster though, as fast as you can and press down hard. Bits of the pad would catch on the fabric, snagging on it, tearing holes. Faster still, as fast as you can. Foam crumbs flying, fabric in tatters, till the hand was reduced to nothing but an ungainly shredded cone, bearing only a distant resemblance to a human limb. Where once had been a right hand all that remained was a bloody stump, already beginning to fester.

"Mommy!"

She looked up toward the path.

"There you are. Where were you all this time?"

The boy burst through the gate and threw his arms around her waist. His heart beat hard, pounding against her belly. The blood was throbbing in his head too, she could tell from the little vein under his chin, which visibly pulsed when he was scared, or ran a long time, or both.

"Is there something wrong?" She held the boy away from her and carefully examined him.

"No, no," he said unconvincingly.

"Then what happened?"

"Nothing. Hungry, I got hungry."

She looked him over one more time. "What's that on your hand?"

"A scratch."

"From you? You scratched yourself? Here, let's see, stop moving around." She reached for his hand, but he slipped out of her grip and was back in the cottage before she knew it.

She stood outside smiling. This is normal resistance.

Normal! There are times I just have to leave him alone, let him learn to read the world for himself, that way I won't have to explain and translate everything.

Hearing him howl in hunger, Bohumila had to laugh. As she listened to the quiet trickle of urine from the other side of the bathroom door, she couldn't stop smiling. He was happy here. Can I be happy here for his sake? she wondered. Then just shook her head.

"I'm coming to heat up your food now."

He walked out of the bathroom, hungrily following her movements with his eyes.

I can, I definitely can, I definitely will be. For his sake.

"Hands!"

He went back to the sink and rinsed off his right hand.

"So where were you?" she asked, taking the pot of sausage goulash from the fridge. It was the only meal she could make with what she bought at Bubble's shop. Permanent special on sausages, potatoes, and goulash seasoning.

"In the meadow."

"Alone?"

"Yes, Mommy, alone." He drilled his eyes into the floor.

She knew he was lying, but let him have his friends. Let him enjoy his dirty little secret bunkers and hideaways. She smiled again. I can hold out for his sake! She felt a swelling feeling of victimhood, indulging it to the point it sent a tingle down her spine. I'm the victim. I'm the sacrifice. And he's going to punish me for one weak moment, a few weak months?

She tried to light the stove but couldn't get it to work. The third match had just gone out. She clenched her fist in rage.

She handed the boy an apple and a cookie. "Go and build something, okay? It'll be a while still."

He put the apple on the table and took an eager bite of cookie. His mother kicked the oven door. Clearly it was time for him to get out of the way.

Bohumila stood over the burners, striking match after match. The oven was old and the knob that controlled the gas kept getting stuck. First she set it too low and the flame went out right away, then she set it too high and had to jump back to keep from getting burned. She cursed. The boy will just have to eat his meal cold. Cold because they live in this cold shithole, where even in the middle of a boiling-hot summer it's still cold at night. When Bohumila climbed out of the tub in the evening, she trembled like a chihuahua. Her teeth chattered so hard it was a wonder they didn't crack. But before she got out she would lie there alone, naked, dissolving into the rust, bandaged arm raised above the water like it was frozen in place.

A flame jubilantly sprang to life but then immediately died again. As the glow flickered through the room, she realized she had forgotten to switch on the lights. It was almost dark. She was starting to get cold. She could hear the boy humming to himself as he built something outside. She was alone. She didn't want to be alone. Where was he? Let him warm the food up himself. The boy could wait. Everyone would just have to wait. She sat down hard on a chair. Looked around. It was waiting here too. The whole village was seething with desire for action, she sensed, but something kept holding them back. As she passed through the village square, she noticed the crusty plastic chairs, the tables decorated with coffee cup circles. Worst of all, though, were the old ladies. They sat on the bench staring off into space. The skinniest one was Maruška, they called her. She lived alone in a low-rise apartment building near the bus stop. In the morning she would put her chair out in front of the fence, affording her a view of the village square, the bus stop, and a slice of the pub across the street. She would sit, nodding off, staring into space. Maruška, you're so old! Wrinkles like cracked paint on a radiator. Maruška, grannie! Old age like a faded piece of blotting paper, tucked into the back of an unneeded notebook.

One time, as she passed the empty bus stop, Bohumila thought she heard a muffled cry from behind her, saying: "Run away!" At first she turned in surprise, then started walking faster. Until at last she slowed down and stopped. Here I stand. This can't go on. There has to be an end to running away at some point.

With her left hand she took the laundry out of the washing machine. Her back was freezing up from the constant overburdening of one side of her body. A hardened rope of muscles ran along her right shoulder blade, for months now she hadn't been able to turn her neck to the right. She kicked the basket of laundry out onto the porch. She had learned to do that like a person with no hands learns to paint with their feet. Three firm kicks and the basket was under the drying rack.

"What's this right here?" She nodded down at some sticks wrapped in animal skin. Why is this crap lying here for me to trip over?

The boy turned in response to her shout and shook his head. Not mine.

"What do you mean not yours? Will you at least do me the favor of looking at it?"

He glanced down at the sticks.

"Not mine," he said, and walked back into the cottage.

She cast a resigned look at the trail. It too rattled

emptily, absent any passersby. She peeked again at her watch, anger building within her. *I can't do it all myself, he practically crippled me!* She looked again at the path to the cottage, littered with firm, succulent burdock.

He ran past so quickly, it didn't even stir the pollen on the windowsill. Bohumila went on standing by the drying rack, wet shirt in hand, once again alone.

Calf. Hm.

He reeked of manure so badly, she couldn't have come near him even if she'd wanted. Which she didn't. She no longer wanted anything from him. *Sure, go ahead, take a shower. I'll hang it all myself. With my left hand, my foot even, why not. We're out of clothespins, but I'll just hold it in my teeth here all night.*

As she tossed the laundry onto the clotheshorse, a chill crept into her. There was a strange creak. She looked around but didn't see anything. Blinded by the lamp above the front door, she couldn't see any farther than the fence. An uninviting coolness blew through the uprooted pickets. She shivered. Something barked near the forest. *I'm going to feed the cats, even the sick hungry kittens with the gnawed-off ears, pour them some milk, tear up a roll, make sure they have a proper feast, but if that stray mutt comes back around, I'm chasing him away.*

She took the empty laundry basket in her left hand, gave the door a shove with her foot, and stepped inside. The sounds outside the cottage grew louder. She called to the boy to come and help her close the gate for the night.

She'd brought her computer with her, on the pretext she needed it for work. But no one wanted her designs anymore. She hadn't worked in months and couldn't muster the courage to tell him. So instead she talked about the boy, the weather, the apples ripening such a short way away from their fence that as far as she was concerned they were theirs. That strudel he'd had for yesterday's breakfast, that was those apples. For days at a time she wandered around the front of the cottage, squinting into the sun and often crying. She had to do something, find some petty job, make some petty talk with people, live a petty life. Jarda had promised. He'd promised! He would definitely let her at least work the tap, she could handle pouring coffee with her left hand.

She sat down on the bed, laid the closed laptop down next to her. Felt around for the needles. The boy had learned to knit as part of his training in motor skills. She pulled one out from his attempt at a wool scarf and thrust it into her wound. Is there anything a person won't do for love? She almost yelped in pain. Slowly, she ran the needle back and forth, but she couldn't stand it. She needed more, more. She worked it in between the stitches, feeling them burst. The needle emerged from under the bandage covered in blood. A trickle of blood leaked out, she let it be. Watched the spot of blood on the sheet as it spread, bit by bit, into the shape of a Christmas star.

She was bathed in sweat, her body shook. She breathed a sigh of relief. How long has she been lying here? She got up and walked to the door. From the other side she could hear the orcs beating their drums, she still had some time.

Lying on the bed, she stares up at the ceiling. She feels so lonely she tries giving herself a hug, cradling herself in her arms. The barking outside the cottage is getting louder. She is cold and a little bit scared. I need a shot, she thinks. Before she goes out, she puts on her glasses.

Now all she has to do is get rid of the child. Shoo, she

feels the urge to shout. So she shouts. Shoo, into bed, little one, sleepy time, shoo, my love for today is exhausted. Reaching my hands out in front of me, I see they could crumble apart at any moment, as if they were made of ash. If you touch them, you're just going to get dirty and burn yourself. Better get some sleep, my child. By morning it'll be fine. Then I'll wrap you in a loving embrace and together we'll sail through the end of our dreams.

She looks over at Bohumil. The gray that's crept into his hair has helped obscure the huge circles under his eyes. The deep blue pools of engorged veins must be incredibly heavy. He is completely wasting away in that moldy old armchair, how long has it been since the last time he ate? She wanted to caress him, wanted to tell him, let's forget the whole thing and just get out of this horrible place, I'll be good from now on. I've been punished enough, haven't I? I can't see to cook because of my allergies and I've got huge itchy bites all over, and I mean all over my body. Plus, have you seen that giant spider in the bathroom? I was in the village today, down at the pub, we've got to get out of here, my love, all that awaits us here is drudgery and frustration. I can sense their stares. There's something fishy going on, something malevolent. I get frightened even during the day. The butterflies in the meadow scare me. The people here scare me. I can sense their shadows creeping along our fence. They tread lightly, but if you sit quietly by yourself, you know they're there, you can hear them. Do you not hear them? Are you not afraid?

I need to give you a hug.

Bohumila, smiling kindly, is just about to lift her arms. But her hands are nothing but ash. Good for dumping into the fireplace and digging the hidden bottle out of them later on, that's about it.

What shall we drink to? Me? Let's drink to me,

because I want to be more than just a ball of sneezing grief, just another woman dried up and empty on the inside.

They sit facing each other, shot glasses in hand. The glow of the TV behind Bohumil shining through his ears. If his hair hadn't been so black, he would have looked like an elf, a crazy, underfed elf.

"Here's to us," he said.

"Thanks," she said. She knows what she's thanking him for, for the time, the chance, for this fucked-up house in a ravine by an equally fucked-up village. She needs to take it slow. Not let it knock her flat on her back. I have to be a good girl, cook, clean, hang the laundry. And then sit politely and wait, for the moment when he forgives me. And when that moment comes, whether in weeks, months, or years, he'll pour her a shot and say: Here's to us.

My dear Bohumil. My dear Bohumila.

The heat is so scorching it hurts even to breathe. You have to take the air in sips. Heavy, sticky heat clogs the lungs, hot gobs of spit come out your throat as you exhale. The wooden gate at U Fandy is on the verge of melting. Splinter after splinter flopping onto the stone threshold, *tsss*, *tsss*, hissing like a nest of vipers. The pub is about to burst into flame. A couple more degrees and *whoosh*. The whole thing will boil away. And this is late afternoon!

Inside, two small windows give onto the cracked road dotted with potholes and ill-fitting sewer covers. Hidden behind a large flowerpot with a single withered flower, the windows are covered over by a grayish-yellow curtain, brittle with lager fumes. The pattern is a brownish batik produced by specks of tobacco. But no one really minds, since the windows serve no purpose. Assuming any thirsty soul is still outside, they're too eager to get in the pub to try to peek through the window. And once they're inside, who cares what's happening on the street? There's nothing going on outside anyway. Podlesí is notorious for its boring atmosphere, overlaying everything like a thick blanket.

The pub was a shadowy place. It extended toward the rear like a long noodle—the swinging doors of the small taproom conveniently opening into the hall of the former sokolovna. It was a spacious hall, with room for twenty tables, and a few years back, they had erected a stage at one end. At the annual ball, the sweaty MC from Hradec stood up there, and when the club had a meeting, they carried one of the tables up there for Sláva, so everyone could hear.

It's Saturday and the pub is packed. Everyone is crammed into the dark and ostensibly cool interior. But even here the sweat trickles down from their ears and slithers under the soiled collars of their shirts like a startled lizard.

Bohumila stepped into the pub, blinking into the dark and smoke. She had to stop in the doorway and let her pupils adjust.

She expected the beer-soaked tables. The floor spattered with reddish vomit. The suffocating smell of overflowing ashtrays. And the eyes of the locals—watery, bloodshot from drink, whites cracked from the steady glow of the TV. But U Fandy was utterly nondescript: six identical tables with advertising tablecloths, the TV droning, the barkeep lighting a smoke as he leaned his belly against the tap. The floor spattered with boredom and apathy.

The moment they spotted her, though, the volume level dropped. Bohumila nervously swallowed. She's being a tease, she thinks, attracting their attention, the men having to fight back the urge to rub their groins. She instinctively drew her shoulders together. As long as I hunch they won't look. But she's wrong. They do look, but with unfeigned disinterest. She isn't turning them on at all. If anything, her presence in the pub slightly annoys them, now they have to watch their tongues. They track her with a hunter's gaze, but a hunter with the grazing roe comfortably in his sights. No need to shoot just yet. They'll hold their fire. They're in no rush. They've already known for a long time which side of the bed she sleeps on, and as of tomorrow they're going to know what she dreams about as well. The locals purr contentedly after an all-day shift at the pig farm: Let the little baby bird from the city settle in, make herself at home. Add one twig to another, spit and droppings and glue it together, caulk it together, you've got your nest. Tidy up, bake up some food. And then we'll come for you.

A pair of men suddenly rose from their seats, blocking her path. She clenched the edge of the table and tried to steer around them. One of the men stepped right in her way. She shrieked softly, preparing to defend herself.

"Excuse us, please. We've got a birth to get to," Michael said politely. Josef, next to him, gave a slight bow.

Bohumila shrugged with a look of befuddlement. The men walked out of the pub and headed up the dusty road to the cowshed.

Jarda Hejl, the bartender and owner, nodded to her. He was on the tall side, with a firm, bulging belly typically damp with slops of beer. Next year he would be fifty and he'd already begun to plan the celebration. He insisted on picking out a few piglets that he was going to personally fatten up himself. Slaughtering them all, on the other hand, was too much work for one. For that he'd arranged a butcher from Hradec, though he did have his own cattle gun. He had a fondness for guns. This one made a soft, hollow sound, like it wasn't even firing, just sighing softly into the cow's brain. He planned to pay for the two large kegs himself, though he was accepting contributions for the pigs. He was surprised how expensive homegrown pork, pampered and raised with care, had become.

Bohumila nodded back to him. Would she find the courage to ask? They'd been here a few weeks now, she had to do something. Even if it was just cleaning. Or doing laundry.

Her sweaty T-shirt stuck to her back.

She was so thirsty her tongue was peeling like the bark on a dead tree. Her eyes flitted over the sign with the three green leaves. An ad for Platan beer. Did that even still exist? Whatever you do, don't start crying. How great would it be if that new girl broke down in tears at the pub! Oo, that'd be nifty. Afterward they would go racing home with the story, holding it tight against their chests as they sprinted down the stony path, so it would still be warm and fresh when they blabbed it all over the village. They might even add a few details to the story. A few extra tears here, some loud moaning there, by the time they reached the convenience store the story would be that she'd flung herself to the ground. And what would the story be like by the time it reached the cowshed, all nicely wrapped and boxed? And then she just lay on the floor, twitching and foaming at the mouth. And then she peed herself.

Marcela, a withered blonde with dark roots, waved to her from the corner table. Bohumila had met her at Bubble's a few times, they had gotten to talking a bit, a tiny bit, about children. Her husband beats her. There is a cowering quality to her body, even her voice. Before she starts to speak, she looks around and hunches in anticipation. She drinks. She has to drink for there to be at least some justice in the world. Because when she's drunk, she's almost happy. And everyone deserves a little piece of happiness. Bohumila sits down across the table from Marcela. The woman rattles on like a coffee grinder. Milan is great, he's just the greatest. Assembly line, odd jobs. He's helping out in the cowshed today. So she was glad to go for a beer. She's got a right to relax a bit too, doesn't she? She's exhausted, so just a little nip, Marcela nods her head. But Bohumila knows that what Marcela's really telling her is how, even just for a little while, vodka and bad beer slow down the steamroller of a life laden with loneliness and desperation. They may not stop it, but at least they slow it down, and that's the point, isn't it, that's what it's about, right? Bohumila even hears what Marcela doesn't say: Sure it hurts when I rub cover cream on my bruises. But what I see in his eyes when he raises his fist hurts me even more. Like he could never love me. No one ever could.

"So, cheers to that, right?"

Then a long time gabbing on about how hot the summer is. Unendingly hot.

Bohumila nods.

Splatter the ugliness with a splash of the hard stuff.

Bohumila nods.

Marcela evidently has been sitting here awhile, she's tripping over her tongue.

"Sorry, guess I'm rambling, huh?" she says, stopping short.

Bohumila shakes her head.

A half-finished beer and an empty shot glass sat in front of Marcela.

"Just make it two of everything?" asked Jarda when he finally made it to their table. Time had slowed down for Bohumila, stuck in the deep, watery wrinkles of Marcela's face. She never would've guessed she had been here only a few minutes.

She couldn't stomach Platan and a shot would've totally floored her in this heat. But the whole reason she'd come was to try to fit in, after all, and maybe get a job. She needed to do something, or she would go out of her mind. She needed to like these people, at least a little, a tiny little bit. It's just that, have you seen them? Bohumila with trembling fingers smoothed out the tablecloth advertising Gambrinus. Why Platan then? She ran her finger over two cigarette holes. The smoking ban didn't count for much around these parts.

Marcela gave her order. "Make it one large and a vodka, then."

"Tea," Bohumila whispered. She had no idea why she said tea. For God's sake, tea in this heat? I've lost my mind, she thought. She swallowed hard, her tongue swelling up even more in anticipation of the hot beverage, expanding in every direction within her oral cavity. Soon it would have to start coming out her ears and nose.

Marcela rolled her eyes. Jarda didn't say a thing.

"He's going to spit in it, you know that, right?" Marcela laughed.

She felt sorry for Bohumila. Her son a retard, her husband in his cute little coat and loafers cruising the village and obviously beating her. She glanced down at Bohumila's hand. She was hiding bandages underneath those long sleeves, everyone in Podlesí knew. Everyone in Podlesí already knew everything.

Gulping down the rest of her beer, Marcela thirstily reached for the shot, but the glass was empty! Jarda hurried over with a large beer and a vodka and set them in front of her. He marked the check with two lines in the beer & shots section, ignoring the order for tea.

He was going to punish her, Bohumila knew that. She could rest assured of that. Punish. Chasten. I am a weary, grieving cow.

Her hand twitched from the heat. She could feel the cigarette smoke seeping under the bandages, tickling and itching between the stitches. Her swollen hand was practically smoked with pub fumes, just peel off a piece and dip it in mustard and horseradish. She really needed to scratch it. She would have to dig under the bandages tonight. With the cooking spoon. No. The knitting needle.

"Go ahead, drink," she urged Marcela, well-manneredly waiting in front of her freshly poured beer.

"No, thanks, I'll wait," said Marcela, and walked off to the ladies' room.

Bohumila thirstily eyed her beer. It had settled just right, the beer still fresh but no longer so much foam it filled your mouth. She could almost feel the bubbles bursting on her tongue. She should take a drink. She must take a drink. She was unbelievably thirsty. Her tongue was stuck to the roof of her mouth like a piece of bread spread with honey. She pounced on the half liter, cramming the glass into her mouth and guzzling and guzzling, choking on the cool liquid, the foam running up her nose, into her hair. Bohumila gagged, spitting beer all over herself.

"Still didn't bring it?" Marcela said, shaking off her wet hands. She went on drinking and talking. Bohumila had to avert her gaze from the beer. It made her sad. She stared at the withered flowers in the window. I'm wilting here too. I'm wilting. She turned to the tap. "One small," she said, a resigned tone in her voice.

"Celebrating, are we?" Jarda set a beer in front of her.

Not a muscle on his face moved. She looked up at him in surprise. Marcela grunted into her glass.

Bohumila shot her a glance. What are you laughing at? I didn't want to. I had to. "When're they coming back?" she asked Marcela.

"Who?"

"The kids."

"Oh, that." Marcela lowered her voice and cautiously peered around. "This weekend, or after the weekend, I dunno. They might stay there a few more days."

"Wait, you don't even know when they're coming back? That's great you've got someone to watch them that long," said Bohumila, nodding in awe.

"Yeah, I guess." Marcela squirmed in her chair. She knocked back the rest of the vodka, closed and opened her eyes. I'm still here.

"So how're you doing here, you holding up?" she said, changing the subject.

Holding up? Am I holding up? If only he at least slept at night, I could let off steam in the kitchen. But he doesn't sleep all the way through the night. She can hear him breathing when he's awake, tossing and turning under the duvet, fully alive even at night. Am I holding up? If only I could at least let off steam in front of the cottage, but the animal is out there at night. "I'm holding up, yeah."

"I get that it must be hard, y'know? Prague, right? So much history."

Bohumila nodded. History, yeah. The village stucco hunters, she knew them well. Pants below the knee, sandals, mom backpack, dad fanny pack. Dashing across the platform to change trains in the Metro, overjoyed they made it.

"But it really is great here, though." Marcela smiled

at her. Why is she so sad all the time? So he beats her, so what, Jesus. She'd come to like her docile nature in the short time since they'd met. The way she sipped her little beer like it was scalding hot. The way she scratched her injured hand, lowering her eyelids like a sleepy kitten. "Beautiful countryside," Marcela added, to cheer her up a bit.

Fuck your countryside. "Yeah, it is. Beautiful," said Bohumila.

Marcela took a long swallow and nodded to Jarda. He deftly drew another and was almost on the way over when Marcela looked up again. He nodded lightly, set the beer down on the wet metal surface, reached behind him for a bottle of vodka, poured a shot, and placed it all on the table in front of Marcela. He looked at the empty glass in front of Bohumila. She smiled faintly.

All right then, bring it on.

The gloom inside the pub was starting to appeal to her. It obscured the faces around them, making the view more tolerable. The TV in the corner illuminated only the first few rows, whose backs were turned to her. Her eyes explored the sweaty hair, hairy ears, faded collars. She studied the men with intrigue. Beer and a glass of Turkish coffee with rum. A pack of cigarettes, swollen fingers resting beside it. The flame of their lighters flashed on the TV screen, the eyes of the stuffed wild boar on the wall reflecting a contorted image of the pub. The men looked like monsters. Her face was missing. She ought to be going. But she had to ask.

Jarda brought Marcela another shot.

"Eh-hem, there's something I wanted to ask," said Bohumila. I wish he wouldn't stare at me like that, please stop looking at me that way. "I don't suppose you're looking for help? Someone to tap the beer, clean up, I dunno."

Jarda glanced at her bandaged hand. She demurely slipped it under the table.

"Hey, thanks, but I'm doing all right."

"Hm." Her head sank.

He kept staring. He could see she was asking for it. The way she twisted and wriggled her ass on the chair. Tossing her hair. Pouting her lips. Acting like she wasn't asking for it when obviously she was. He smiled. She was like a mouse sniffing cheese in a trap, testing it out with its whiskers to see if it'll snap shut, then when nothing happens, sticking in its whole head. Doesn't even notice the trap swishing past its ears.

"Look, I actually am gonna need someone behind the tap, the next time we have a party. Stop by next week, we'll work something out."

Marcela closed her lips tight and gently shook her head. Bohumila didn't see.

"All right, thanks a lot," she said.

"No problem." *Peep peep peep*, look at our little baby bird thanking us, look at her smile, look how delighted she is to have friends around her again, Jarda thought. Maybe he'll invite her back to the nest, for some coffee and a bilberry tart, you're always out looking for bilberries anyway, you're completely obsessed with them, I see you out there every day, squatting down in the bilberry bush like you were taking a pee, but you're picking berries and baking tarts and filling dumplings, and if you knew how to make jam, which you don't, since you're a city cow, then you'd have a good few jars of it put up in the pantry by now.

He walked out in front of the cottage. Looked around. He was alone. He stood awhile, stretched his back, then headed along the big moss-covered rocks up to the meadow. A couple of times his feet slipped out from under him and he fell, smudging his hands brown and green. He walked for a while. Caught a glimpse of the cows in the distance. Looked around. He was alone. The blades of dry grass cracked beneath his feet, snapping like brittle needles against the hard skin of his heels. To while away the time, he picked walnuts, chased butterflies, and gathered whatever flowers he found for a bouquet. Every now and then he stooped down to look at a grasshopper.

Here's one, there's another. So many grasshoppers!

Suddenly he spied a strange-looking creature on a burdock. He squatted down and prodded it with a stick. Turned on its back, it looked like a beetle.

Looks like a beetle, he thought.

Its belly was covered with red hairs. He'd never seen a beetle like that. He stooped down even closer, smelled a pungent odor. The beetle fluttered its legs and a thin yellowish fluid oozed from its behind. He dipped a stick in it, the fluid stretched like honey.

Hearing footsteps behind him, he turned his head.

"Howdy," said Sláva. He had been watching him for a long time. He didn't want to rush. He stood over the boy, examining him. A little person. He looked like a person but wasn't. Still just a pup. No longer drinking from his mama's breast, but not yet tall enough to reach the bottle in the pantry. Worst age of all, Sláva thought. He peered into his wavy brown hair. The boy had nits, for sure. And every morning wakes with his undies stuck to the duvet. How old could he be? Twelve, thirteen? It's hard to guess with retards.

"What you got there?" He nodded to the creature on the leaf.

"Oh, a bug." The boy poked it again with the stick. "It's bleeding."

Sláva leaned in closer, turned his head away.

"Stinks," said Sláva.

"Stinks," nodded the boy.

Won't be stepping in that, I'd never get it off my shoes.

"Where are your mom and dad?" He already knew the answer. Bohumila was in the pub, with Marcela. Bohumil was in the cowshed. He knew the boy was alone. He'd come to check him out. He'd seen him only a few times before, standing outside the store, waiting for his mom. He would stare off into space, kick rocks, then sit down on the steps, stare off into space, toss rocks into the gutter. From a distance there was nothing suspicious about him, you had to see him up close, talk with him awhile. Sláva knew he wouldn't be of any use to them but wanted to find out what kind of person he was.

"Oh, out."

He studied the boy. He'd expected him to be smaller. When something develops wrong, it's usually small. Diminished intelligence was expressed in the face. But he couldn't quite pinpoint where and how. The number of eyes was right, nose and mouth in a straight line. Still, at first glance you could tell something was wrong. But what? No nervous tics, placid eyes, maybe his mouth, the left corner drooped slightly to the left. Like the gravity on that side was stronger. Yes, that was the abnormality, the deficiency, the mistake. Being so near the creature was making him uncomfortable.

Jesus, that stinks.

The boy stood quietly facing him.

"You want to see something?" he asked the boy. What exactly is he supposed to tell him? What should he be showing him? A cloudiness came over his eyes, could he even see that they were standing in a meadow? Does he even know who I am? And who he is?

"Yes."

Uh-oh. All I wanted to do was get a look at him up close. "You promise you won't be scared?" Sláva laughed.

"Promise," said the boy. "I won't be scared."

"You're already scared now." Sláva grinned.

He was taken aback by the look in the boy's eyes. Is he scared or isn't he? What kind of person is this?

"All right then, come with me." He took the boy by the arm. His hand slipped on a moist sheen of sweat. Disgusted, he wiped his hand on his pants and moved it to the boy's shoulder.

They set out toward the woods. The boy didn't resist.

Sláva peppered him with questions. What did they do back in Prague? How long did they plan to stay here?

What about his mom? What was she like? Mom? He shook his head in exasperation. The boy gave him words, phrases. Instead of answers, all he had was questions. He was incapable of putting together a sentence. Either that or he didn't want to. There he goes, answering with a question again. The boy is relentless.

"What's wrong with her hand?" Sláva finally asked. He had expected the boy to mention it right away.

His question was met with silence. The boy trotted along beside him through the withered grass, not saying a word.

The natural anger that resided in Sláva clawed its way to the surface. His eyes darkened.

The boy didn't even look at him, quietly stumbling over the drought-cracked earth. If it went on like this, they'd have to start killing off sheep again. The grass was yellow as rapeseed, there was nothing to feed them. The flock had been bleating hungrily for several days now, half the village couldn't sleep at night because of it, and Pepa had started to sharpen his knives. One female still in heat, another already dropped calves, how is this even possible? Confusion reigned within the flock, never before had lambs been born at such a large time interval.

When is it finally going to rain? wondered Sláva, shielding his eyes from the sun.

Dry branches snapped beneath their feet, crunching so loudly you would have thought there were at least four people walking. Every so often the boy slowed down and listened. Looked at Sláva. He didn't have his rifle. Just a large pack on his back with something inside that jingled whenever he tripped on a stump.

The heat was building. It was closing in on noon. The sun stung, nibbling at the boy's reddened shoulders. With that red blot on the scruff of his neck, he'd be whining by afternoon. And that evening, when he walked into the cottage, he would be shaking like someone in the midst of a howling blizzard, trembling from the bitter cold. His palms would be burning, but he would allow only his sunburned shoulders to be rubbed with cream after putting on a show of denial. He wouldn't tell his parents a thing. It wouldn't take him long to fall asleep, but he wouldn't be able to roll over, so he'd have to lie on his belly, head stuffed in the pillow to stifle the moans. With the cotton-polyester mix sucking the tears from his eye sockets, no one would know the boy cried at night. So in the morning no one would ask, what in God's name are you bawling for? What are you bawling about this time? Sunburned skin will do that to a person.

At the edge of the woods, the boy came to a stop.

"What are you standing there for?" Sláva asked.

"Because," said the boy, kicking at the moss. "I'm not allowed in the woods alone."

A little baby bird on a plate, defenseless, just waiting to be plucked clean. Sláva smiled.

"But you aren't going in alone. I'm with you, aren't I?"

The boy hesitated.

Sláva nudged his shoulder. Oh, come on. I'll show you something. I'll show you the corral. But he didn't say it out loud.

"Are we almost there?"

"Almost."

The boy slows down again. Almost standing still. Sláva doesn't even want to look at him, just no more questions. Sweat snakes down his face. The heavy odor of the summertime woods weighs on his lungs. The past few days he hasn't been feeling too well. Running a fever and having a hard time breathing.

The boy stands awhile just staring, then looks around. Woods on every side. Despite being tall and sturdy, the trees provide no shade or cooling. As if the heat slipped off of them like a child slipping out of a swing, and, screaming in delight, squealing higher higher higher, Mommy, harder, Mommy, I wanna fly, Mommy, I wanna fly, before landing on their sweat-soaked shirts and heat-addled heads.

They continue on their way. No longer speaking, they are too exhausted, thirsty. Amid the powerful fragrance of bilberries, the odor of overripe forest fruits only heightens their thirst.

Nevertheless, Sláva quickens his pace, the boy can hardly keep up. Perhaps he has forgotten he has a child with him. As the boy yet again came to a stop, Sláva looked down at him, almost surprised.

"I wanna go home," said the boy.

But they aren't at the corral yet.

"Seriously, Uncle, home," he said, blowing his nose.

Uncle. Uncle? Sláva felt a piercing pain in his stomach, go fuck a cow with that uncle stuff.

"We're almost there, stop whining," he said, seizing the boy by the hand. He gave it a rough squeeze, the way he liked.

Now he was practically dragging him. Stumbling over the tree roots, the boy noticed two lovely boletes. He wanted to pick them, but Sláva refused to let him go. He dragged him deeper into the woods. Five miles' trudge through the forest; do not leave the path because of the bears, the wild boar, the starving wolves.

He walked and kept his mouth shut.

They came to a stop at a wooden corral, huddled behind it a stand of small, freshly planted spruce. Even though he came to see the corral almost every day, the saplings never ceased to bring him joy. He resisted the desire to open the gate, wound round with barbed wire, and burrow down into the moss beneath the trees. Amid the fragrant boletes. Fresh and crunchy. Inhaling their aroma. The boy, at his side, regarded the corral. Why is there a corral here? He didn't ask.

As long as he'd dragged him all the way here, he might as well go in. And not just in the corral, but all the way back, into the little shed, hidden behind the thick clump of bushes. What do you mean you don't see it? I know you can't see it from here. But it's there, right over there!

"Go ahead, what are you waiting for?" said Sláva, nudging him forward.

"Where?" He pointed to the corral. "In there?"

"Sure, just climb over."

"Why?"

"Because." Just because. Sláva clicked his teeth. Stay away from the wolf, man's enemy.

The boy stands there, not moving. Turns red in the face, for a moment not breathing. Now look, he's choking back tears. Cough, cough cough. Snot hangs out his nose, he wipes it all over his face with his hand. Jesus, it stinks.

Sláva observes him with satisfaction. This is fear. The transparent film around the nostrils. The moist, blinking eyes. The flushed cheeks, coursing with blood. The parted lips and the jerky, rapid breath. The muscles on the back of the neck painfully clenched, the whole body bent forward, ready to escape. This is fear.

He turned onto the path back, losing interest in the boy. Besides, what next? He won't be any use to us, on the contrary, Sláva could tell. He didn't even bother to look at him again. He wanted to remember the quiver at the left corner of his mouth, the vein throbbing on his neck, the restlessly flitting eyes, the hyperventilation, as if at any moment the air was about to run out. The fear.

They make their way back. Neither one speaks. The boy has no comprehension of what happened, but he knows something is wrong. He wants to go home. Sláva is no longer smiling, lips clenched tight, he is in pain, stomach heaving, but I can't just puke here, he thinks. As they emerge from the woods into the meadow, into the direct sunlight, he sees how unfairly he judged the trees. They were caressing him with shade. Now the sun is directly overhead, once again biting hungrily into their sunburned shoulders. He squints into the blinding light, but he can't close his eyes any further, they're almost all the way closed as is!

He glanced at his watch, he'd better get going, the birth at the cowshed must be underway by now, he was hoping to see the calf still fresh. He always enjoyed watching it fall helplessly into the straw, struggling to its feet, then falling down again. If it was a bullock, they would shoot it in the head as soon as it was born, since it wouldn't give any milk.

As they neared the first cottages, he was aware they were being watched. He sensed their impatience and understood it. Though he himself wasn't impatient, even he found the waiting suffocating, like a plastic bag over the head. It wouldn't be easy in this case, though. In this case they had to wait. He hadn't yet accepted that she, she especially, was going to be part of the game. When he staggered in front of the pub yesterday, when the pain again betrayed him and all his attention was focused on not screaming out, she took him by the forearm and sat him down on the steps. Even once he was sitting, she didn't let go of his arm. He saw her bandage up close, the green loop of a stitch poking out the edge.

I don't know if it was shared pain or not, Sláva thought. Honestly, at that moment, I didn't care what she felt. Yesterday, when I was cutting the grass and a couple of blades stuck to the sweat on my forearm, I brushed them off without thinking. But then I ran my hand over the spot on my arm again. The spot where she was holding me.

E ven before he fired he knew he was on target. He had been watching her for months now, week after week. He knew the exact order of her movements, the crouch, then the flick of the ears, then the long leap steered by her tail. He wouldn't be fooled. He had to aim in the opposite direction. Her tail swished one way, but she fled the other!

At the start of the summer, it had been almost impossible to spot her through the grain. All he saw was the swollen stalks rippling back and forth as she raced across the field. But now it was all mowed. There was nothing left of the golden wheat but a bare stubble field, the skeletons of the blades scraping and pricking. Even the fox at times felt them pressing against the soft pads of her hind feet.

He could see the fox all the way from the woods. Running around the field naked.

Of course he had attempted to lure her. He carried a hare call in his pants pocket; even when he was just out for a walk with no dog or rifle, alone, with no intention of hunting, he would tempt the blasted fox with the cry of a wounded hare.

The fox marked its territory from the woods almost all the way to the pond. He regularly found fox droppings with glandular secretions by the big rock a short way from the lake, where the water reached in times of thaw. In summer, though, the rock was dry and warmed from the sun, and the water snakes lay out on it to dry their stiffened necks. He had spotted her by the lake several times. A bushy tail flitting against the sunlight two or three times, a few hairs from the tail snagged on an old stump. His hunter's instinct told him it was a vixen.

Even before he fired, he knew where he would hit her. In the leg. The fox let out a shrill cry and, tail between her legs, limped off through the trees as fast as her three legs could carry her, leaving behind a trail of blood. She tried not to whine, assuming the hunter would follow. The pain was severe, she did her best to move at a swift clip, but after a while she had to slow down. Her leg was bleeding heavily, he probably hit a vein. Her head was spinning and her vision was fading in and out. *Am I still in the forest, or am I at the lake?* Looking for an empty den, dug precisely for moments like this, she headed in the opposite direction from where she'd hidden her pups. *In the slope overlooking the lake, not under that stump, you bastard! Go ahead and come for me if you want, skin my hide, tear out my guts, if you want to eat me or stuff me. And if you don't need me for anything and the only reason you killed me is we've known each other awhile, watching each other, chasing each other, wanting each other, then leave me to rot here in this den, racked with spasms and all alone, because I know,* the fox smiled despite the pain, *that the same fate is also inscribed on your dirty paws.*

The fox crawls, bleeding, into the den with the hunter right behind. The pain has slowed her down so much that even though Sláva is moving at a walk, the distance between hunter and fox is shrinking. No one is going to play games with me, he thinks, hefting the rifle onto his shoulder. No one is going to play games with me unless I want them to. I've been trailing you for weeks, you laughing at me under your rust-colored whiskers. Teasing and taunting and playing tricks, but I'm going to win. My binoculars must have a screw loose, I thought I saw her raise her right paw and wave. I must have imagined it, Sláva thinks, I thought I saw you waving, flashing me a smile with your yellow, rotten teeth as you leaped out of range. But my aim is true, it always is. When the bullet dinged the bone, you recoiled your paw. As if you were embarrassed, hiding it under your tummy. This is me waving, my dear. Standing here, looking down at you. I'm smiling under my beard. I know I'm old. My wrinkles are like cave paintings, my legs look like a mummy's when I crawl out of bed in the morning. But never underestimate an old hunter, dear fox! It isn't just experience and endurance, it's the whole history of killing. Stuffed trophies and a double order of glass eyes when the hunt is a success. It isn't just wetting twigs in the wound, that's disrespect for death, contempt for pain. Your hot blood smells to me like the rohlíky at Bubble's shop, ordinary and cheap. I'm waving at you, hunched on the ground like a squirrel caught stealing. My eyes may be old, but the rifle is new.

He stands over the fox, the fox losing consciousness, doing her best to keep crawling, but finally she just lies down exhausted, breathing heavily in and out. Whimpering. Sláva steps back a little bit, then frowns in dismay and steps closer again. It can't be. He bends down and lays a hand on her flank, rising and falling in rhythm. He can feel her heart under his palm, but the rhythm is intermittent, it falters, resumes, falls silent again. He runs his hand down to her belly, clasps one of her teats in his hand. Silky as the cap of a king bolete. The fox tries to snap at his palm but is paralyzed. She bares her teeth, grass getting in her mouth, but she's no longer able to raise her head. Her tongue, wilted and dry, hangs from her jaws, her fur is covered in dust, two thistles cling to the hairs on her belly.

He pulls on the teat, a sharp spray of milk grazing his boot. Sláva shakes his head. It doesn't make sense. The teat is packed with milk, even once he stops squeezing, the milk continues to drip. Finally it stops, one last white drop running down the fox's tit and vanishing into the parched soil as if it never existed. She must have been hurrying back to her pups, he thinks. The vixen is in full lactation, her pups can't be more than two weeks old. But how can that be, in late summer? She must have not mated till May.

Is she sick? Sláva wonders. He sits down in the grass beside her. The fox rasps for breath.

"Are you sick?"

The fox remains silent.

"They're goners. Either they'll die of hunger, or they'll crawl out of the den and get eaten by a hungry bird," he says.

The fox remains silent. She doesn't understand what the hunter is telling her. She watches the movements of his mouth, but her thoughts are on her pups, she wants to give them a drink.

They are crying for her. They are hungry, taking risks. They play outside, keeping a lookout for her, and whenever a fish leaps from the water making a loud noise, they fly squealing back into the den. Out of all the gorges, cliffs, escarpments, trenches, rifts, gulleys, rocky crevices, and abandoned human structures, she chose a den by the lake. She knew a den among the tree roots could be inhabited for decades. And not just any roots! These roots were thick and hard. One encircled the entrance, a small tunnel with a chamber lined with grass and leaves, where they squeezed in one on top of the other. In spring the walls drank in the underground waters, swelling and crowding in on them. There were times when there was very little room inside the den, but in summer, especially a hot summer like this, even the root languished, drying up. Its fat, swollen fingers turned into withered claws, breaking and falling off without a fuss, quietly and acceptingly, whenever the fox's snout brushed against them. The den was so roomy now! The pups could even play inside. It was a good den. The fox had been unerring in her selection and given the den a thorough cleaning in the spring, flicking away the accumulated dirt with her front paws, painstakingly trampling down the hillside—the kits are playing on it at this very moment, hungrily watching out for their mama. They squeal, pressing up against each other at night, shivering, too hungry even to close their eyes.

Sláva set out to find them the very next day. Chrastík obediently trotted along at his heels, his belly wet after disobeying his master's command a few minutes ago and charging into the lake, tongue burning with thirst. He wasn't an earth dog, but he was clever. When Sláva led him to the den by the rock, he vanished down the hole even before he got the command. The pups had no chance to hide. The den was so roomy now. Roomy enough even for a large dog.

He carried out several pups and laid them at Sláva's feet, some still breathing. Sláva stared at them impassively. Had he eaten yet today? Probably, he couldn't remember. But that was a lie, of course he remembered. He knew he hadn't eaten. For several days now he had avoided food. The pain after he ate was excruciating. For a while, nothing would happen. He had the almost-pleasant feeling of a full stomach. He used to drink beer with lunch, then go take a nap in the garden. Over the past few weeks, though, everything had changed. Now when he closed his eyes after lunch, his stomach rippled with cramps. Followed by a stabbing pain and two slashing cuts. Before long his whole body was locked in a spiral of staggering pain, he had to bend over and breathe deeply, then sharply exhale, then squat down on his haunches and breathe deeply again.

I know I'm sick and I know I have what my dad had. I just figured it'd come later. And I thought it'd hurt less. But what do I do now? Sláva thought. I'm all alone. Everyone down at the pub is oozing sympathy. I'm smeared all over with pity, from all the slaps on the back. No one will ever ask me again what I want. Because when they talk to me, all they see is a swift end, eaten away by old age and death.

He studies one of the broken-necked kits, eyes half open, doesn't look like it's asleep. He pokes it with the toe of his boot. Looks dead. He peers around, nobody here. He lowers himself into the grass beside the broken-necked pups. Keeps his eyes half-open, looking at his reflection in the eyes of one of the pups. It's still warm. He lifts it up and slams it against the rock. The skull is nice and soft, no loud crack, just a soft swoosh, like the sound of a deflating balloon. He stares at the shards of bone mixed with the mush from the head, one of the eyes popped out into the grass under the force of the blow. Chrastík runs over and licks at it, wagging his tail. Help yourself, thinks Sláva, eat up. Still holding on to the carcass, he lifts it up in front of his face, intending to tell the soupy head how terribly lonely he feels. If only I could tell you how alone I am, he whispers. He looks at the kit, at himself in the kit. Picks himself up off the ground, flings the corpse toward the lake, but only makes it as far as the mud on the bank. Chrastík runs squealing after it, taking it for a game of fetch. Sláva stares at the mess in front of him. Predators are an important link in the biological chain, he tells himself, nodding his head. Ridding nature of the weak, the elderly, and the ill. I know. And he turns to go home.

Winter and cold weather.

Go and visit grandmother, who has been sick. Take her the oatcakes I've baked for her on the hearthstone and a little pot of butter. The good child does as her mother bids—five miles' trudge through the forest; do not leave the path because of the bears, the wild boar, the starving wolves. Here, take your father's hunting knife; you know how to use it.

The child had a scabby coat of sheepskin to keep out the cold, she knew the forest too well to fear it but she must always be on her guard. When she heard that freezing howl of a wolf, she dropped her gifts, seized her knife and turned on the beast. It was a huge one, with red eyes and running, grizzled chops; any but a mountaineer's child would have died of fright at the sight of it. It went for her throat, as wolves do, but she made a great swipe at it with her father's knife and slashed off its right forepaw. The wolf let out a gulp, almost a sob, when it saw what had happened to it; wolves are less brave than they seem. It went lolloping off disconsolately between the trees as well as it could on three legs, leaving a trail of blood behind it. The child wiped the blade of her knife clean on her apron, wrapped up the wolf's paw in the cloth in which her mother had packed the oatcakes and went on towards her grandmother's house. Soon it came on to snow so thickly that the path and any footsteps, track or spoor that might have been upon it were obscured. She found her grandmother was so sick she had taken to her bed and fallen into a fretful sleep, moaning and shaking so that the child guessed she had a fever. She felt the forehead, it burned. She shook out the cloth from her basket, to use it to make the old woman a cold compress, and the wolf's paw fell to the floor. But it was no longer a wolf's paw. It was a hand, chopped off at the wrist, a hand toughened with work and freckled with old age. There was a wedding ring on the third finger and a wart on the index finger. By the wart, she knew it for her grandmother's hand. She pulled back the sheet but the old woman woke up, at that, and began to struggle, squawking and shrieking like a thing possessed. But the child was strong, and armed with her father's hunting knife; she managed to hold her grandmother down long enough to see the cause of her fever. There was a bloody stump where her right hand should have been, festering already. The child crossed herself and cried out so loud the neighbours heard her and come rushing in. They knew the wart on the hand at once for a witch's nipple; they drove the old woman, in her shift as she was, out into the snow with sticks, beating her old carcass as far as the edge of the forest, and pelted her with stones until she fell down dead.

Now the child lived in her grandmother's house; she prospered.

In the memory the boy is about three years old. Maybe four. Mentally how old? They didn't know that yet.

"It burns," he said. Sitting on the toilet like a girl, he swung his legs, twisting up a piece of toilet paper. The repeated synkinesia of his thumb and index finger gave him trouble, so he used his other hand to help. The scrunched-up little roll of paper tore in two. He spread his legs and tossed it in the toilet bowl. The paper made no sound.

"No, it doesn't," Bohumila said. She stood over the boy, observing him impassively.

"When a person pees," she corrected him, "it's warm but it doesn't burn."

"It burns." He didn't look up at her, just stared straight ahead.

Leaning against the sink, she cast a fleeting glance at herself in the mirror, ruffled her hair with her hand. A few strands fell out of her ponytail, she clipped them up in back.

It was just before Christmas. The city, shrouded in

mist, had been drinking in a salty drizzle since morning. Bohumila sits out in front of the cottage. Why is she remembering that now? She shades her eyes, the sun is burning like a barn on fire today. Why now?

"No, it doesn't," said Bohumila. Her lips smiled faintly, but her eyes remained impassive.
"When you pee, it doesn't burn, it's just warm. And then, after that, it isn't warm anymore."
"It burns," said the boy.
She stood over him for a minute or two, glanced at herself in the mirror again. Shook her head.
"It burns," he repeated.
Kicking his legs in front of him, head tipped slightly right. It was quiet, he was done peeing.
"It doesn't burn. Now it's just right," said the boy.
There he goes, the little guy, mixing things up again. Bohumila couldn't help but smile.
She lifted him off the toilet, pulled up his pants. He could usually hop off by himself now, but every once in a while he would get tangled up in his sweatpants and fall. Coordinating his hands and feet was complicated, walking down the street he looked like a poorly assembled action figure. One day he went running off after a sparrow perched on a half-eaten rohlík.
"Mine, mine, mine," he shouted, chasing after it.
One aspect of his deficiency was a delayed phase of hysterical insistence that everything in the world belonged to him. At his age, this provoked nothing but indignation on the part of passersby. No faintly indulgent smiles. Just sheer disgust.
The sparrow continued hopping along, the boy didn't seem to constitute a threat. Still, it held fast to the piece

of rohlík in its beak, not taking any chances by setting it down. Hop, hop, dodging warily back and forth, like it was playing with the boy. Until the boy fell down and started screaming. The sparrow, taken aback, fluttered up to the tree, put off by the uncalled-for noise, the unpleasant falsetto, which agitated the fine feathers covering its ears. Finally it flapped its wings and flew off with its prey to a tree on the other side of the road. It dropped a poop along the way without even noticing.

Bohumila watched the bird with a pensive look on her face. Then bent down to the boy.

"Meow." He thrashed his arms and legs angrily. "Meow." He kicked his feet so hard one of his rubber boots flew off and landed in a puddle next to a trash can.

He had been meowing for a week now. Instead of a simple "no" he said "meow." At first she didn't notice. Then she smiled at it. After a few days, every new meow of disagreement caused her face to break out in bright red spots. The moment he started in, her breath began to race. Bohumil didn't see what she was getting so angry about. He hadn't been paying the boy as much attention. When she pointed out the meowing, he didn't say a thing. If only that were his only problem, he thought.

"He probably saw it on TV," he said.

"Probably." She nodded.

The boy rolled around on the sidewalk in a fit of rage. As soon as he caught enough breath to speak, he fired out in rapid succession "Meow, meow, meow."

She gripped him firmly by the hand and tried to lift him up.

"Meow," he objected.

Quietly and slowly she tightened her grip. She could feel her nails digging into his skin, pressing through the fat on his arm almost all the way to the bone. The boy's face was red from screaming. Saliva, mucus, and tears melded into a gooey mask as a foul smell issued from his mouth. He couldn't stand brushing his teeth and hid his face in his hands whenever she tried to hand him the toothbrush.

Bohumila's lips were pressed together so tightly they were turning white. Then, closing her eyes almost imperceptibly, she held her breath and tightened her grip even more. She could feel the eyes of the passersby on her body like hanging lanterns. The wax of condemnation dripped from their eyes, burning her skin.

She looked at her son. There was something shady, almost evil, about children. The grimy hands, the sugar from candy stuck under the nails. The chubby, dirty cheeks. The moist lips. The snot.

"It huuurrrts," he screamed, falling onto his back again. His body jerked like he was having an epileptic seizure. She never ceased to be amazed at the force of the anger that seized control of his limbs. Bohumila stood transfixed, absentmindedly wiping away her tears with her scarf, watching his hands wave in the air. They were surprisingly synchronized. You may flop around like a carrot top when you walk, she thought, but your arms dance when you throw a fit. A modern dance, jerky and fast. But graceful in its own way.

When they returned home, she put a pot on the stove. Spaghetti. Again. They can all go to hell.

The boy stood watching her.

"Poo-poo," he said.

She still had her coat on, moving around the kitchen in her shoes. The apartment was overheated, she could feel the sweat under her breasts. She knelt next to the boy and soaked up some tea spilled on the floor with a corner of her coat. She didn't pay much attention to it, just noticed the tea was sweet. She took off the boy's clothes. Sat him down on the toilet and went back to the kitchen.

"It burns," he called from the bathroom. She dropped the pack of spaghetti into the water, turned up the flame. Outside the window she heard the purr of the city, the squealing of brakes, a bubbling argument. My city. My house, where written in marker on a metal tag labeled Elevator Oversight is the name Mr. Butthole.

She rubbed her tired eyes.

"It burns." The voice demanded a reaction.

"No, it doesn't," she replied without a second thought. She stood awhile leaning against the counter, took a deep breath in and out. One more time.

She attempted to open a can of crushed tomatoes, but her hand was shaking too much. It slipped out of her grip and the can opener's hook sank deep under her nail. She gave only a little yelp, but her sudden movement swept the can off the counter and onto the floor. She watched as the blood ran into the half-open can, forming a dark glaze on the bright red tomatoes. A few drops of puree happily embraced the puddle of tea. She looked down at her coat, the left side was covered in a red stain, beads of crimson dripping obediently to the floor, as if on command.

"It burns," said the voice from the bathroom again.

"It burns," she shouted back.

And left the apartment.

Why was she remembering that now? She carried the tub of potatoes out in front of the cottage, head down over the water, peeling them in the shade. They had never spoken about that night. She still didn't know what time Bohumil had come home. It occurred to her the neighbor might have called, what with the boy shrieking, kicking, howling, choking, coughing nonstop. But did she? The boy couldn't leave the apartment, they had a safety door that couldn't be opened without a key. So was it the neighbor who called him? Mrs. Hrázká, did you call my husband? Did he come home that evening, or not till later that night? Did the boy fall asleep in the puddle of tea and tomatoes, or still on the toilet?

The two of them had never spoken about it.

She didn't know his fingers were trembling when he unlocked the door. Bohumil unlocked the door quickly, fingers trembling. Found the boy on the floor in a bath of blood. Screamed. It took him a moment to notice the can of tomatoes, lying impassively in the corner of the kitchen, as if the mess had nothing to do with it. On the stove sat a pot of overcooked spaghetti. When the water boiled over, the cooktop had switched off. Christ! The boy had a beaming smile plastered on his face. His teeth were black. Nestled between his legs was a jar of Nutella, which he sat happily dipping his fingers into.

He gave the boy something to drink and walked through the apartment. She wasn't here. Exhausted, he sat down on the floor next to the boy. She wasn't here anywhere. A puddle of whitish water from the spaghetti had formed at the foot of the stove. He inserted a finger like a seasoned police detective: The water was cold, almost crusted over. It was getting dark. The boy smacked his lips. He even had Nutella in his hair, it looked a little bit like trampled cow droppings. The lashes over his right eye were stuck together, from a certain angle it looked like he had makeup on. Bohumil sat like that for a while, then got up for a spoon and plunged it into the jar. Scooped himself a mouthful. It was so sweet it practically burned his tongue.

Then he ran a bath for the boy. Undressed him slowly, carefully folding his things in a pile next to the sink. He felt old and tired. The rash that had broken out around his nipples a few weeks ago had spread all the way to his armpits. It itched like crazy. Sometimes he couldn't take it anymore. He had to scratch it lightly. Then even more, again. He was probably spreading the itchy seeds to his other skin surfaces under his nails. The roll of fat around his navel, his armpits, his groin. A red stripe dotted with whiteheads spread up the sides of his torso. He didn't care, he never took off his clothes in front of anyone anyway. But the itching, which came in sporadic attacks, almost always at the least convenient time, he couldn't take anymore. Walking down the street he squirmed like he had worms. That he knew. What he wasn't aware of was the sweet purring interlaced with contented sighs that issued from him whenever he scratched himself in public restrooms.

The bath was pleasantly warm. He tossed in the boy's toy car and a Lego dog with a firefighter's helmet on its head. The boy happily skittered it along the surface. Bohumil saw the bruise on his arm but didn't ask. He sat quietly next to the tub, resisting the urge to scratch. Then all of a sudden his torso brushed against the edge of the tub. All of a sudden he was rubbing it back and forth, scratching himself. All of a sudden he felt really good.

He set the table for dinner in the living room. He didn't have the energy to clean the kitchen. They ate a meal of bread and ham in silence. He turned on the TV. When they were done, he tried to force the boy to brush his teeth. The boy took the toothbrush, licked off the toothpaste flavored like forest strawberries, and handed it back to Bohumil.

"You have to brush your teeth," Bohumil said calmly.

"Meow," said the boy.

Bohumil stepped toward him, grabbed the boy's hands with his left hand, with his right forced the toothbrush into his mouth, and ran it over his yellowing teeth till the boy started to gag. He made himself sick. It wasn't supposed to be this way. He was so tired, he felt a constant pressure weighing on his shoulders, pressing him down to the ground. It wasn't supposed to be this way.

"Fairy tale?" the boy pleaded once he was in bed.

"All right." He wanted to make the boy happy. He studied him searchingly as he climbed into bed and took out his book. That bruise. Had she hurt him? The boy hadn't said a thing, didn't ask about his mom, not a word. Bohumil took off his glasses, rubbed his eyes. He needed a drink.

He lay down next to the boy, switched on the bedside lamp, and began to read. The boy wove his hands together. Then took them apart. Finally he wrapped his left fist in his right palm, like it was a soggy puppy that needed warming up. He ran his palm lightly over his knuckles. Stroking his hands.

Then he caught his father's look and hid them under the duvet. But kept on rubbing them.

"Are you listening, what're you doing?"

The boy nodded. The movement under the covers stopped.

"All right, now quiet and let's read." A fairy tale about a dad who makes a new boy for himself by carving him out of wood.

The cold wet tongue of the morning alarm clock wriggled in her ears. Marcela reached for the nightstand, groped around till she found the alarm, and pressed the button. Didn't even open her eyes. Not yet, just one more drop of night, tucked away behind the eyelids, snuggling in the toasty warmth between dreams and waking. But she already had a migraine pounding away in her head. She opened her eyes, smudged with eyeliner, she had wanted to look nice yesterday. She gazed up at the crack on the ceiling, the chipped chandelier, the empty space beside her. Alone. She put off sitting up, she had a hunch she'd feel sick. Lying down she didn't yet know how much or how little.

She sat up, belched. Loudly. Poked the soles of her feet around under the bed and slid them into her slippers. Got up. Her head reeled. She bent over and leaned her hands on her knees like a wrestler.

———

Yesterday she drank. Even though she'd said she wouldn't, she did. And how! Even the four hundred she'd brought with her wasn't enough. She dragged herself into the bathroom and sat down on the toilet seat. Then went to turn on the coffeepot and fished a cigarette out of the pack. She hungrily inhaled. Two teaspoons of Jihlavanka in a glass. The last of her coffee, she needed to go to Bubble's, she thought, squeezing her lips.

She attempted to eat breakfast, but her stomach refused to accept any food. Finally she gave up and went to stick her finger down her throat. She sobbed convulsively over the toilet. She shouldn't have drunk, she shouldn't have. She had told herself she wouldn't. Or only a little, just one beer, small. And definitely not a shot. No hard stuff. One beer and home.

She grabbed a dry white houska and drank the rest of the cola. That would settle her stomach. She looked around the apartment. I'll take a shower, wash my hair, one more cup of coffee, dammit, I'm out, all right at least a smoke, then I'll go pay Jarda back the rest of what I owe before Milan comes home. But what'm I supposed to pay with?

Milan's going to beat the shit out of me, Marcela thought.

She sat on the balcony, looking out over the railing. Her fingers began to shake, the ash at the end of her cigarette flying away before she could tap it into the ashtray.

She rested her elbows on her thighs, smoking and looking around. A plastic bag was caught on the apartment building's door knocker. Hanging down from its handles like a rabbit knocked out before gutting. The bag would dissolve soon in this heat. Logo running down the rusty metal like hot wax.

The heat crept in through her mouth to her stomach like a pesky fly, making her feel sick again. She really ought to have a drink of water and a shower.

Milan was going to beat the shit out of her. When he came back and found out how much money she had spent, he was going to scream, Marcela thought.

One time he locked her in the apartment. When she ran out of cigarettes, she had to call down from the balcony for someone to come and let her out. Three days. She even smoked the filters, waiting for him to come back.

I try not to let him hit me where it shows. But when it lands on bone, I can't help it. I can't not cry or scream. Owwww! Anybody would. Wham with a bar of soap in a nylon. Anybody would. My arm didn't mend right, how're you gonna explain that? I told people I fell.

Marcela sat in the chair thinking. Nobody wants to loan me money anymore, since they know I have no way to pay it back. Maybe I could ask Bohuna. Sláva warned me not to talk to her so much. I get drunk and tell her everything. Have you seen her, though? She's pretty banged up herself. That man of hers wriggles around the village like a worm. Loafers, collared shirt, thin as a thread. Maybe that other guy smacked her around, everyone here knows the story. There must've been another guy, I bet even two. There always is.

She exhaled a puff of smoke and stabbed the butt out in the ashtray under the chair. Fished around for another. It's always the same.

The tobacco softly caressed the inside of her mouth. Marcela loved to smoke. She went back inside the apartment. Opened the fridge: one hard piece of cheese, couple eggs from the Kadeřábeks, mayonnaise, pickles, ketchup. I'll have to go by Bubble's, that settles that.

But first she went and knocked on the gate at the pub. Lowered her hand and waited. She heard footsteps and the tinkling of glass. He must be inside, cleaning the tables. The fragrance of dish detergent tickled the hairs on the inside of her nose. Why didn't he open up? She banged again. Nothing. No one. Her fist was red from pounding by the time he opened the door.

"Howdy," said Jarda, giving her a sizing-up.

"Hi, you mind?" Marcela indicated that she wanted to come in.

"I just mopped the floor," he muttered through his cigarette. But he stepped out of the way. Glanced at the clock over the tap. Almost three.

"The meeting's at four. But I still gotta unpack the supplies and close out the register. What's up?"

Shallow patches of water clung to the stone floor. The water had probably already dried over the linoleum sections, either that or you just couldn't see it. She fixed her eyes on the floor. Marcela fidgeted, rubbing her fingers together. Peering around the room like a trapped lizard. She knew she couldn't save her tail, but there might still be a crack she could slip through to freedom. Her eyes searched the pub, which she'd closed down the night before. She still felt kind of sick. The detergent. The smoke. The hangover.

The television purred into the silence but she didn't bother to look. It was always the same anyway.

"I was just wondering, how much have I got on my tab?"

Jarda was taking down the chairs and wiping off the tables. She waited patiently at the counter by the tap. Once he had taken down the last chair, he walked slowly past her to the cigarette display and opened a small drawer. Flipped through a notebook, took out a pencil, and wrote something in. Her bill for yesterday.

"Thirteen hundred since the start of the month." He laid the notebook down and started unpacking a box of corn puffs.

She nodded imperceptibly. Today was the sixteenth.

He stomped down on the box, she flinched.

Skinny as a chihuahua, but her cheeks were all puffed up, like she was still workin away on the pack of cream rolls she had for breakfast, thought Jarda. He could smell her shampoo. He set the washcloth aside on the counter. Rubbed the corners of his mouth, half closing his eyes, a bit prematurely, it'll be nice. He can think about Bohumila. That chick is askin for it. One small beer, peep peep, but first a little cup of tea, peep, peep, little baby birdie. Who do you think you're foolin out here in the woods with that camouflage? You little nestling, you little squab!

"So how bout it?" He nodded to her.

She was hoping to chat still awhile.

He glanced at the door. I probably locked it, he thought, but if not, it's not like anyone's gonna come creepin around here this early. I don't have the lights on and I came on foot, don't have my bike outside.

He did step a little farther back behind the counter, though, just in case.

He gave her a hundred-crown note to pick up some food at Bubble's place, to help stop the shakes at least. But the store had almost nothing right now. Nothing she could eat. Nothing she'd want to eat. She needed something to wash out her mouth.

She crept along the shelves. Grabbed some rohlíks. Lunch meat. Put it back on the shelf. Canned goulash, on sale. There was a sale on Primus too. The beer display was right next to the shelf with the vodka.

She swallowed, nervously shifting her weight. The two bottled beers clinked sadly against each other.

Bubble's chubby hands raked through her purchase.

I'm not going to say hello, why should I, thought Marcela. I know she saw me go into the pub. I'm not going to say hello.

"Sixty-seven," said Bubble.

Marcela handed her the hundred. Dammit, I thought it was gonna be more. I might have enough for that small vodka. Stupid goulash. Fuck, and the coffee. She took a quick peek at the sign behind her. Jihlavanka: 36 Kč.

"Thirty-three," said Bubble, handing back her change. Marcela eyed the coffee. Lemme throw in a bag of that coffee too, she wanted to say. I'll bring the change by later, or wait, just don't add in the deposit on the bottles, I'll be droppin them off with you in a while anyway, she wanted to say. But you know what? I'm not gonna say a thing, why should I.

"Thirty-three," Bubble repeated.

Marcela stood there in silence.

"Jesus, here." Bubble held out the change with a nod.

Marcela dumped the coins in her pocket. *Clinkity-clink.*

Oh sure, you know how to count, she thought. She had to grab hold of the counter. Her mouth was working like a fish out of water. She stood staring at Bubble, a miserable girl who was seriously overweight and gorged herself every night on a stack of expired yogurts. Oh sure, thought Marcela, you know how to count, but you're disgusting, Bubble. Covered in eczema from all that fatback. You stink. You stink. When you talk, you gasp and hack like the fat's dripping back down your throat. Your eyes are greasy white balls of lard. You're fat and treat everyone like shit. Bubble, that's why you're Bubble! Just be glad we don't call you shithole.

Sláva impatiently cleared his throat. The meeting had been called for four o'clock, but it was five minutes to and only a handful of seats were occupied in the former Sokol hall. He sat behind the table onstage, peering around the room. Where is everyone? He snorted loudly through his nose, the sigh sliding down his sweaty chin, getting trapped in the poorly shaved hollow of his throat. I do it all for their sake. And who appreciates it? Who?! True, a week ago they'd brought him a piece of roast duck, but what was he going to do with that? He hadn't had a thing in his mouth for three days. Imagine giving food to someone with his diagnosis. And greasy no less—in this heat! He mixed it in with Chrastík's dog food, and as he saw the next morning, it didn't sit well with him either.

He wearily scanned the hall as it slowly began to fill. A couple fellas in back had dozed off, Maruška had brought her knitting. The clinking needles made him want to go to sleep. Her red scarf was wrapped around her almost down to her ankles. Who wears things that long around their neck?

He began to get nervous. It was almost quarter past four. I'm going to have to get started, thought Sláva. He had the plan written down on a scrap of paper. He had gone through the whole thing over and over again. But now he was here all alone, only him. Sitting across from them like they were the judges and he was on trial. The truth was, he wasn't convinced his loneliness was a choice. He could have lied to himself that he wanted it to be this way, sitting in the quiet gloom, bathing a párek in yellow and red and swearing when a shred of casing got caught in his teeth. But it wasn't.

The hall was slowly filling. He faced the hungry mouths of the hoarse, nose-blowing mass alone. Wobbly stools, creaky parquets. Mouths gaping impassively, open wide not with the urge to bite and chew but to yawn. Lips chapped with boredom. At the sight of their dull indifference, he couldn't help but think of how all alone he was. How does a man come to an understanding with his fate, enveloped in such unpleasant and disconcerting loneliness, he wondered secretly.

He nervously rubbed his thumb against his fingers, like he was salting them.

"Eh-hem," he cleared his throat. He could hear his voice vibrating, coming back to his mouth with a delay, the words getting tied up in knots, the syllables doubling, his tongue beginning to stutter. Lolling around his mouth like a swollen snail. He couldn't bring it under control to form the words correctly. All that came out of his mouth was bleh, ehhh, ooahhh.

My stomach hurts, thinks Sláva. My stomach is hurting me bad. And you just sit there gawking at me. Hiding behind the back of the person in front of you, hunched down in the shadow of the person next to you, huddled in a mass of drink-besotted eyes. I want to howl my pain at you, scream into the grubby air of the hall, so finally someone will come and give me a hug. To hell with it all.

He batted at a fly. He would have to start over again. On top of that, his shirt was totally drenched in sweat. He sat glued to the chair, his rear end squishing like a full baby diaper. It seemed like this summer would never end. He was well prepared, he knew that. He'd spent several evenings working on his talk. Drinking and smoking heavily, why cut back now? There was no point in that! His gums bled, he had to change the pillow covers every morning. The stains all tidily stacked up, one under the other on one side only, did he really not roll over even once? Once again he'd eaten almost nothing all day long. It was better not to think about it. Food just wrenched and cut and burned. How many times had he unbuttoned his shirt and lifted up his T-shirt to see his guts spilling out, a piece of his intestine unwinding like Maruška's scarf, all yellowy green and infested. I don't understand why I don't have rusty blood dripping out of me, a gaping scar on my belly at least, a boil, a torn freckle. Because that's what it felt like.

He had the same thing as his mom.

He thought about her often, mornings as he was stirring milk into his coffee, it was a ritual he was loath to give up. He needed coffee at least, even if it did eat away at his insides. His mother used to drop bits of houska into hers. Over the holidays she would dunk in a hardened piece of vánočka, which took a while to realize it could drink in all the hot brownish liquid that it wanted. She had gray hair, cut short. A year after his dad's death, she still gently shook her head when she was cooking. A sort of gentle no no no she never said to him. Her body took a deep breath to speak the word, which she for years refused to voice. Staggering, losing her balance, withering away. One time he caught her by the arm and his fingers pressed clear through to the bone. Muscles reduced to a swath of messily sewn curtains. The body has a memory all its own that can't be deceived, swayed, erased. He can feel the mush in his hands to this day. There were times, when he was alone and walking through the woods and his stomach ceased to hurt for a while, he remembered the person he had been before he had the pain.

He rubbed his eyes. He was badly sleep-deprived, barely smoked. At night Chrastík would bark, he had to go out to the kennel and beat him. That made him feel better, and finally, toward morning, he managed to fall asleep. He tried to shift the way he sat, but the wet chair refused to let go. Clinging to him from his drenched hairy back to the opening of his bottom. He suddenly got an urge to go to the bathroom. He had to get started or he was going to completely dissolve in the chair. Pain throbbed in his temples. Now it alternated between an urge to go to the bathroom and an urge to throw up.

He rose to his feet. The hall fell silent, the pale blue gaze of the mass coming to rest on him. A sinister glint flashed across the audience's eyes when he mentioned Bohumila and Bohumil. From the moment those three moved in, he'd had everything figured out, definitely better this time than the last. They would do it in September, there was still enough light to see then and it wasn't cold yet in the woods. He was fond of early fall. The needles still held the summer's warmth, the summer sweat running down the tree bark onto the fallen cones. And to top it all off the mushrooms, fragrant and hard, that crunched under your knife.

Jarda burst into the hall with a full tray of beers, flinging open the swinging doors from the tap with an expert thrust of the back.

"Eh-hem," said Sláva, clearing his throat again. He paused. The sight of the cold half-liter glasses disrupted his train of thought. He could feel the chill on his hand, the ginger swigs cooling his throat. He waved to Jarda, I'll take one too, but Jarda, busy scribbling down orders, just waved back, hey, sorry to interrupt, and dashed back into the pub. The swinging doors gently creaked in sync with the gulping of the thirsty patrons in front of him. *Creak creak.* He stood watching as the beer caressed their shriveled tongues, moistening their dry-corroded vocal cords, sliding deep into their bellies, causing them to bulge a bit, just a little bit, more. I could really do with a draft right now, Sláva thought.

He began to speak, leaving his notes on the table, hands shaking as the pain descended into his groin.

"So then, so much for introduction," he concluded.

The blush of his suppressed pain ascended through his neck into his cheeks, coloring them a tender purple, like a young lady receiving roses from a man for the first time. He couldn't swallow, like his tongue was coated with velcro and stuck to the roof of his mouth. He tried to take a sip of water, but his hands trembled like a soggy whippet, uh-oh, spilled on himself, hopefully no one will notice.

The crowd was dead silent. Everyone noticed.

"So, to go on, eh-hem, as you all know, we were recently hit, thankfully this time less seriously, by an epidemic of bird flu."

The audience's hungry eye looked down at the pamphlets everyone had been given when they walked into the hall.

"You can find all of this information printed in the pamphlet," he said.

They read: *How does bird flu spread? What are the symptoms? How do I protect my breed?*

That last part he'd had printed in red. Really it's mainly about the breed. About keeping it going, about the plan, its execution, survival, the polis, my place in the polis, it's about me, my place among the people, it's really mainly about me.

"It often happens that part of the flock perishes in the course of breeding, the resistant portion survives. The point is to focus on this part of the flock that's resistant," he said, continuing with his comments. The room was silent. He swallowed, looking in surprise at the notes on the table. He picked them up, but it still wasn't clear. Like it had been written by someone else.

Part of the flock perishes, the resistant portion survives, he had written in ballpoint pen, but then there was a note added in in pencil: *Tell about the dog.*

He balked.

Tell about the dog. Now, in the section on birds and their illnesses? He still wanted to tell them about the hen experiment. Blood draws had shown the tagged hens had a certain type of flu one year, but not the next. Only that year, apparently due to weakness, did they fail to produce young. He still felt sick to his stomach, remembering the blood draws. Do you have any idea how damn hard it is to take blood from a hen?

Tell about the dog.

He didn't want to talk about some stupid chihuahua! He wanted to tell them about the hen, since everyone had a hen out back. They didn't even deliver eggs to Bubble's anymore, since they just went bad and cracked and then the whole place stank like a cowshed, so Bubble told them to take their eggs and go fuck themselves.

He wanted to tell them about the hen.

But now he was talking about the dog. Now he was talking about the wolf. The hall lit up with energy, smiles.

People jumping out of their seats, hair on end, carrying their eager bodies closer to Sláva. They stood at the foot of the stage, bubbling over with joy. Now he had them, now they were his, one big ravenous mass.

Jarda Hejl, pink-cheeked, well-rested, right arm ever so slightly thicker than his left from carrying half-liter drafts. Maruška, a hundred years old, a thousand years old, white-haired, gray-haired, nutty as a fruitcake. She had dozed off. Look, everyone, someone had kicked the ball of yarn under her table, it was tangled around her chair like a beginner spider's web.

Will someone turn off that cell phone? It just keeps ringing and ringing. It's driving him insane.

It rang again.

Milan, cold blue eyes and a sport coat too small in the shoulders. It kept on ringing. And that drunken little whore over there, huddled next to him.

Marcela clutched the string bag holding her purchases, two drained Primuses next to her and a large vodka shot in her hand, which Jarda brought over without her even having to ask. Didn't even mark it down, just stuck it in her hand. No need to pay. On the house! Guess why, Milan, you jackass!

Summer had been clutching them all in its sweaty embrace for several long weeks. Breathing hotly into their hair, nuzzling their earlobes, dry and bitter. The air shimmering in layers as they made their way uphill to the cowshed in the morning. An endlessly long summer. Endlessly long hair. She had long brown hair. In Podlesí the women all wore their hair short and curly, in home-made perms. He didn't like that. Endlessly long hair. She was skinny, collarbones peeking out the neckline of her T-shirt, thin skin stretched so tight he felt like he could see through it to the structure of her bones. She waddled like a duck when she walked. Teeter-totter here, whoops, not that way, teeter-totter there. Quack quack, come here, little duckie, let me give you a cuddle. It turned him on. Especially her eyes. He couldn't remember what color they were, brown maybe, but it wasn't that. There was something in Bohumila's eyes you didn't want, some off intensity or something. Whatever it was, you didn't want to get too close, like in a movie—I saw it, I lived through it, and I'm here to tell you about it.

Only I've been alone for so long now, Sláva thought. When I open my eyes in the morning, the stove isn't lit and the cesspit stinks from outside.

Jarda was bringing out the third round, tacking through the crowd with his grease-stained tray of green shots and beer. He fished under his T-shirt and handed Maruška a bag of corn puffs. She looked up from her daydream in shock. Set aside her needles and struggled to open the package. Her scarf lay coiled around the table leg like a python, done in after a full day of street performances. The snake's tamer refused it milk and not only that but beat it at night.

Bohumila and Bohumil, now he was mainly on about them. What were they looking for here? Why, it was obvious to everyone. It's always the same, said Marcela. Just fix the place up a bit and it'll be lovely. And Sláva, with a smile, thought: And the countryside! The aura of tradition, of honesty and authenticity. Friendly people, cheap beer, homegrown eggs and milk still warm from the udder. He smiled. He knew how it ended. The cottage eats up twice the budget. It's impossible to find anything here, you have to drive to Hradec. Or else stock up in Prague. Eggs? We're low this week, the locals say. Meat? Just enough for ourselves, unless you can pay. And a lot. Currants, sure. Loads of them. Jams, preserves. Only who can eat that all the time?

When Sláva returned from the men's room, Bohumila was sitting with the boy at a table in the corner. The boy was stuffing his face with goulash. The moment he spotted Sláva, he stopped chewing. Sláva just smiled the other way. Shaking off his still-wet hands. He could have wiped them off in her hair, that's how close to her he walked. Wrapped them like hemp ropes around her wrists. Gave a hard tug. Dragged her down the length of the hall and back and forth a couple of times over the threshold.

The morning after Bohumila disappeared, the boy woke him with his cries. A sharp, sawing sound that broke into Bohumil's dream in the form of a falling tree. Mommy, Mommy, Mommy, he wailed. Bohumil got up and leaned over his bed. Laid a hand on his back. The boy settled down but wouldn't stop whining away like a wounded wolf cub. His eyes were shut tight the whole time. Who's chasing you in your dreams, little fella? Bohumil wondered softly. He glanced at the clock, just a few minutes after 4:00 a.m. Darkness. Another wintry day awaited them.

The day she left, he just sat sadly on the bed, resting his hand on her side of the bed. A void. He rose and went to the kitchen. His mouth was dry. Ran himself a glass of water and sat on the couch in the living room. Here too he rested his hand on the place she used to sit. She was nowhere. She was nowhere around and he didn't know how to cope with that absence. He was unsettled, yet not once did he feel anything resembling fear. She hadn't called. Didn't pick up the phone. He had no idea where she was. Where was she? Did he even care? He still did.

He rubbed his hands together. The heating had switched off for the night, the room was cold. He stood at the window. Cold and raw. It was lightly snowing outside, thousands of elated snowflakes drifting down through the light from the streetlamp. He felt alone. He went back to bed but first decided to wipe up the floor. The tomato puree had dried. He had to bend down over the floor and clean the seams between the tiles using a small sponge. The next morning his fingers were still red. The boy cried out twice more over the course of the night, but he went in and gently calmed him down both times.

Morning. She was nowhere. Not there.

"Get up, get up." He gently prodded him. "We need to get to school."

"No," said the boy, burrowing back into the duvet. "I don't want to." He kicked off the duvet, hoisted his legs, and pulled off his socks. Tossed them on the ground next to the bed. Keeping a wary eye on Bohumil the whole time.

Bohumil didn't react, walking off into the kitchen. Made tea and buttered a piece of bread. Took out a yogurt.

"Teatime," he called out.

"No."

"Get up, we need to go soon."

"I don't want to."

Bohumil lifted him out of bed. The boy started to squawk. He carried him to the dining room table and sat him in a chair. The boy was screeching now.

He sat down across from him. It was like he was seeing the boy for the first time. What big shoulders you have! What long nails you have! What big teeth you have! He rose from his seat and went to get his clothes ready. The boy didn't even touch his food or drink.

"You want the green T-shirt, or the blue one?" He remembered that Bohu always let him pick.

"Blue," said the boy.

He pulled the blue shirt on over the boy's head, laid out his briefs and pants. Once the boy had gotten dressed, he went to get his toothbrush. The boy skipped along behind him.

"Sweet!" he shouted, seeing the caterpillar of menthol toothpaste emerge onto the brush. Bohumil faintly nodded. He flicked the glob into the sink and instead squeezed out a tidy dab of pink Perlička.

"It burns," said the boy, handing the toothbrush back.

He flicked the pink toothpaste into the sink as well, rinsed off the brush. Squeezed Perlička onto the toothbrush with the mouse. He impatiently eyed the clock. We're not going to make it.

The boy held the brush in his hand, not running it back and forth over his teeth, but eating the toothpaste instead.

"We need to get going, you can eat something in the stroller." They still had to push him when it came to longer distances, he refused to walk.

"Green," said the boy, winding himself up in the bedroom.

"You wanted blue. You got blue."

"Green."

"You're wearing blue."

"Green."

"Now you've got the blue one." I will control myself, Bohumil thought. "It looks good on you. Really." I'm an idiot.

The boy studied him.

"Ga-reen," he emphasized.

In a single rapid motion, Bohumil slipped the green T-shirt on over the blue one. They were woefully late.

He thrust a Kofila bar into the boy's hand, you got a problem with that? He dashed down the sidewalk like a runaway horse, the stroller wheels spinning in the thinning snow. It started snowing again. No, rain mixed with snow.

"I'll carry the stroller, you can go down the stairs on your own," he told the boy at the entrance to the Metro.

Snow and water and mud and salt dripped from the stroller. Just keep it away from my pants, Bohumil thought. It'll wash out, either that or I'll have permanent salt stains on them.

He turned to look behind him. The boy sat at the top of the stairs, mouth full of chocolate. He looked like a bloated rat. Bohumil went back for him.

"Did you have to stuff it all in at once?"

The boy nodded. He gagged. Bohumil led him down the stairs by the hand. As the crowd swept them aside, the boy spit bits of the Kofila into the palm of Bohumil's hand, the mix of spit and chocolate running through his fingers. Oh, look, some pink, a little bit of Perlička.

"Hold on a sec, you can't go down these stairs alone," said Bohumil, stopping the boy from stepping onto the escalator.

"We'll take the elevator, come on."

"I don't want to."

He picked up the stroller in his right hand, heavy, had to prop it against his hip. A cold stain spread across his thigh. With his left hand he held the boy, tottering a bit. Hold on tight. He felt the hot breath of the crowd on his neck as a line of people went racing past, caught up in their daily sprint to the office. The left side of the escalator is supposed to be kept clear, the left side is supposed to be clear.

Excuse me, but the left is supposed to be clear.

Go fuck yourself.

At the bottom he squeezed the boy back into the stroller.

"Choo-choo train."

"That's right, choo-choo train."

"Mine."

"Yours."

"Mine," the boy huffed.

"Yeah-yeah."

They boarded the car. An old grandmotherly type smiled at the boy. What're you smiling at, bitch?

He could feel the chill from the stain on his pants, a streak of toothpaste and chocolate remained on his hand. Oblivious, he wearily raked his hand through his hair. The chocolate dissolved, but the Perlička stuck his dark-colored hair together like marshmallow.

He sat down, put the stroller brake on. He needed to be kind. I need to be kind to the boy, Bohumil thought. Kinder. The boy sat across from him. There was chocolate on his eyebrows and his lashes. Yet again. Why do you always stick it in your eyes?

The boy paid him no attention. He sat looking curiously around the car, thrashing his legs.

"Stop kicking me."

Kick.

"Stop kicking me, please. These are clean pants." It might dry, it might wash out.

Kick.

"Are you excited to see your friends? You're going to have a nice time playing together, it'll be nice, really nice." I'm acting like an idiot again, he sighed.

The boy nodded. Kick.
"Stop kicking."
Kick.
"Stop kicking, please."
Kick.
"Seriously, please."
Two stops.
"Please."
Kick.
"Pretty please."
Two long stops.
"Please."
"Poo-poo."

Sláva reread the conclusion one more time: *They knew the wart on the hand at once for a witch's nipple; they drove the old woman, in her shift as she was, out into the snow with sticks, beating her old carcass as far as the edge of the forest, and pelted her with stones until she fell down dead. Now the child lived in her grandmother's house; she prospered.*

For several years now he had been collecting books like this, but they didn't all tell the story of the little girl with the red bonnet. At first he had simply enjoyed reading them, then he started to underline. Whatever he found on the internet, he printed out and added to his red folder. The ones that he found most suggestive he retyped into his computer. It never ceased to amaze him how much the stories differed. He was sorry to see that the hunter only rarely appeared in the earliest ones. But he forgave the authors the brutal violence, they all had plenty of that. The insatiable thirst for blood. The inexplicable, instinctive lust for chopping off limbs, devouring flesh still warm, hot and bloody, the fibers sticking between the teeth like fine threads of yarn.

He broke into a cough. Stood up from the table, opened the secretary desk, and poured himself a drink. Thoughtfully scanned the books on the shelf. Went back to the table. Reflected. The wart in this version intrigued him. He remembered the warts his mother had had. In summer she walked around barefoot in slippers, all shabby and rotting. Her knuckles were blue and distended, as old people's often are. But his attention was always drawn more to the two black warts by her toenail. On the day the pity he felt for his mother's warts and boils turned to disgust, the boy became a man.

He closely examined his hands. They were mottled with sunspots, red and chapped. Am I old? he wondered. I am. Do I smell like an old person too? He was afraid to ask. His mother did. She smelled sweet, like when you left a roasted piglet out in the sun the day after a drunken party. I don't know, thought Sláva, maybe not. I shower in cold water, with soap, every morning and evening. Shave every other day. Since she's been here, every day. I've got an iron, and a scale I never step on, for the opposite reason from most people. Turning doughy isn't my problem. What worries me is the decline, the way I'm sinking, fading away, being eaten away from inside.

As a matter of fact, Sláva's hands smell of soap and his shirt collars are clean and unfrayed. He'd bought himself a new one, green-and-brown plaid, in Hradec just last week. Although yesterday, when he put it on, the shirt searched in vain for a belly and shoulders that corresponded to its size. Disappointed, it hung down his sides, sadly flopping in time with his stride. He furiously tucked it into his pants and tightened his belt, but the tightest hole wasn't tight enough anymore.

He went out to the shed. Laid the belt down on the stump and hammered a nail through the leather. This was the third time already. The other times he had first carefully measured, then marked it with a pencil, and only then laid down the belt and drove the nail through. This was the third time already. How far would he have to roll up the belt before this thing was through? Sláva closed his eyes. Seeing her in the lake, I wanted to jump in after her. Quietly, though, unobserved, slipping in and feeling her body through the shoots of flowering water and the bubbles from the catfish rub up against the fence of my skin. And then jump right over it. There's only so much lust a person can take. How long had it been since he last felt this? The suffocating need to have her, combined with the sweet desire to do violence to her. After love, violence was the only way to still feel something. How long had it been since he felt anything?

I stood there watching the water lap at her shoulders, he recalls. Then she fully submerged herself and the lake will remain forever warm. From her body. That wet, hot body. When was the last time I wanted someone so badly as this? I've never wanted someone so badly as this.

I would like to lock her up at home, run a hot bath, and watch her bathe. But I would only watch for a while. That isn't a body for watching.

When she ran out of the lake nude, I had to pull my shirt down over my pants. She was plucked clean as a chicken, hairless as a piglet, pink and a little bit flushed. Her smooth body glistened like a fish scale in the sun, I can see the sparkles to this day. I am still there, Sláva realized. In that reflection. My wanderings ended there, I am still there in the reflection of Bledá Lake—Bledá, the Pale Lady. Sláva swallowed.

The temperatures in recent days had climbed high above thirty. The quiet of the baking-hot afternoons was disturbed only by the intermittent cracking of desiccated tree bark. The animals lazed about, dumbstruck by the heat. Painfully the birds managed to unglue their scorching beaks, peeping faintly and solely when absolutely necessary. Without moisture to deliver the scent of the moldy undergrowth, the forest no longer smelled sweet. Practically all the senses were killed, the drought was so extreme. People moved slowly, but even so, every lift of the hand, every step, made them break out in sweat. Their armpits pooled with sweat, but their foreheads were bone-dry. The sun drank up every drop. Only under their hair and in the rolls of fat on the backs of their necks did a greasy sweat condense, stained grayish black by the dirt on their skin or the collar of their shirts.

The only place Bohumil and Bohumila could breathe was at home. Along with the secrets of the dwelling's former inhabitants, the thick walls retained the chill of long, hard winters from days gone by. When Bohumil laid his hand on them, he had the impression he felt a gentle shiver. It was only an illusion, though, a trick played on the senses by the outdoor temperature running up against the heavy bricks. Even this heat was no threat to them, yet because it had lasted now for so many weeks, it was encroaching despite the additional layers of plaster to the point they could practically touch it. The bricks seemed almost to be wriggling, smirking. Their faint laughter was the dark shiver he felt tickling the palm of his hand, or his whole back, glued to the wall in an effort to cool off a bit.

They had heard it said their house was sick. But they didn't know in what way or with what. Some claimed it was only because it was built at the ravine's bottom. A bumpy road led to it, plunging down into damp burdocks and tick-infested ferns after the last cottages.

It's a sick home where the sun doesn't shine. The cottage sat so deep in the ravine it had never even heard of the sun. An old spruce tree stood blocking out the sun's rays. No one had ever attempted to chop it down. Its roots stretched too deep, beyond a depth safe for the human intrusion of pickaxes and shovels. Those centuries-old, twisted claws, sheltering clusters of earthworms, speedy centipedes, and lazy blind beetles, alongside thigh bones and human skulls, formed the home's foundations. The roots *were* the home. Those fleshy shoots were the home's vascular system, and if they had been torn out, the house would have dried up and crumbled to dust. Even if someone had mustered the courage and ruthlessly felled the tree, so deep was it positioned within the ravine that no one in the cottage would have had to shield their eyes. Perhaps only in the morning, at the fleeting blink of daybreak, when even the sun was still half-asleep and didn't rightly know itself which way it was looking, it might have boyishly licked at the rusty ledge outside the bedroom window.

But the old spruce is still there, its thick, heavy branches quietly birthing male and female cones. The pollination drop flows lazily down the cones, the pollen penetrating the ovule with cool deliberation. What's the rush? The cone haltingly unfolds its scales and the winged seeds go helicoptering off in the wind. There were new saplings growing around the cottage all the time. They would dry out or rot away. The home's current inhabitants occasionally beheaded them all at a single swoop, with a single feeble blow. So weak were the stems that even the mere push of a child's hand was enough to break them.

The home received its occupants with sleepy indifference. No one told Bohumil the house was sick. They kept it a secret from Bohumila that anyone who unpacked their duvets and chipped mugs onto the shelves here fell ill, passed away, or had to start playing the game.

His eyes were clouded with a dogged case of insomnia. For weeks now his eyelids had been painfully wide open. Occasionally he managed to sink into the soothing waves of slumber, but it offered no repose. Just feverish dreams accompanied by a twitching of the lips until his whole body was consumed by the ravenous insomnia. A sharp jerk in his right leg and he was wide awake.

Bohumil studied the cracks in the ceiling, drinking in the rhythmic breathing of his wife and son. His weariness wound a wrathful crown of thorns around his aching head, sowing contempt for the sleepers. He despised their easy escape into unconsciousness. So spineless, he thought. So limited. Opening your eyes with the coming of the light, talk about a farce. Peeling them open in the depths of the night, now that took courage. It took courage to listen to the scratching on the metal gate, the long-drawn-out howls drifting from the woods. Was it a single animal or an entire clan? Either way. Which was more dangerous, a hungry pack or a lone wolf, surviving only thanks to his cold-blooded ruthlessness?

He got up and quietly walked into the kitchen. The stone floor chilled his feet even in the summer heat. Winter here would be impossible. But increasingly he had the feeling that come winter they would be gone. They would have to go back. Their escape had been a mere escape. A condition she had been forced to accept. She'd had no choice in the matter, just nodded, packed up, and went. But neither of them had found any respite here. Their fingers trembled in isolation, pointing in opposite directions whenever they had to decide together which way to go.

Where did you disappear, my dear? Down which path, which track, in which field, which bed?

Our silent nights. I'm drowning alone in anxiety here.

He shuddered. He longed for the touches of the city. Hand over hand on a grimy handrail. Bodies in the Metro. Somewhere out there at this very moment the jingling tramway cars were breathing people in and out, unwashed armpits launching a full-force attack on lonely days without human contact and winning. Remembering the outrageously hot summer in the city was a healing salve for his torn soul here in the midst of this wasteland. No one even bumps into me, Bohumil mused. I wander the woods alone, and when I want to be hugged I curl up in the titillating embrace of a bilberry bush. The purple stains on my T-shirt serve as reminders of my afternoon assignations.

I am alone, Bohumil felt distinctly, and I am afraid that nobody loves me. And I will never convince anyone to love me again.

He stood in his boxers and T-shirt in the middle of the kitchen. He didn't want to switch on the lights, but he would have to. The haze of light from the city street was missing here. Nothing but sheer darkness, inside and out. No streetlight staring in the window, no headlights crowding into the room from passing cars. The pure essential darkness of solitude, deep and uncompromising. His temples throbbed. He didn't want to admit that at night he felt afraid here. He groped in front of himself, bumped into the table, walked another few steps, and found the kitchen sink. Everything here injures me. He switched on the light over the kitchen counter, it stabbed him in the eyes. Bohumil hung his head like a repentant little boy. He felt deeply hurt. A middle-aged rag doll tottering through life with a companion he didn't trust.

When the boy was still crawling backward at age one and a half, they both suspected something was wrong. One day she called him from the car, holding a piece of a paper from a doctor somewhere outside Prague. She was sobbing so hard she stopped breathing. There was a heavy rain. She was delirious. Screaming in a high falsetto he had never heard before and never heard again. The voice of a ruined life. He convinced her to pull over at a gas station just before Zahradní Město, called a taxi, and went to meet her. His driver was a woman, he still remembered her. She had long, curly hair, wound in a bun. The color was brilliant red, and it might have been the light from the oncoming cars, but it looked like it was on fire. Watching the flames from the back seat, he had half a mind to tell the dazzling beauty, Don't stop. He remembers to this day the odd sensation of trying to catch a whiff of her hair as he paid the bill.

That was the night his insomnia began, probably. He wasn't exactly sure. Once she finally fell asleep, the boy in her arms, he walked around the apartment, draping the wet sweaters and shirts on the radiators. All night long. Reflecting on what love can withstand.

Then came morning. Coffee, bread, butter, cheese, teeth, shirt, pants, work. The mechanics that keep even a gasping fish alive.

I know I'm feeling sorry for myself, thought Bohumil, but nobody else is going to do it for me.

It was light in the room, but the darkness outside was growing. It was unsettling. He groped around under the counter and pulled out a bottle. The corners of his mouth stretched wide. This'll do the trick. I'll drink myself to sleep. He downed the first shot in a single go, such a waste. This is good stuff, he ought to slow down. He sat on the sofa awhile, blinking into the light, sipping from the glass, then reached straight for the bottle. The transfer via the glass was causing delays. He drank, descending slowly into the depths of Bohumil Novotný's existence. Sinking down, further and further, to the bottom of a solitude that would be all he knew for the rest of his life. He sat alone in the middle of the kitchen, listening to his own lonely bleating.

"And also I'm going to build, a house," the boy said, announcing his plans in the morning. The aroma of freshly poured-over coffee filled the kitchen. Bohumila was eating a piece of bread with honey, they had a pantry full of it. So much honey!

She nodded to the boy absently, as in yes, build a house.

"And a roof, a house and a roof." The boy glued together two metal tiles.

"The crap that you drag in. Who knows what it is."

"A roof."

She topped up her coffee, sat watching him. He was happy. All this junk that upset her was part of his special kingdom. At night he collapsed into bed, knees scraped, hands scratched, not one word about where or what from. Or who? He's a regular mystery box, I can see it behind his eyes. Sometimes I spend hours calling him, then suddenly he comes racing in, burned to a crisp, red in the face, hungry but happy. Apparently. The yard was full of little houses, bits of animal skin and little sticks he dragged in from someplace or other. At first she threw it away, but why bother cleaning up here? The cottage's innards were working their way to the surface, the rusty gutters lapped at by the summer wind. As if everything were all right. Only it wasn't. There's no way something this disgusting can be all right, thought Bohumila. The whole place is infested. You can't live here. You can't even walk past without being affected, she sighed.

She stood with her mug at the window, studying the hillside across the way. Nothing left but a couple of bricks. Once upon a time, a long, long time ago, there had been a fire there, the villagers told her. By the time they reached the blaze, all they found were ruins and two bodies baked together. Of the whole house all that remained was a fire-scorched wall.

She slurped the last of her coffee. When was he going to get out of bed?

He had already gotten out of bed and was puking outside the cottage. Rather than humiliating himself by running into the bathroom, turning the water on—just taking a shower!—and quietly gagging, it was better to go outside, but the hot summer morning had prodded him in the stomach sooner than he expected. He leaned against the bench he had long been meaning to give a new coat of paint and puked. Then wiped his mouth and contemplated the partially digested bits of food. It was actually morning by the time he'd eaten dinner, his stomach had barely had a chance to warm the houska up.

He hears the clatter of dishes from the kitchen, the sounds of breakfast, a new day, two well-rested people fortifying themselves with coffee, bread, eggs. Fortifying, thinks Bohumil. I am exhaustion, I am the weary, limping, sleepless night. I want eggs, butter, bread, sugar. I need coffee bad. He glanced toward the meadow. He despised the morning's energetic sounds. Nature was roaring at full tilt, his head was splitting in two. Summer was reaching its climax, the whole countryside shrieking and buzzing in preparation for winter. Pollinating, copulating, mating in every direction, eggs and spawn deposited all over the place. He glanced at the sky overhead. Another sunny day. An aggressively blue morning. The ubiquitousness of the rutting was nauseating. He stood, bent over double, walloped by stomach cramps and fatigue, alone, next to his vomit.

I'll duck inside for the bucket and a washcloth, so I don't get any bullshit, Bohumil thought. Or looks, even worse. Meaningful looks.

He ran some water into the bucket, tossed in a cloth. Then went back for a broom. He sure isn't going to use his hands. He came out of the house and stopped in his tracks. A tabby cat stood crouched over the chunks of his morning supper, greedily inhaling them. It arched its back spotting him, but hunger is stronger than fear. It squatted back down and continued to snarf up the bits of soggy bread, eagerly licking the gastric juices from the cracks between the rocks.

Putting the bucket on the ground and leaning the broom against the wall, Bohumil stood watching quietly, a faint grin on his face. The thing was going to get plastered.

"What no good are you up to?" said Bohumila, stepping outside from behind him.

"Oh, nothing." He pointed. "Just feeding a cat."

"Are you planning to wash the floor for her before she eats?" she said, lifting her chin toward the bucket.

"No, just want to make sure she doesn't catch something, you know?"

"Funny, very funny." I know I should probably be nice, but how are you supposed to be nice to that, Bohumila thought.

Bohumil barely heard her. To him she was a distant creature in the mist, opening and closing her mouth, hand cocked on her hip like it was her final gesture. He followed her into the kitchen, nodding to the boy who paid him no attention, and poured some milk into a dish. So the cat would have something to wash it down with.

I don't want to be so sad all the time, Bohumil thought. I need something pure white. Someone is eating my life turned inside out before my eyes.

"Excuse me, but since when do you feed hungry animals?" She followed him back out in front of the house again.

Since they started breakfasting on my vomit. He kept the thought to himself.

"I'm just going to give the cat some milk, nothing wrong with that, is there?"

"You can do whatever you want, but when all the cats in the village come creeping around here looking for milk, you're on your own."

"On my own is fine by me." He walked out the door.

He glanced down at the rocks in front of the cottage. Not a trace left, just a blue spot fading away in the rising heat before his eyes. The cat lay a short way away, licking itself clean paw by paw, purring the whole time. He set the dish of milk down on the ground. The cat lifted its head, took a peek, sniffed, but didn't move.

You're just overfed. You aren't a cat, you're a pig. I'm going to call you Pig.

"Aaw, she's beautiful," the boy shouted from behind him, and rushed toward the cat.

She bolted for the fence, paused there, bristled and hissed.

"Is she ours, Daddy?"

"Sure, now that's our cat."

"Ooh, can I pet her when she stops growling?" The boy squealed in delight.

"Cats don't growl."

"What do they do?"

"This one snorts, because she's a Pig."

"Are you crazy?" said Bohumila from behind him. "Do you have any idea how long it's going to take me to explain that?" You and your stupid jokes, she thought. Only they aren't even jokes. You think you're funny, but you're just embarrassing. You're so embarrassing it hurts, it actually physically causes me pain.

"Explain what, Daddy?"

"Later, son. Later. And pick up these sticks, so Mommy doesn't get angry." He gave the sticks a kick.

"They aren't mine," said the boy.

Once upon a time there was a village girl, the prettiest you can imagine. Her mother adored her. Her grandmother adored her even more and made a little red hood for her. The hood suited the child so much that everywhere she went she was known by the name Little Red Riding Hood. One day, her mother baked some cakes and said to her: "I want you to go and see how your grandmother is faring, for I've heard that she is ill. Take her some cakes and this little pot of butter."

He paused. This part was too long and the story had no spring to it. Who cared about some silly pot of melted butter? He picked up copying from the scene with the wolf.

The wolf ran as fast as he could on the shorter path, and the little girl continued on her way along the longer path. She had a good time gathering nuts, chasing butterflies, and picking bunches of flowers that she found. [. . .] The wolf pulled the bolt, and the door opened wide. He threw himself on the good woman and devoured her in no time, for he had eaten nothing in the last three days. Then he closed the door and lay down on Grandmother's bed, waiting for Little Red Riding Hood, who, before long, came knocking at the door: Rat-a-tat-tat. [. . .] Upon saying these words, the wicked wolf threw himself on Little Red Riding Hood and gobbled her up.

<u>Moral</u>

*From this story one learns that children,
Especially young girls,
Pretty, well-bred, and genteel,
Are wrong to listen to just anyone,
And it's not at all strange,
If a wolf ends up eating them.
I say a wolf, but not all wolves
Are exactly the same.
Some are perfectly charming,
Not loud, brutal, or angry,
But tame, pleasant, and gentle,*

*Following young ladies
Right into their homes, into their chambers,
But watch out if you haven't learned that tame wolves
Are the most dangerous of all.*

Bohumila came home to find the boy seated on the doorstep, holding a pair of scissors. He was cutting up something, some brochures or pamphlets, and gluing them into a notebook. From the paper's uneven edges she could tell his hands were shaking. At least he was using them. She tended to smile at him a smidge more than you would at a healthy child. She thought often about where he would end up. An institution? Supportive housing? Maybe he'll turn out just fine. She watched him awhile. Hey, how's it goin? How's things? And his New Year's card: *Hi hapy birtday wisshing you al the besst helth hapines love piece end good chear.*

What do you know of the world, my dear lost love, thought Bohumila. You came out of my body cracked and bruised. He'll turn out just fine, I know. Muddied blood of my blood, a man who'll never find out who I am. I speak to him in our made-up language, whistling loud and clear at the agreed-upon frequencies. My dear little boy, you have no idea who I am, but do I know who you are? Maybe you were sent down to earth to watch over the eggs laid by creatures from another planet. Pick a nest and hide it carefully. Keep it warm. No one would ever suspect you, a little broken toy, a wounded bird, a sick cat, a limping veteran who had his leg blown off when he made the mistake of lighting up a smoke. Deficiency, imperfection, towering negativity, the opposite of a miracle. A system error that destroys the system.

The boy smeared glue on a page from one of the pamphlets and stuck it in the notebook. He liked the colors, and he'd tried to read it too. He read slow and not that well. Sounding out the fairy tale. The one about the wolf.

Absorbed in his work, when he saw his mom, all he did was nod. She didn't ask what he was cutting out. Watching her son, she felt overwhelmed with love. Out of that whole entire day, out of that whole entire story, that was the only thing that made sense. She quietly sat down next to him and took a sniff. Just let me stay here in this salty, sweat-drenched child's body smell.

"What do you want?" he squawked. He didn't like it when she looked at him that way.

Usually what came next was her trying to give him a hug and a wet kiss on the cheek. Here it comes. She snuggled up to him, stroking his hair, then fluffing it up. It was light brown and wavy, like his dad's. She ought to trim it.

She pressed her lips to his head:

"So which one're you?"

"The beloved," he replied as he had been taught, without even lifting his head.

Pepa sat in the pub across from Sláva, drinking a beer and watching TV. Jarda had put on a tennis match. Women's, though, Pepa huffed. It was too slow, it had no zing, and all the players were black women, who frightened him. Not that he would ever admit it to anyone. They were bigger than he was, maybe not in height but they definitely weighed more. And those nostrils! So big they could hide a scout troop in a storm. On the other hand he liked their pink palms. And the pink tongues! They stuck them out whenever they were trying to concentrate. Just like monkeys, Pepa thought. Really big monkeys. With really big asses.

He took a swig of beer, went on watching the match. Smoking.

He turned to Sláva. When were they going to go through with it? he wanted to ask, but he kept his mouth shut. He was enjoying it. There was something almost tender about the whole thing, he would have said if he had known how to use the word *tender* in a sentence. It was great. He ran a hand over his face, time I had a shave. Tipped his head to his armpit. I stink. Son of a bitch summer. Raked a hand through his hair. He was going gray. And his hair was thinning too, but he didn't say that to himself. All he had left on his forehead now, instead of the bangs he used to have, were two thin wisps. Gone were the days when they billowed in waves, now the sweat streaming down had stretched them out like two grass snakes, still barely alive but too beaten down to smack their tail, flick their tongue, hiss, and lick the bald spot at the back of his head.

He enjoyed working with Sláva. Apart from that, there was nothing else but the cowshed, beers, a shot, and staggering home to bed. And now that they had a TV here in the pub, why go home? Sure, it cost something, but who was he saving up for, Pepa thought, blowing his nose.

He glanced again at Sláva, sitting quietly over his beer, staring up at the black women, the green ball, the white skirts. Pepa really liked him, he felt sorry for him, wasting away like a shot rabbit over the past few weeks. Better not to burden him with doubts. He was just curious what it was going to look like. I mean, have you seen the chick? She must be forty. Thin as a goat. Still, her hair was nice, brown, like a young mare. One time, when she didn't notice, he'd managed to get a good look at her eyes. Dark, with long lashes, like that calf he'd birthed a few weeks back. How could a chick over forty have such pretty eyes?

He finished his cigarette, stubbed it out, and smiled. Her bike seat was still damp when she stopped in at the pub. She came straight from the lake, her hair almost dry by then, but the ponytail had left an uneven wet spot on her T-shirt, from the bumpy roads tossing her around on the bike. She walked into the pub a few minutes before him, wet and docile. So docile it made him hungry.

He bent down under the table and pulled a jar of utopenci out of a plastic bag. As the heavy glass thudded against the table, Sláva gave him a look.

He didn't say a word.

"Bubble had a sale, so I bought two," Pepa explained. "They expired day before yesterday, but they're pickled, they won't go bad."

He banged the jar lid to break the seal.

Jarda watched from the counter. He won't open it, he won't. He can't just open his own food right here in the pub, Jarda fumed.

The smell of vinegar and onions wafted from the table.

He actually opened it!

Sláva screwed up his eyes. The onion with the vinegar was harsh as hell. If I narrow my eyes, I don't see Bohumila, I don't see the lake. I see sausages with white specks of fat. A ring of onion, a bay leaf, a carrot stick.

"So you're seriously going to eat that in here?" Jarda stood over the table. He couldn't stand watching it play out from behind the counter.

"What's your problem, Jarda?" Pepa held the bitten sausage in his hand, having nowhere to put it down. Some bread with it would be nice. Can you bring me a piece of bread, Jarda? But he didn't ask out loud.

"If you want a sausage, just order one, why don't you?"

"You get em from Bubble too, don't you? What's the big deal?"

"My buddy drives em in from Makro, jackass."

It really would be better with bread. He knew they couldn't be bad yet, even if they were expired, but they were a bit on the sweet side. He swallowed hard on the aftertaste, the brine lingered a bit too long. His tongue felt like fur and he'd taken only two bites. I need to wash it down with something, gargle. He reached for his glass with his other hand, but he'd already drained it. Can you bring me another, Jarda? But he didn't ask out loud.

"You clear that off the table or I don't know what I'll do." Jarda snapped the table with his dishcloth, since he couldn't whip a man. Sláva sat quietly on the other side of the table, breathing in the stinging pepper. His nostrils filled with pellets of allspice. If he sneezed, they would look like mouse turds in his handkerchief.

Jarda got his sausages and onion from Bubble too. She usually brought him one load, through the storage room out back, but yesterday he'd bought three loads from her. Fifty jars! He opened them up, poured them out into plastic tubs, wrapped them in cling wrap, and lined them up in two rows in the big fridge in the corner. No consume-by date, price, manufacturer. Time for the annual ball, time for salty and pickled.

Bubble just awkwardly stood there after he had paid. She probably wanted to make out. Jarda felt sorry for her. But he knew feeling sorry means you only do things that people can see, that look good and don't cost much. Plus I treat her nice, he told himself. I wait till she leaves to air the place out, so she doesn't see.

Bohumila pushed her bike to the top of the ravine. Climbed on and rode to the village square. Passing Maruška, she thought she heard it again. The whisper. "Run away." Soft but clear: "Run away." She braked a little but stayed on the bike. Looking around her, it all seemed like some weird game. Were they strange, or were they just local?

She pedaled through the empty village. How could they not have even a church? Just a little church, or a chapel at least?

Maruška sits out on a plastic chair in front of the apartment building, drinking an herbal infusion. A sour odor wafts from her mouth, her whole apartment is steeped in it. One day, as she was lugging her groceries home, Bohumila offered to help. The old woman just nodded, handed her a bag, and plodded up the stairs to the third floor. Bohumila got an up-close look at the rotting grooves in the old woman's heels, the blue veins on her calves. Maruška's pulse slowed to the point it almost disappeared. Eventually there wouldn't be a drizzle left in her body. Soon the rain would stop entirely and the old woman would fall quiet to death. That was how it had to happen, Bohumila knew. That's how it happens when it comes.

They sat down at the table and Maruška started talking.

Her stories jumped all over the place. Glimmers of tucked-away memory, roses from the county fair, sugarplums. But who to tell it all to? She stared off into space, somewhere past Bohumila. Maruška had been lucky enough to find her Josef, big, broad shoulders, soft heart. Melted like butter when their Janek died, only a few months old, poor thing. And the time she smuggled a goose on her bike, this was during the war, child, Maruška said. She stuffed its neck but not to the point that it would perish. If a person was lucky, a goose might have six, even eight kilos of fat. Antonín didn't survive his first year either, gave him a beautiful little white coffin, she'd been saving up for it ever since the first spots broke out on his face. Růženka was born dead. The old woman knit her story like a scarf in winter. Would she live to see the end?

As they sat facing each other, Maruška fell silent.

The apartment shrank, you couldn't breathe, the walls were weighed down with old photographs of people and animals. Who takes pictures of wild animals? Bohumila thought. That necklace over there on the chest, that old blanket chest, were those pearls? Their shape was oddly irregular.

They sat facing each other, neither woman saying a word. The air in here hadn't moved in weeks, Bohumila's back was wet, she was starting to suffocate. Her head was in a whirl. It was that tea—after the second gulp, the flaking walls revealed their secrets. She was on the verge of fainting. It was those rotten cookies—that white layer on top wasn't frosting, it was mold.

But only here, only now could she too tell her story. Finally spill her guts. If you really want to know, why not, Bohumila thought. You're the only one I can tell, since your head is completely mired in a jumble of scenes from the past. You won't remember a thing, and even if you did, no one would believe you. I won't tell anyone but you the way it really was. The truth about me and him. And on top of that I'll throw in what I do every night when Bohumil sneaks into the kitchen for a drink. He thinks we're all asleep, but I know how to breathe so it sounds like I'm asleep. I won't tell anyone but you. My family limps on both legs and drools with a terrible cold affliction that freezes every joy, every laugh. I'll tell you my whole story right here and now. There isn't a writer or filmmaker alive who wouldn't pounce on it, it's got love, betrayal, sex, and long-drawn-out howls coming from the forest at night.

Maruška, you shriveled little apple, left in the grass forgotten during the harvest, worm-eaten, mold-infested. Covered in scabs, bitterly freckled. Shining through from underneath your paper-thin skin is the blue-gray flesh of an old person.

It's like you're dying before my eyes, old woman, Bohumila thought, turning to her as she walked out the door.

Her breathing and pedaling were more relaxed. She reflected on her life in the ravine. Our house remains silent. Our life in the house at the bottom of the ravine is quiet but unsettled, Bohumila thought. Sometimes I want to say something so badly. I bite down on my glass, the words dripping into my drink. But instead I just toss it back and go to sleep.

Run away. Did she whisper those words behind my back or not? Riding through the gravel, the bike frame creaked, pebbles sprayed, cracking, out from under the tires. Bohumila shook her head.

She continued along the dusty road until she reached the meadow in back, behind the beet field. The chain had fallen off again, she had grease all over her. That morning she had tried to tempt the boy to go swimming. He said no. Took two pieces of bread and headed up to the meadow. What did he do out there all day? She had no idea, and when she asked he wouldn't say.

She pedaled through the field. The ground squirrels stiffened, caught in the act of stealing grain. Their cheeks were crammed so full that a grain fell out with every hop. It was nearing noon and the sun was beating down again. Bohumila had a bathing suit on beneath her T-shirt, towel thrown over her shoulder. Her hand under the bandage itched. She'd put a plastic protector on and wrapped the edges around with tape. Still it would get wet, though, and at night it would swell and hurt.

The road to the pond was well-worn but narrow and covered with rocks. As the bike jolted up and down, Bohumila reflected. Podlesí. The signs of petty lies she sensed in every other sentence. The constant inquiring, nodding, shrugging. Where were those two she'd met in the pub? The two guys from Prague? No one had seen them in weeks. In response to her questions, they just shrugged. Not a word.

She reached the shore, hopped off the bike, sat down on the sandy grass. Watched the dragonflies hover over the surface, the fish catching them from the water. Lay on her back awhile, squinting into the sky. Her shoulders were red from the sun. She took off her T-shirt, then her swimsuit top as well. She couldn't stand having untanned stripes on her body all the way into fall. She looked around. Part of the pond extended up into the bushes and stunted trees, but she seemed to be alone. She removed the lower part of her swimsuit and laid it on a big flat rock. A whistle, she heard it distinctly, but she must have been imagining things. There couldn't be anyone whistling from under the rock.

Bohumila basked in the sun like a water snake. She'd noticed a snake a while ago, swimming only a short way from shore, strangely enough she wasn't afraid. It rippled through the ripples, paying her no attention. A few Aesculapian snakes lived in the trees around the pond. They thrived here. Their bodies were firm and slender and they had special angled scales on their bellies that helped them climb trees. They lived on birds, mostly their young.

The heat was too much for her. She stepped into the water like it was a dress, wrapping tightly around her, silky cool with lace ripples. She slipped beneath the surface, holding her breath. As she felt around for the bottom, she buried her foot in slimy mud, got startled, and let out her breath. She didn't panic, though, instead pushing up against the water with her arms so she could stay down in the dark. Her eyes were wide open, but the pond was murky, she couldn't see a thing. She spread her hands wide and closed her eyes. She couldn't breathe, her lungs were crying out for air. A little while longer, Bohumila told herself. A little while longer.

She could feel the eggs laid in the furrows of her skin. She sat down on the rock and scraped the mud off her toes with a stick. In the distance she saw the village. She could feel the chill from here. It was dangerous. Not even disguised as tomatoes and a shiny greenhouse full of basil still in mid-December, it was visible in the locals' drink-soaked eyes, the rancid pond she had emerged from, the muck stuck under her toenails. A dangerous evil. But how to name an evil I'm not familiar with? Bohumila wondered.

Bohumil had a dream that it was pouring outside. The parched, dry-cracked field thirstily lapped it up. He lay on his back with his mouth open wide, dreaming about running out of the house to soak up the water until he was so heavy he sank to his knees. He needed the weight to fend off the constant shaking and quiet moans. But if he had gotten up in the middle of the night and walked out in front of the cottage to get a gulp of rain, he wouldn't have been able to go on pretending nothing was wrong, everything was fine, he hadn't lost his mind.

He opened his eyes. Sighed in disappointment. Even at night the heat crackled outside. No rain. Nocturnal animals were all that he could hear. He remained lying down, staring up at the ceiling, imagining what it would be like to splash naked around the meadow in the sweet flag and ribwort. Alone in the meadow, at night, naked in the rain, *wahooo*, he would have shouted had he not been surrounded by sleepers. *Wahooo.*

When he woke in the morning, all he had left to show for it was a feeling of regret. A wet dream but not a trace of water. Nothing but withered blades of grass around the cottage, the oak trunks sticky with heat. Just a few drops of dew, barely enough to water a hedgehog. The morning sun had already greedily slurped it up. Never before had he seen such an insatiable sun. He had a feeling that one of these red-hot days it was going to swallow up the cottage and the family with it.

I ate your mom, I ate your dad, and now I'm eating you.

But some water still remained. In front of the cottage stood a small willow with a fishpond beside it, a romantic little pool, as the classified ad said. Except the water under the tree was spoiled and never dried out. Why? What creature reigned over its roots but didn't drink? He thought at most the pool might be hiding a little disabled water sprite, which no one would have tolerated in a pond of adequate depth and size. So instead it was resigned to the puddle in front of the cottage. Looking after the oily water, the muck, the flies, rotten crickets.

Yesterday he had found a footprint by the puddle. He missed it at first, on his way to the pub, but then doubled back and stood staring down at it for a while. As he looked at the footprint, he thought about the wolf. He'd heard them talk. They may not have said the word directly, but it sure looked like they were talking about a wolf. Their eyes went gray and their heads shrank down between their shoulders. He already knew there was a wolf living here. It lay whimpering in a small rusty cage somewhere, claws gnawed to the bone, trying to dig itself out of its prison. One of its hind paws had grown through part of the cage. The poor thing couldn't move. A depressed animal locked in a cage so low it had to bow its back even when it stood. He threw it some scraps every now and then, when they grilled out on the propane-butane stove in front of the cottage. But no one dared get near the cage. That strange gathering of theirs in the Sokol hall may have looked like an amateur theater club, but he knew they had a wolf here. An actual wolf.

He wasn't sure why it occurred to him now but he hadn't seen Michael and Josef for weeks. Their cottage was empty. He politely knocked whenever he walked by, politely hoping to try a cup of that good coffee.

He stood over the footprint, unwinding his ball of thoughts.

The wolf was not in a cage. It lived in the woods. It came out to the meadow at night. From the meadow to their cottage was no more than a few steps. And there was always something barking outside their cottage at night. When he told them down at the pub, nobody believed him. They just looked at each other and jeered: What, are you crazy? No way. In Podlesí? A wolf?

So he decided to bring them the footprint.

But how to make a cast? He went back into the cottage for his tablet. The Wi-Fi was working for once. He typed into the search bar *how to cast a footprint*, then added a question mark. He skipped the first suggested link, for a YouTube video: Vagabonders. Pimply little brats. He clicked: *Wondering how to cast footprints?*

I am.

All right then, let's begin. To make sure everything comes out the way it should, you'll need plaster of paris, a bowl and some water, something to mix the plaster with—say, a spatula or a stick—and if you want a cast for connoisseurs, so to speak, a piece of cardboard to make a barrier around it.

No, not for connoisseurs.

First, find the footprint you want and sprinkle it with a touch of plaster. You don't need much, just enough so you won't have any problem lifting the cast out when it's done.

All set.

Then take your bowl and pour some plaster into it. Add a little water. But careful, not too much, or you'll ruin it!

I'll be careful.

Then give the mixture a good stir. You want to end up with a consistency that's not too thin but also not too dense either. Kind of like mashed potatoes.

I'm hungry.

Once you've got everything ready, pour the plaster into the footprint. Wait awhile for the plaster to harden. It takes about fifteen minutes. But be careful. The plaster underneath dries more slowly, so it's better to wait than ruin the whole thing just when you're almost doen.

Proofreader!

There, the cast is out. Now just clean it off. The best way is with a brush, but you can use a stick if you have to. As soon as you think the plaster is hard, lift the cast out of the ground. Again, you can also use a stick, or a spatula, just be careful.

Pff.

No one at the pub wants to hear a word about it. And the cast came out so well! Four toes with a fifth in back. A thumb. Not a thumb. A pad? Ah!

"Look, this animal is walking around my cottage at night," he said, pointing to the footprint. "So I'd be curious to know if it's yours, or whether it's some wild animal from the forest that ought to be shot." Bohumil slammed his half liter down on the table more forcefully than usual to emphasize he was serious. It startled even him. Everyone at the table snapped to attention. He could smell the odor of hunters on them, they were hot on the trail. His trail.

A shot landed next to his glass of beer.

"It isn't that simple," Sláva said. "You can't just walk into the forest and start shooting, you need permission for that."

"All right, fine, no shooting, but how about at least finding out what it is? I don't know anything when it comes to animals."

"Allergic, are you?" Pepa gurgled into his beer.

Bohumil ignored him. He actually was allergic to animal fur. But if they had a dangerous animal living here that was out of control, he needed to know. The second he found that out, they were packing up and heading home. He said so out loud. No one reacted.

"Are you guys listening to me?" Bohumil insistently returned to the footprint. "This looks like a big paw, don't you think?" He showed the plaster cast to everyone one more time. A bit of white dust crumbled onto the table. Sláva rolled it around in his hand, lost in thought.

"Wolves are protected," he said, sweeping the crumbs of plaster off the table like caraway seeds from a crust of bread.

"So in your opinion is it a wolf?" Bohumil laid the footprint down in the middle of the table again. He wasn't about to give up.

"Yes, in my opinion it's a wolf," Sláva said in a near whisper. He felt incredibly tired. They couldn't leave. They wouldn't.

Pepa squirmed in his chair. "It is pretty big," he said, nodding to the cast. "But maybe something fell in the mud, maybe it isn't a footprint, just a branch or a nest that looks like one."

Sláva raised his head. Pepa cowered down.

"Christ, what kind of nest?" Bohumil shook his head in disbelief. "You want me to take this thing to an ornithologist?" Now he was mad. "This is obviously from some big animal, and it's been roaming around my cottage for weeks."

Milan whispered to Pepa: "An ornithologist is an expert in birds."

The chair went flying. Pepa grabbed him by the shirt. The cast shattered against the edge of the table and broke into two almost equal-sized pieces. By the time it landed on the floor, there was nothing left of it but a few lumps of plaster. If someone had walked into the pub right now, they would have thought it was a children's playground or a school.

They sat back down in their chairs. Pepa brought his racing breath under control. Sláva gave him a look. Then shook his head.

If you were smart, you would be sad right now, thought Sláva, looking at Bohumil.

"And not only my cottage." Bohumil was relentless. "The other day I went by the farm to see Michael, and something there seemed off."

"What Michal is that?" Pepa laughed.

The others around the table smirked. What Michal, ha ha ha!

Sláva stayed out of the rest of the debate. He sat over his small beer, watching Bohumil and thinking about Bohumila. The way she went under the water. He kept seeing the image again and again like it was on a loop—the body already wet, the hair hesitating a moment, clinging to the surface like a reluctant octopus's tentacles before being pulled down by the body's momentum into the green depths of Bledá Lake. Then swimming back to shore. Then stepping onto shore.

Then she stepped onto shore, Sláva thought.

For days now he had been thinking about that hair. Her wet face, her wet body. Was it still desire, or was it more like love now? Did he have to distinguish between them? He felt so good being in those images of the young girl and the old man, who she wants too, since how could she possibly not want him. She was naked after all. Nude!

He was alone. He had a pension, gray hair, and old eyes pulling him toward her.

He studied Bohumil. Guy would not shut his mouth. Talking his head off, can't hold his drink. Sláva felt revulsion, an intense hatred for him. For the fact that she was his, that he fell asleep next to her, could sniff her hair whenever he wanted. He studied Bohumil's fingers, fingers that could touch her up and down. Studied his mouth and tongue that could lick her inside and out. And meanwhile all this numbskull was doing with it was rattling on about a wolf, a dog, and a swollen paw.

"I'm goin to take a leak," said Pepa, getting up.

"So will you do something or not?" said Bohumil, waiting for a verdict.

"Sure, I'll write to our fellow hunting associations that we might have a wild animal roaming freely about the residential areas here. We'll take care of it, for sure," said Sláva.

He could tell him any bullshit he wanted. Dumbass from Prague. Fellow hunting associations, yeah right. The Podlesí Hunting Association is me. I'm also registered for a secondary business in the sale of fermented spirits, consumer spirits, and other alcoholic beverages, so we can have our ball every year and get a grant for it. And our top decision-making body is the member's meeting, which you were at, you nitwit. A person has to make do with what little he's got around here, but I enjoy it. Keeping the folklore going. Only everything is different now, since you showed up with her. You come in here waving around some grit off a trilobite, like you figured something out, thought Sláva, smiling. But you didn't figure out squat. You don't understand a damn thing. And in fact they already told you that, they didn't just hint at it, they came right out and said so. But meanwhile you're goin around casting footprints and don't even recognize the danger. You're too stupid to be afraid. Even a little bunny rabbit that hasn't been out of the den more than a couple of days, mother's milk still drying on its nostrils, squeals when it sees me.

"The main thing I care about," said Bohumil, attempting to take a conciliatory tone, "is whether some danger is threatening us."

Sláva was quiet a long time. Then he grinned and said slowly: "There's no danger threatening us."

A few days later, out in the woods, Bohumil would recall this conversation. And even have a little laugh at his foolish trust.

Sláva followed Pepa into the men's room. Pepa leaned his head against the wall as he urinated.

"Which moron?"

"Sláva, it was just a joke. We thought it would be funny."

"Who we?"

"Okay, me."

"So you're the moron."

"Well, I . . ." Pepa said haltingly.

"That wasn't a question!" Sláva lowered his voice. "Didn't I tell you all not to do anything?" His heart pounded in his chest. The unventilated room, filled with the odor of urine and cigarette smoke, was making him dizzy.

"Is it so hard not to do anything?"

"No, it's not hard." Pepa shook himself off and zipped up his fly. "So when's it gonna be?" He was horny as a bitch in heat. "He said they were leavin. Matter of fact, he talks about it all the time. They both do."

Sláva gave no reply.

"When?"

Sláva turned to leave. He wanted to be alone. He wanted to think about the lake.

"After the ball."

"Mommy, does it hurt?" he asked. He eyed her hand.
Around the house she usually just wore a T-shirt. But more often her swimsuit bra. Every once in a while, she went out in front of the cottage and splashed a tub of cold water on herself. It sizzled on her skin. Is it possible to die of heat? Bohumila asked herself. Here in Podlesí, anything is possible, she answered herself.

"It's nothing," she said.

He stared at her arm, she followed his gaze. The hand! It twitched. It was a hand cut off at the wrist, a hand hardened by work, covered in aging spots. On the middle finger was a wedding ring, on the index finger a wart.

"Does it hurt?"

Everything on me hurts, son. I could melt in pain here on the spot. But you don't see my pain, just this rotting claw. The hand had started to fester, bleeding through the bandage, which was now loosened almost all the way up to her elbow. The wound had opened up. How was that possible? Like it had never been stitched shut. The edges had turned away from each other like two children after a playground argument. I'll never be friends with you again, ever! She walked back into the cottage and looked for the first-aid kit. But all she could get her hands on was a couple of bandages. Anti-itch drops, anti-itch gel, anti-itch powder. At least she was able to rebandage the wound, the touch of the gauze on the fresh flesh made her exhale sharply. *Tss, tss, tss.* She broke out in a sweat. It's nothing, she reassured herself. If the wound was infected, she'd go to the hospital, get some antibiotics or an injection. The hand had a bit of a sweetish smell, how had she not noticed that? Unable to resist, she loosened the bandage again and examined the wound by the window. The red edges were coated on the inside with a greenish crust, like fresh corn sprouts. It stank. So bad it made her cry. The hand wasn't hers anymore, even her limbs refused to obey her here in this house. She smeared the edges of the wound with Fenistil. Once it falls off, she said to herself, once the beetles, large and small, sink their jaws into it, once the ticks attach themselves, once the ants lay eggs in it, then it'll stop itching.

Now dressed, she went back out to check on the boy. Skirt and long-sleeved T-shirt. A little bit of black pencil liner. The line was shaky, she didn't know how to apply makeup with her left hand and she couldn't even lift her right. How was she going to tap the beer? She had a packet of Brufen in her handbag. She swallowed two, then took out a third. Pink happiness. Happiness, after all, is when it doesn't hurt.

She and the boy ate their supper in silence. Bohumil had been helping out with the ball all afternoon, delivering food, raffle prizes, and, toward evening, visitors from Hradec. Would he eat in the pub or not? She had no idea.

It had been several days since the last time they spoke. Yes, they were together, they still ate breakfast together, but one day he would go help at the cowshed, the next he would be down at the pub, then another he would be off somewhere digging something or other. He had a tan and at night she could see the twitching in his overexerted muscles. Bohumila spent days at a time by herself, the boy either out racing around the meadow or cutting things up in the bedroom. At midday, when the heat was too much to take, when even Bohumila couldn't cry anymore, they would sit in the dusky kitchen together, each doing their own thing and neither saying a word.

"You're a brave boy," she said, ruffling his hair. She cleared off the table, it was time for her to get going.

"There's an ice cream bar in the freezer for you, as a reward."

The boy nodded.

She poured him another glass of water from the sink.

"And your PJs are on the bed."

Their three beds were pushed together side by side, allowing them to move freely back and forth. With the need for intimacy gone, it was just a question of how to get some sleep.

Before she left, she put on a movie for him. Gave him a kiss on the hair. She didn't notice him sadly shut his eyes in front of the TV. When she reached the gate, she turned and looked back one more time. It would be getting dark soon.

Brave boy.

Bohumila stands behind the tap. Lukewarm foam runs down her hand. Please don't let it get under the bandage, she thinks. The wound is infected. With every contraction of her heart her hand twitches in pain. There. With every pump. Why is it foaming so much? She eyes the glass. Foam gushes, oozing from the pipe like lava from a volcano. She expects the metal to burst under the pressure at any moment, producing a drip of poorly chilled beer from the ceiling into the next day. A soft splutter is the only sound as she raises the glass to the nozzle. *Splut.* Bohumila keeps a close eye on the fill line, opting for a slight overpour, she doesn't want any hassles. The evening is just getting started and they're already crowding in, already slamming them down, already sweating. She tries to ignore the pain in her hand.

The pub is full, with still more people crowded into the hall. It seems like everyone from the surrounding villages came out tonight, the sokolovna's packed to the gills. The hired band is just getting tuned up, but an older couple is already dancing at the foot of the stage, the man's eyes glassy with drink, the woman almost asleep on his shoulder.

Bohumil is busy getting the raffle together, arranging the terry towels next to the pig's head. Bohumila works the tap, passing out beers, hand twitch and all. You're mine till midnight, for fifteen hundred, Jarda laughed. She has two scars. One runs up the underside of her forearm, where the door's glass panel slashed through a tendon. The wound runs deep. The other scar, which she got swinging her arm up as she fell, is right on top of her hand, a deep, saturated red and gaping wide open. It hurts something fierce. Ever since she was little she's gotten colloidal scars. She has a thick red line across her lower abdomen from giving birth, like someone cut her open with a dull saber. To this day it burns whenever it's about to rain.

The men are dressed in suits or at least collared shirts. They ironed out the creases in their pants. Whoever could find a tie wore it. But before too long, the sweaty hands will loosen it, the neck demanding space to breathe. Someone open the windows, you can hardly breathe in here! They doused themselves in cologne, smoked excessively. The blend of nicotine and blue men's fragrance from Bubble's shop lapped at the ceiling, doing its best to stay away from the windows. Someone needs to open those windows! It finally looks like rain outside.

She wiped her hands on her apron. What time is it? Still early. Her hand is throbbing, sweating. She needed to get some fresh air and stretch a bit at least, but no way. Not with this long, thirsty line. The summer had dried everyone out, people looked like shriveled plums, like desiccated heating chips. She's tired and wants to go home. Curl up with the boy and sniff his hair. He still smells like a baby. Maybe he'll wake up when she snuggles up to him later that night. She's dying to give him a call. Where did I put my phone? Bohumila wonders. The boy was supposed to text her, let her know he's all right. The pub was a brisk twenty minutes' walk from their cottage, but he was forbidden to come see them on his own. If he got scared, he could call and Bohumil would pick him up. Around 10:00 p.m. she grabbed her phone and pressed the number 1. The boy's photo appeared on the display and the green phone icon. It didn't ring. The signal had dropped. That happened often. With the storm approaching, it was practically a given.

Pepa hung a poster with the program for the evening on the door of the hall.

Program:
21:00 Opening ceremony
23:00 Raffle drawing

He put a flyer on every table with a breakdown of the prizes.

Prizes:
Towel and washcloth gift set
Tea set
English for 40 and over—ten free lessons
Pig head (grand prize)

He shook his head. At least the food looked good. Fourth through tenth place was all grub. Smoked meats and homemade pickles. And reigning over the table in the middle of the hall was the grand prize. He and the flies eyed it greedily. One especially persistent fly kept nipping off into the ear every minute or two, then scooting back out on its thin hairy legs, wide-eyed in shock—it would never tell a soul what it saw in that pig's head. Pepa fingered the raffle ticket in his pocket. Last year he won second prize, a five-kilo leg of pork. He ate part of it the very next day, froze the rest, and cooked up the last bits with cabbage in the spring. Sláva brought in a wild boar every now and then, but the meat was tough and took ages to cook. Who wanted to bother with that? Pepa thought. Leave it out in the barn to age, till the meat turns black inside and green around the edges, Sláva insisted. Wild game isn't chicken, freshly killed it hardens on the tongue.

"Lookin shallow there, Bohouš," Pepa hoots at Bohumil as he urinates into the sand outside the pub.

He contemplates the scantily clad village square. Dusk is falling, the sky is growing dark. His wife is tapping beer, he is officially jobless, his son is at home watching *Lord of the Rings* on repeat, either that or playing some shooting game for six-year-olds. September is drawing near. They'd arranged a school in Hradec for him but were worried the special school there wouldn't be special enough. The plan to rescue the family with the warmhearted atmosphere of the Czech countryside and deep-orange-yolked eggs was about to be terminated. They were dwelling in limbo here, their bodies mere shadows, their souls the leaking cesspit they could smell every morning from out in front of the cottage. They needed to leave, they were slowly rotting away like dead leaves here. They might still leave together, but soon this family would be nothing but a memory, Bohumil was certain of that.

He looked around the square.

"You don't even have a church here?" He'd been wanting to ask for a while.

"We need hoes, not prayers, Bohouš."

"Not even a chapel, a place to go on Sundays?"

"Jarda opens early on Sundays." Pepa smiled. "What, do you miss the crosses?"

Bohumil remained silent.

"Here." Pepa handed him a small plastic bottle. "From my brother in Slovakia."

He took a swig. Homemade, good stuff. A touch of fruit and a touch of gratitude. He took another swig, without even asking.

When they went back to the pub, he walked straight through to the hall. The heat wrapped around him like a pungent fur coat. There were a few couples dancing, some youngsters messing around in front of the stage. The band was playing, a poorly placed mike squealing feedback. He was pulled into a circle by a teenage girl. Bohumil could see that her friends were goading her on. Maybe they had a bet who could go for the most exhausted, careworn, run-down guy? It won't change a thing for me anyway if you give me a big kiss and press up so hard against me it feels like you're trying to bore right through me. And I'm feeling sad, so I'll give you a kiss. It means nothing to me.

How fast does time go by? Some minutes don't even brush against the hairs on the skin, bursting like a bubble of foam in a beer as the next rush in to take their place. Then the hour will hit like a swig of hard liquor, just two small steps and one big hop till midnight. Just hang in there a little while longer, don't be impatient like Bohumila, fidgeting as she wearily tracks the hands on the plastic clock beside the TV. And here it is. The big hand has finally caught up, after keeping its younger sister waiting. Midnight. The winner of the pig's head was a blond girl from Hradec. She accepted it with reluctance, lugging the heavy tray back to her friends. Jesus, keep away with that, that's disgusting, squealed the girls. Pepa eyed them with hatred. I'm pissed as clover, he thought.

Bohumila sighed in relief. Nodded yes to the cigarette offered her. She rarely smoked. She sucked in deeply, then exhaled the warm smoke with relish. Bohumila was drunk.

All night long she had been tapping beers, pouring shots. The tap had been howling. She smiled. She couldn't wipe the smile off her face, pinned on by the beers she'd drunk. A cracking noise came from under her hair, the sound of her stiff neck giving way. At one point she felt a warm drop of sweat running down between her buttocks. She was thawing. For several weeks now she hadn't been able to turn her head to the right without pulling up short due to a sharp pain in her neck. She stood smoking, smiling, turning her head from side to side. For a while she felt happy. Why are you filming me? she laughed. Stop filming me, she shouted at Pepa, aiming his phone at her. Oh, never mind, go ahead, it's a party. Her dress was all wet from leaning against the tap counter. She had a big damp spot on her belly running all the way down to her crotch. It felt pleasantly cooling amid the sweat-drenched pub filled with the fumes of liquor, smoke, and pickled sausages. One for ten, two for fifteen. She had pickle juice under her nails, and her fingertips were covered in wrinkles like a child whose parents had left them in the bath while they softly made love in the bedroom.

As she walked out of the pub, the rush of fresh air made her weak in the knees. She stumbled on the steps. Two shots. That was it. She took a pass on the zelená.

They drank it with milk here. She checked her phone, no texts, no calls. She hadn't seen Bohumil anywhere. He was probably already home, eyes wide open looking at another sleepless night. Either that or still making out with that girl by the toilets. Her father had a fruit and vegetable shop in Hradec and she was helping him out for the summer. She had bits of carrot between her teeth, smelled of apricots.

Bohumila leaned against the railing for a moment. She couldn't stop smiling, like someone had carved a smile in her face with one of those little fish pocketknives, and anyway where was that one they used to keep in the bathroom? She hadn't been able to find it for weeks. But that wasn't what was on her mind now. Now she had a smirk on her face, like the goose that thinks the apples in the roasting pan are to feed her, not cook her. Tomorrow she was leaving Podlesí, she smiled.

There was still a streetlamp shining on the village square, but after the bus stop she stepped into darkness. She was glad he had joined her. He'd flashed her a smile. Surely she wasn't walking alone. She was already smiling. He offered his shoulder and she leaned on it like it was the most natural thing in the world.

Are those roots slippery? They are.

He glanced at the wet stain on her dress.

A person shouldn't walk in the ravine alone at night. She laughed when he said that. There are plants that turn their leaves into stinging tentacles after dark. Before a rain, on nights like tonight, the animals wake up hungry after being asleep all day. She shook her head, nonsense. Who ever saw a wild animal eat at night?

They walk side by side, he's so tall. The wolf's song is

the sound of tortures to come, a murder song. She laughs, that's the silliest thing I ever heard! A wolf that sings?

They strode along the road to the woods. He wove his hand into hers, she gently stroked his thumb. It all seemed totally natural to her. She staggered and stumbled. He had to guide her, keeping a firm grip on her. Steering her. The roots were wet with dew, like they were coated in butter. Bohumila stumbled and staggered. Giggling. Sláva told her the story about the fox cubs he and Chrastík had flushed out a few days before. Why would he tell me a story about dead children now? Bohumila wondered.

She matched his stride, quiet and meek.

Sláva could sense how fragile she was. He held her skinny hand, afraid to squeeze too hard, since he knew she had a cut. They walked in silence side by side till they came to the small clearing, where the old pine tree stood. A few minutes from now, as the tree bark painfully digs into the crack in her lip, Bohumila will taste the sticky secretion of resin.

"Tell me something about our house. Who lived there before us?" she asked. It couldn't have been people.

"It's an ordinary house," he said. "Just old is all."

"How old would you guess?"

"I don't know exactly."

He looked at her. How tall is that little baby bird anyway?

"But seriously, for real, what do you know about it? Did something bad happen there? I get this strange feeling sometimes . . ."

"I have no idea, but it was one of the first houses in the village."

"You build your first house in a ravine? It doesn't make any sense."

"It takes all kinds . . ." Sláva sighed. "Some just don't want to be around anyone else. I think whoever lived in your house, it was always someone who wanted to be as far away from folks as they could. Hidden."

"From what?"

Sláva shook his head.

Bohumila looked him straight in the face. She demanded an answer.

"Themselves, I guess. I don't know. From whatever's out there, maybe." He was feeling older than usual today.

"Not a bad idea, is it? Holing up deep in the darkness, hiding."

This was no ordinary land here, this was no ordinary house. Life here pulsated with inanimate objects and creatures, and any human who lived here had to be tamed, naturalized, ritualized. But he didn't tell her all that.

Her fingers were clenched firmly together. She was afraid, he could see it. He grinned. He liked a woman's fear, it had the light scent of herbs.

He told her only what she wanted to hear. She settled down.

The clearing was the last place where you could park a car. There was the road, the clearing, then the ravine. And in the ravine their house. Normally they left the car by the tree, but today it was parked at the pub. Bohumil had helped all afternoon, driving over decorations for the ball. A short distance away, on the dirt road past the clearing, where they usually turned the car around, a van stood parked.

Sláva slowed his pace a bit, Bohumila came to a stop.

They were standing right near the pine tree. A part of her wanted to cry, she felt sorry for herself, unhugged for so many weeks, months. All of a sudden he sensed that she wanted him to touch her.

He was standing next to her. That water in the lake, Sláva thought, those were my hands. That water snake was my tongue.

"I'm leaving Podlesí," she said. "Tomorrow."

Sláva shook his head vehemently. She looked at him in surprise. She wasn't going anywhere. He knew she wouldn't leave. Bohumila smiled. Tomorrow morning she would remember his disapproval and not know what to think of it.

She stood looking him in the face, holding his hands. Be the wind in my eyes, hunter, she laughed. She was being playful again, covering up her anxiety. Touch me. She looked stupid and the mascara in the corner of her right eye was smudged. Sláva had no idea what she was babbling on about. The cigarette smell coming off of her was extremely unpleasant.

Bohumila rambled on, head in a whirl. None of it made sense.

Sláva, already right next to her, took another step closer. He kept a firm grip on her shoulders, so she couldn't slip off like a fawn or a partridge into the night. A sharp pain cut through his stomach, but that only spurred his excitement. He was prolonging the moment until they touched, though only as long as was bearable.

Where did you lose me, my dear? In the dark woods with the hunter.

He kissed her, deep and slow. She abandoned herself to his hairy arms, sinking into him. They were still dressed at that point, but why wait? She was open to destruction, he sensed, her body wasn't putting up the slightest resistance. It was asleep. He had no intention of waking the dreamer from her dreams, let her go on snoring under the covers, as long as she let him do what he pleased.

He turned her back to face him and leaned her against the tree. As long as she's letting me.

She wrapped her arms tightly around the trunk, her bandage snagging on the bark. It hurt.

"Go slow," she whispered, but he didn't hear.

All of a sudden he clutched her roughly against him. She yelped. The wound on her hand began to bleed, she could smell the tang of blood soaking through the bandage. Her face was pressed against the bark, pine pitch stuck to her hair. He flung her violently to the right, her lip tore and she hissed in pain. His teeth were so big. She tried to turn her head toward him. She tried to turn her head.

A bird lifted off from the tree top and quietly flew away. It had something in its beak, a piece of bark, probably.

She didn't have to clean up after him. One quick move and everything was back in place. She pushed herself away from the tree. Cold. She shuddered with the chill of the approaching storm. Her crusty lips quivered, her teeth chattered in bursts. She spat a mouthful of blood. Squatted down in the grass and took a long pee.

She needed to warm herself up. Chase the cold away with some fire, from her head down to her toes. It was still too early for sleep, for cuddling up with a child, she still wanted to drink. She headed back to the pub, as if she'd never left. How long had she been gone? A few minutes, a couple of nights? Time was no good to her anymore, it had ceased to make its mark on a body she felt was no longer hers.

She stepped into the pub and didn't look back.

Sláva remained standing by the tree in the dark. Waited for his heartbeat to quiet down. Then sat on the ground, leaned his back against the tree, and thought.

They held each other's hand on the way back to the cottage. The path was steep and they couldn't see even a step ahead. The clearing was far behind them now. Bohumila grinned as the two of them passed the pine tree. Bohumil stumbled, she let go his hand, he'll only pull me down with him, Bohumila thought. She was already edging toward her escape, the soil would turn to mud in a while. He'll only pull me down with him, she repeated to herself.

He regained his balance and searched for her hand again, so close and warm. Bohumil's teeth chattered in the chilly nighttime air. He stopped and listened. Silence. The quiet rasp of his drunken thoughts was all he could hear. I wonder where that animal went? Probably off somewhere mating. Or had it breathed its last? Would he find its bloated carcass a couple of days from now? Fur absorbs water, the body would swell in the rain.

But in my sad story the animal gets eaten by an even bigger animal, Bohumil had a hunch.

They headed down toward the ravine. He shone a

light on the path with his phone. The boy had messaged earlier, he showed Bohumila the text, sent at 11:00 p.m.: Going 2 sleep good niht. He was a brave boy, they had to give him that. They'd been told to show him trust. As the child psychologist said, treat him the age he is in his body, not in his head. Bohumil didn't agree, but he didn't want to fight anymore.

His foot slipped again. This time Bohumila didn't manage to let his hand go and got yanked to the ground. It was the closest they'd been to each other in months. As she attempted to pick herself up, she leaned against his chest. He took it as a touch. Please please touch me, please. As she rose to her feet, he grabbed her hand and pulled her back onto his chest. He gazed into her eyes but couldn't see anything in the dark. He imagined her eyes were quiet, coated over with a crust of blue ice. Let her make the effort, he thought. She owed him.

He lifted his head toward her, lips parted, but she was farther away than he realized.

"What do you think you're doing?" she spat.

"Give me a kiss."

She pulled away. Leave me alone, she said in her mind, just leave me alone. They were only a short distance from the cottage now. But he didn't want to stop. He managed to get to his feet without letting her go. He leaned her up against the gate. He didn't dare push up her skirt, but he ran his hands back and forth over her breasts.

"Be nicer to me," he begged. She'd had enough of him.

She shoved him away, he tripped. The metal bucket rolled off toward the wooden bench. They both froze, listening for the voice of their child from inside. Mommy? Nothing, just silence.

They were a short way from the front door now, the bulb over the entrance should have come on automatically.

Bohumila glanced up, expecting light any moment. But she was enveloped in darkness. The sensor definitely worked, he just hadn't changed the bulb after the last one burst, even though she'd asked him to do it a thousand times. She was substantially shorter than him, to change the bulb herself she would have had to use a chair, which wobbled perilously on the uneven stones outside. Whereas all he had to do was reach up his hand, unscrew the old bulb and screw in the new one. A few quick turns, that's it. Even in her drunken state and her feelings of utter futility, that nothing made any sense, she felt a growing wave of anger that there wasn't any light. She blamed the darkness enveloping her squarely on him. It was his fault! And on top of everything else, he had his hands glued to her body. As he tried to give her a hug, she didn't resist but instinctively crossed her arms over her breasts. She finally shooed his hands away like pesky insects, thinking: We already did this once. Bohumila felt a near-paralyzing exhaustion, her right hand, with which she had been clutching her left shoulder to keep him from groping her breasts, peeled away and dangled loosely, bumping against her right hip. He had her all tangled up in her dress, trying to pull it over her head while they were still outside, still on the doorstep, so everyone could see how beaten down, crushed, she was. Bohumila thought, he wants to belittle me, hurt me, and punish me all over again. He didn't consider the fact that the motivation for his behavior might be sheer lust, stirred up by sucking face with that girl by the toilets. His sleeve caught on the bandage, Bohumila shrieked in pain, but he didn't slow down for one second. Maybe it was this petty lack of willingness to wait and see if maybe she was in too much pain, to ask if she was all right, if maybe he had hurt her. It may well have been this silence, broken only by his heavy breathing, that acted as the signal she was waiting for. For months, long months, she had thought, you can't break me, because I know what I did, I know what I'm guilty of. I was knocked flat on my back, you know it as well as I do, yeah, I went to see him that night, and I regret that I did. But I was already broken a long time ago, you can't break me, because dammit I know what I did. From this moment on, though, it's your fault too.

"Come here," he said, his voice cracking. Bohumila ceased moving, she wanted to be an observer, nothing but an impartial witness. She almost felt like smiling, knowing he would never in his life weasel out of the blame for this moment of coercion, for these hands running all over her against her will.

He slammed her into the door hinges, this time she didn't shriek. But maybe he had no intention of hurting her. She didn't want to misjudge him, she knew it was too dark for him to know they were so close to the door. Bohumil deeply inhaled her scent, holding her, hugging her tight. Bohumila stood quietly. When he grabbed her violently by the arm, she only sank deeper into her pain. She so badly wanted the light, so badly needed to look into his eyes and tell him: I see you, I know what you're doing to me, and I know exactly why you're doing it. What looks like pure vengeance and another attempt to humiliate me is nothing but an upwelling of pain you can no longer control, thought Bohumila. Her whole life she had thought shitty things like this happened only to other people. Her whole life, up until the moment she was driving home with the boy from that first checkup, where they gave her no indication of anything, no reassurance, but simply stated where the situation stood. That was the moment when shitty things started happening to me, said Bohumila to herself. When I look at him, I feel a twinge of sympathy. It's happening to you too, after all. For months on end you tried to forget about the whole thing, filling in potholes, helping out on the cattle farm, drinking lousy beer, making an attempt to feel love and lust again. But the way you fling me into the cottage, knowingly grabbing my right hand, when you know, I know you know, how much it hurts, is just evidence of the stored-up rage and the desire to pay it all back with an even more painful blow.

Bohumila knew he thought that he was better than her. She suspected he was banking on her generosity, and it almost made her feel sorry that in the morning, when the first heavy wave of his hangover swept over him, he would have to admit how badly he had failed not to harm her, how badly he had failed to resist, like a fruit fly when it gets a whiff of rotten fruit from the kitchen.

As Bohumil steered her into the bedroom, Bohumila managed to pull herself together, trying with all her might to shove him away and quietly close the door. It was the middle of the night, the boy was asleep, they had to make sure not to wake him up. She listened a moment at the other side of the door, the boy didn't even roll over or she would have heard the bed creak.

He pulled her into the kitchen. They slammed into the counter's sharp corner along the way, only this time it was his turn. He swore in pain and backed off of her for a moment. Bohumila calmed her breathing, you can't break me, you can't, what you're about to do will only break yourself. The revulsion she felt for him mixed again with a twinge of pity as she felt how skinny he was. She could have hung herself on him like a coat on a peg. And she decided not to wipe that crumb of pity off the table, and made an attempt to bring it all to a stop while she still could.

"Wait a minute," she said softly. "Don't do it, please, I'm begging you, don't do it."

He threw her onto the unfolded couch, she bounced off the springs and landed to the side. A long pause followed. Bohumila took advantage of it to move her throbbing hand as far away from her body as she could. I can take more of any other pain except this one, she thought.

Bohumil lay unmoving for a while. She felt like he was so close she sensed, she knew, what was going on inside his head. She could hear the quiet purr of his brain. He was conscious, knew what he was doing, and knew he shouldn't be doing it.

"We'll leave, is that what you want?" Bohumil suddenly whispered.

"Yeah, I want to go home."

"Good God," said Bohumil.

Bohumila was silent.

"What is going on?" he asked, though it didn't sound like a question. "I mean how can this be, dammit, Bohu, tell me, what is actually going on? I'm so sad I can hardly breathe. I don't want it to be this way, I didn't want any of it to be this way at all." He leaned back, the springs howled in protest.

"I want to go home," she whispered.

"For fuck's sake, so do I. How can anyone live like this. Have you ever been more miserable? I doubt it, I doubt it. Oh sure, you say, the usual drunken bullshit, but I am so entirely alone. I don't have a clue what we're doing here. Every morning, and I mean every single morning, when it's stupid hot yet again, I get up and say to myself, over and over and over again, what are we actually doing here? And you know what?"

Bohumila lay on the couch, eyes open, now used to the dark, she could clearly make out the beams on the ceiling.

"I have no idea what I'm doing here. But the thing is

not only here, and this is the most terrifying part, I don't have a clue about anything anymore. Like some sorry-ass middle-age crisis or whatever. You know, there are times, and I know I'm gonna sound like a moron now, when I just stretch my arms out in front of me, like this," he said, reaching his hands forward. The sudden movement gave Bohumila a bit of a start. "And I look at them like, those are my arms, they belong to me, or what they belong to is me, I'm this big lump of warm flesh, somehow I'm alive, I'm here, but that's pretty much it, after that I have no idea. What to do with those arms I don't have a clue, get it?" And he gripped her tight in those arms and she took a deep breath in his grip. A soft whimper issued from her throat. Even if he didn't say so out loud, Bohumila knew he exaggerated her guilt. She lay slightly beside him, slightly on top of him, and had no idea what she felt or what she should be feeling now. Her head was pounding, she should get up and have a proper drink of water. Instead she kept lying there, listening as Bohumil's breathing became regular. She pulled away from him, lying on her back, feeling a bit of an urge to make fun of his glaring crisis. Darling, she wanted to whisper to him, only clear-cutting confirms the importance of the woods, only a chain saw allows a tree to breathe.

She had an urge to get up and check on the boy in the bedroom. Whisper in his ear that they were leaving. But she was too tired even to turn her head. She cast a glance at the foreign object in the corner of the bed, as if her hand was no longer hers.

Outside it was quiet. No animals snuffling around, it seemed even the cat was at the ball, stuffing its face on sausage scraps. A rat quietly ran past underneath the table. It stopped, perked up its ears, scratched at the two ticks attached to its belly. One would fall off a few moments later and remain lying limp, legs in the air. From a distance it looked like an overripe bilberry.

As the rain outside began to howl, she pulled the duvet up to her chin and fell fast asleep. A storm is a thorough eraser of footprints. In the morning there would be nothing but a whole lot of mud everywhere, no tracks, no footprints, and if any blood had spilled in the night, it would be washed with the rain into the gutter and run into the cesspit.

In the morning there was a downpour. As long heavy drops of rain pelted the metal roof, the trees rustled with pleasure, wet branches rocking in rhythm with the storm. The wind joined in, wailing through the chimney.

She awoke to the sound of water gushing from the roof gutter into the rusty tub in front of the cottage. Bohumil was still asleep, turned to the wall. She rose from bed, crumpled her panties into a ball, and threw them in the wastebasket. She needed a shower.

But there he was, waiting for her in the tub. Slut, whore, the arachnid spat, wiggling his fuzzy legs. She splashed him with a spray of water, whirling him in a circle, washing him down the drain. He struggled back, crawling out again and again. Fleeing behind the faucet, he almost managed to slip into the hole between the tiles. She didn't want to, couldn't let him get away. She reached for a towel and crushed him against the edge of the tub. She felt a soft crunch, but kept pressing down firmly, her arm quivering with the strain. Now, at last, she burst into tears.

She swathed herself in a bathrobe and wrapped her hair in a towel. In the kitchen she had to switch on the lights, a gloomy mist hovered outside, the rain falling now in a thick curtain. She put the kettle on the stove. Bohumil slumbered on. She had never seen him sleep as deeply as this. She stood over him, watching as he slept.

The aroma of coffee filled the kitchen. Toast. She started the eggs so they would be hot by the time the boy got up. He liked them scrambled with butter.

The door to the bedroom creaked, careful, she didn't want to wake him yet. She liked watching the boy as he slept. Mouth closed, breath steady, an occasional twitch of the hand.

Bohumila put a smile on her face. Prepared for the smell of a stuffy room with a child asleep inside.

Part Two

Once a little girl was told by her mother to bring some bread and milk to her grandmother. As the girl was walking through the forest, a wolf came up to her and asked where she was going.

"To grandmother's house," she replied.

"Which path are you taking, the path of the pins or the path of the needles?"

"The path of the needles."

So the wolf took the path of the pins and arrived first at the house. He killed grandmother, poured her blood into a bottle, and sliced her flesh onto a platter. Then he got into her nightclothes and waited in bed.

Knock, knock.

"Come in, my dear."

"Hello, grandmother. I've brought you some bread and milk."

"Have something yourself, my dear. There is meat and wine in the pantry."

So the little girl ate what was offered, and as she did, a

little cat said, "Slut! To eat the flesh and drink the blood of your grandmother!"

Then the wolf said, "Undress and get into bed with me."

"Where shall I put my apron?"

"Throw it on the fire; you won't need it anymore."

For each garment—bodice, skirt, petticoat, and stockings—the girl asked the same question; and each time the wolf answered, "Throw it on the fire; you won't need it anymore."

When the girl got in bed, she said, "Oh grandmother! How hairy you are!"

"It's to keep me warmer, my dear."

"Oh, grandmother! What big shoulders you have!"

"It's for better carrying firewood, my dear."

"Oh, grandmother! What long nails you have!"

"It's for scratching myself better, my dear."

"Oh, grandmother! What big teeth you have!"

"It's for eating you better, my dear."

And he ate her.

She let out a quiet croak, like a frog still underwater. Just a gurgle. Seeking the strength for a voice. For a minute or two nothing happened. She cleared her throat. Sat on the bed, lips pursed in an attempt at articulated expression. But all that came out of her mouth were the cries of a wounded animal, desperate to lose consciousness and escape the crippling pain.

She whispered a word. And again lost her voice. She gripped the boy's notebook, hands trembling. Suddenly she was no longer whispering but screaming.

"Bohu, Bohumil, Bohumiiiil," as if drawing out the syllables might create a warm cozy den where she could curl up inside, contentedly fall asleep, and wake with her child in her arms. She kept calling and calling for him to come home. She didn't want to be alone near such a cruel animal, who before he killed his victims destroyed their dignity. Why in God's name did the little girl have to be naked?

Clutching the boy's scrapbook, she rattled her fingers against it. Knees nervously shaking. He shakes the sand off when he comes into the bedroom, Bohumil thought. It spills all over the house, she grumbles about having to sweep all the time. The sharp grains on his soles bothered him too when he went to the bathroom barefoot at night.

She was screaming even though he was almost right beside her. Why is she screaming like that? wondered Bohumil. But she couldn't help it. The needles were digging under her skin. A faint prick, almost tender. At first. The needles sliding into the flesh like a pebble slipping under the calm surface of a lake, for a while it had been fine. Until now. Now a sharp, uncontrollable pain shot through her whole body.

She looked over at Bohumil, she wanted him to read it too, she knew the boy cut things out and glued them into the notebook, and so did he. She didn't want to read it alone. She handed the notebook to him. It had been two days now since the boy disappeared.

The morning after the ball, when he had been woken by her screams, he immediately knew the animal had gotten inside the house. He ran into the bedroom naked, holding a pillow against his crotch. He took a quick look around for his pants, but without his glasses on he couldn't find anything. He didn't want the boy to see him naked, and confronting the animal without any clothes on seemed somehow inappropriate. He assumed, first and foremost, and entirely realistically, that the animal was going to badly wound him. Of course he harbored some faint hope of also wounding the animal, but given the state of his body, that was hardly a given. Though he did regard himself as more pathetic than he actually was. Yes, he was skinny and his face had begun to swell up as the result of regular alcohol intake and irregular meals. But his skin had a healthy bronze tone, the sun had lightened his hair. Plus, with all his work in the ditches, his arms had firmed up and the muscles on his hands stood out when he reached across the table to pour himself a drink. He hadn't noticed the transformation. When he looked at himself in the mirror, which he did only begrudgingly and rarely, he saw nothing but the wasted body of the beast that was devouring him from inside. It changed shapes, and species, but in recent days it had settled into the form of a fox. An infected, spitting fox wandering restlessly inside of him, chafing his stomach and throat with its rust-colored fur. He always felt like he was on the verge of throwing up. He could see in the mirror that the fox was doing well, growing fat on Bohumil's bilious fear, the drippings of his desperation. If he had been able to look beyond it, he would have seen a tan, slender man with a receding hairline and gray hair, an ordinary forty-five-year-old. But he couldn't see beyond the fox.

When he had come running in to the screams of his wife on the empty bed yesterday, he knew as well as she did that the boy hadn't just gone for a walk. Out to have a run through the dew and get soaking wet before breakfast. He wasn't playing out in the meadow, wouldn't come bursting through the gate hungry, thirsty, needing to pee. Bohumil knew it had finally happened. The village boil, which for months he had been watching grow, filling up with white pus, had finally burst, swamping their lives with sticky, foul-smelling misery. The stress and itching he had been feeling all summer long suddenly stopped. He was enveloped in the pleasantly calming, healing quiet of the village that had brought them here in the first place. Looking at the empty bed, he could almost hear the locals' loud sigh of relief, mixed with the joyful banging of pots in the kitchen, the jars merrily bubbling away, it was pickling season. He stared at the bed and knew it had begun. The wolf, the meeting, the footprint, the fairy tale. He didn't know yet how, but he had a hunch it was all connected. All the pieces in Podlesí fit together, it was exquisitely thought through, orchestrated. He too felt a strange sense of relief now that his worst expectations had finally come true. A feeling that nothing worse could happen anymore, because the worst was already happening now, accompanied by a tiny smile over his small victory. I told you, I knew it the whole time—something awful is going to happen. Of course he had no way of knowing that it would be the boy, but when he thought about it later, he realized it couldn't have been otherwise. For his fear to come true, for the animal to eat its fill, it had to get the leanest prey. A small child. It was impossible to miss that the animal had gone quiet.

Eyeing the notebook in Bohumila's hand, he touched a hand to his heart. He felt it brush past. Awakening inside of him, stretching, sleepily blinking its eyes as it triggered the poison sacs behind its fangs, surely his fox must have those. Even if it was contrary to nature. He had a beast inside of him, on the border between species. Sometimes it had fins and no teeth, other times it had poison sacs and a sharp tongue—today it had fangs. The moment he picked up the notebook, the fox bit in, releasing a rancid surge of muddy complaints and snotty misery into his stomach.

Bohumil flips through the notebook. He recognizes

the writing. The loopy childish script, the abundance of missing letters. And then there are the drawings again, the doodles, the cutout figures. The pamphlets from the pub. Hybrid animals with two tails, three eyes, four horns. Pieced together, patched together, cut out, added on to. Fictitious beings, neither fish nor fowl. And mixed in with it all, the fairy tale.

"Does any of this make sense to you?" she asked. She was strangely animated. Juiced up on fear. Her cheeks, white with panic the day before, bags under her eyes, had taken on a rosy flush. The blood was freely circulating through her cheeks again.

He shook his head. He had read it and it didn't make sense. He handed the notebook back to her, he had no desire to hang on to it. What for? I want my son, not a fairy tale.

"Should I take it to the police?" she wondered aloud. "I have no idea what it means."

He nodded. Neither did he.

"I don't understand," she said. Like Bohumil she had a hunch they had become part of something malevolent. Who would print such stories? And give them out to children? Where was the boy? Was it some silly village game, modern folklore? Were they in danger?

He remained silent.

"Maybe it doesn't mean anything at all," she said. "Why does the wolf even bother with putting on a disguise when he's just going to eat the girl anyway? He could have eaten Red Riding Hood and then the grandmother. It comes out the same in the end." He paused. "Plus, where's the hunter?"

She froze, staring at him. The red in her face exploded into her forehead. He could see the welling of hatred, the intensity of it still never failed to surprise him.

"Are you an idiot?" Now she was screaming again.

"Seriously, is that all you care about now? Our child's been cutting pages out of some creepy filth, we have no idea who he got it from or what the hell it all means, and all you care about is some minor plot point?" She wanted to slug him so bad. She rose from the bed, stepped toward him. But there wasn't going to be any more hitting in their house, not anymore. Exhausted, she dropped back down on the bed and rested her head on the pillow. The fragrance of the child's body had long since dissipated. The imprint of the forehead was missing, the drool had dried without a trace. The duvet smelled stale and moldy, it had been pouring now for two days.

Bohumil sat down beside her, flipping through more of the notebook. He felt stupid, but looking at it again, it still didn't make any sense. It must be some older version, he thought, maybe French. He understood why it wound her up, she couldn't stand anything French. She considered the language to be a personal attack on her. When the boy was little, she used to parody an old nursery rhyme with a fake French accent: Ze docteur tahps on ze boo-boo, zen writes a prescreepsion, sree times daily take zis pill ahnd you will be like new. The boy would bray with glee. Don't laugh, honey, ze French docteur doesn't know how to treat even an ant. Ze Frrrench doc-teurrr, she would repeat, the boy howling with laughter. The author of the nursery rhyme was a Czech poet named Kožíšek. What did he have to do with France? Bohumil had no idea but wasn't about to ask.

"Did you see those pictures?" he asked.

"Of course, I read through the whole thing. Over and over again it's the same: a dog, a wolf, some larvas and butterflies. I couldn't even tell what it all was."

It's a mantis. But he doesn't say "It's a mantis" out

loud, instead he just thinks, it's a mantis. If he tried to correct her, it would only piss her off. If he said it wasn't a butterfly but a mantis, she would hit him. He looked over at her. She would get pissed off, hit him, then burst into tears. When had that wasps' nest of hatred taken shape inside her eyes? Did it only appear now, or had it been there all along, growing and buzzing since back in the days when he still regarded her with trust and affection as she made dinner, stacked building blocks, fed the baby? When he tickled her feet at night? When he loved her, in short, was that terrible hatred already there?

"It isn't a larva or a butterfly," he said. She gave him a look. "I mean, as far as I can tell," he hastened to add. "Of course, that's not what's important here," he reassured her, though it was kind of important to him. Precision.

She paused and thought a moment. Opened the notebook again, read through it again: "Another thing I don't get is, why pins or needles? Isn't it pretty much the same? It hurts either way, right?" They both froze when she mentioned hurt. Neither one of them looked at the other. It wasn't a coincidence, or a slip.

It hurts—she'd said it intentionally. She wanted him to oppose her, to claim it didn't hurt at all. Like soft kittens rubbing against the soles of your feet, like the caress of your mommy's hand, so say it, say it's like the caress of my hand, say it's like petting a kitten!

"We have to go look for him. Comb through every inch of the village, the meadows, the fields, and we need to find out who gave him those cutouts. What about these other ones here, have you read them too?"

"Excuse me, you think I'm gonna sit here reading fairy tales right now?"

"There might be a clue."

"For God's sake, what kind of clue?"

"I don't know, but at least it's something, or what do you suggest? Nothing?"

"So this is my fault?" She felt the urge to argue.

"That's not what I said."

"No, but you obviously think so and as a matter of fact you're saying it pretty obviously too," she said, raising her voice. "You and your stupid allegories, your stupid logic."

"Linguistics."

"You're a dork. You think it makes you a better person knowing what a dactyl is?"

"A little bit, yes."

"A little bit, yes," she said, mimicking him. "And meanwhile you're just a dork. A dactyldork. It isn't my fault what happened."

"I never said it was."

"But you think it."

"You have no idea what I think."

"I don't want to, either." She felt like she was losing. "This whole thing is exactly the opposite of what you think. You destroyed everything. It's your fault the boy disappeared, your fault and yours alone." She could feel that she herself didn't believe it. "So take your intellectual bullshit and shove it up your ass. Because you screwed it all up and now he's not here, he's just gone." Her voice broke, she burst into tears.

He was convinced the fairy tale was a clue. But to what? How did stories like this end? The boy face down in the mud. Always the face, so you know he's not breathing. And if the director was really slick, he set up the shot so the camera moved from his feet up to his eaten-away eyes, then a caterpillar came running out of his half-open mouth. How did they shoot that?

He looked at the pamphlet again. The irrationality of the stories, no moral, just terror. The little girl consumes the flesh of her own grandmother, drinks it down with her blood, and lies down naked in bed with the big hairy wolf. What to make of it? It was oozing violence. And to find it here, in the countryside. He had to admit, the fact that the brutality was so straightforward was in many ways refreshing. The blood, the raw flesh, wolf or human. Poke around in it with a pitchfork, devour it, bathe in it, whatever you want. He felt a growing need to punch someone, to feel a clump of hair, some blood, a tooth, or at least a piece of tooth in his fist. He longed to be part of those blood-soaked orgies. In such pure evil he sensed a hope that he could break free of the cycle of endless failure and quiet suffering. His small world had become even smaller here. What was the point of it all? He had gained the unique ability to observe his world but lost the ability to live in it. The impossibility of change weighed down on him with full force, the awareness that his life decisions had been exhausted. This is it now, this is my life. He kept treading over the same ground, days and gestures looping back around like the grimy rubber handrail that always lags a little behind on the Metro escalators.

This was the second day now the boy had not been home. They looked for him the same way they had the day before. Calling and calling, the light was growing dim now, soon it would be dark. She got up and went to the kitchen, we have to eat and drink after all. Another day without him. Another evening and then night. The police in Hradec had promised they'd announce an all-points bulletin today. They were supposed to stay at home, in case the boy came back. One of them was enough, but where would the other one go? For the first time in years they had no desire to leave each other.

Tomorrow they would comb the woods, the same as they had yesterday. Calling his name. Again they would go to the village and ask, the same as they had yesterday. Call the police, no, not call, go in person. Right now, though, they were pouring themselves a drink. The lamp was on in the kitchen, how could it be so dark in here?

Bohumila sat in the tattered armchair. It snapped and creaked with the slightest shift in weight. Her legs were crossed, as she often enjoyed, the folding of a familiar body around her offered at least some comfort and a slight feeling of safety. She was wrapped in a big, tattered sweater, likely unearthed from one of the wardrobes someone had left behind here. She normally never wore orange, her face looked even paler, her eyes almost invisible, sunken like the sun behind the grizzled clouds. She clutched a glass in her hand, running her fingers nervously up and down the side. Staring at the ground. Bohumil sat across from her, watching. One of the hardest parts of the sadness stirring inside him was how much this evening was just like all the rest. The child was missing, but otherwise it was exactly the same, every bit of it. How could that be? They drank in silence, neither one looking the other in the eye. He was somewhat less frightened now about what had happened. Fright is a short-term feeling. In its place a sense of hopelessness was slowly settling in, but at least he wasn't shaking so much anymore. The hysteria of the first morning, when he'd had a terrible hangover on top of everything else, was gone. The frantic forays into the woods, hollering at the top of his lungs, the scrap with Pepa after he claimed the boy'd just gone out mushrooming, the screaming at the pub, the broken bottle on the steps of

Bubble's place, all unavoidable reactions of the first day. The next day he calmed down. He didn't know about her, but he was slowly starting to feel like the most important thing was for the boy not to be hurt. The thought of his child in physical pain was unbearable. He sat across from his wife, for a single instant bereft of all hope his son was alive. The animal had been quiet this second day. It was definitely out there somewhere, safely out of the rain, eyes narrowed, breathing softly in and out. It had overeaten. A small bubble formed at its moist nostrils, bursting when it yelped in its sleep.

The lamp in the corner flickered through the empty glass clutched in Bohumil's hand. They should have been talking, having a conversation. But instead he just sat silently, wondering whether the whole thing might have been prevented. If only, years ago, it felt like centuries, he hadn't shown up for that party, if only after a few shots he hadn't said they should go for one more. Followed by an awkward series of sloppy kisses. He was struck by the pointlessness of it all. The existence of Bohumil Novotný meant as little as the dandelions in a meadow. He watched his wife, feeling nothing at all. This wasn't the time for honesty. But when the time came, he would have to admit that what he felt that evening, amid all the fear and anxiety, was also relief. God, so much relief. He had been granted a choice. The choice to walk away. To toss a match on the web they had spun together over the years. The mutual friends, the roast goose on Christmas with one family, meatloaf the next day with the other, then a visit to see his stepfather before New Year's. The grandmothers and grandfathers thankfully were no longer alive, the only other obligation was an uncle in Pelhřimov. Every year! Without the boy, he could be rid of all those interwoven threads, cut them off, torch them, tear them to shreds. He would have the chance to exist on his own again, start his story differently. Because you don't leave the mother of a disabled child, but everyone would understand if they couldn't go on as a couple without the boy. And part of his coming to terms with it, even if he didn't know it yet, was a relief that he must not, could not, and never wanted to express aloud: relief that the boy was gone.

Her voice almost startled him when she began to speak. He settled down once she began to level accusations. The sudden shifts in volume, the gesticulating, the palm of her hand pushed into the air indicating stop, these were all familiar to him. He didn't rush or crowd her, just rose from his seat to pour himself another drink. When he sat back down, he heard the same thoughts that had also occurred to him, but in reverse. It was always the other person's fault. They drank too much, kissed too much.

If you hadn't fucked around with that guy, we never would've ended up in this shithole.

He rubbed his eyes with his fingers, smarting with fatigue.

"What do you think happened?" she said, interrupting his thoughts. Her tone was cool and matter-of-fact, her exhaustion actually helping move her closer toward acceptance. He wanted that for her, the feeling was a relief.

"I don't know, I really don't." He took a long pause. "I think they did it. We underestimated them. I mean, we had a hunch there was something going on, something not quite right."

She nodded faintly. Tears spilled from her eyes, she wiped them away like an annoying stream of snot. No quivering shoulders, nothing.

"I guess."

"But what did they do?" said Bohumil.

Since his insomnia hit full on, he'd spent almost every night listening to the animal pad around outside, sniffing at a forgotten shoe, exploring the garden, circling the cesspit. Bohumil lay on his back, studying a spot on the ceiling where the plaster had dried into an irregular-shaped scar. Every night he pictured the animal differently. Sometimes it was a female, a proud kalon kakon with eyes that bewitched you into being her servant, which you were all too glad to become. Other times it took the form of a werewolf. Striding across the porch upright like a human, its tail nearly knocking the planters off the windowsill. It had long, dirty claws and the dull gaze of a suffering beast, cursed between two species. Miserable brute by night, miserable man by day. He suddenly felt a strange pity for the animal, vividly imagining himself in its place, trapped in the position of husband and father against his nature. It was him at night roaming around the humans in their sleep, it was him who was sad and so awfully alone.

One night the animal was late. When at last Bohumil thought he finally heard the velvet paws, the poorly fastened porch boards sagging under their weight, he burst into sobs of relief. But he never told anyone that.

Bohumila sat across from him, tears pouring out of her eyes.

"They did it," she repeated.

"Did what?" He was relentless. He demanded an answer. Let her say it, let her name it!

Her voice was choked. "I don't know, the animal. They did something to him with that animal. What do I know? You're the one who found those stupid footprints, you researched it or whatever. I never went into the woods."

"No such animal exists." Maybe it only exists between us.

"So where is he then?"

"The boy or the animal?"

"The boy, dammit. Forget the animal."

"You tell me where he is. I'm sure you have your own ideas, right?" said Bohumil.

She shook her head.

He stood up and shook her. "Say it!" He hoisted her up by her sweater, then flung her back into the chair. "Say what happened," he was shouting now, "go ahead."

"What I think," she said, looking him right in the eye, "is the wolf ate the boy."

The wolf is a righteous animal. Strong, determined, loyal. And brutal. In that regard it's like a child.

Put a kitten in the hands of a child, it will start to suffocate it, tug on its tail, lure it into a bag and swing it against a jagged rock. A child knows exactly which animals can run away and which ones can't. Any animal that seems determined to fight back is of no interest to them. Their favorite target is insects, especially butterflies, since they don't sting. Or say anything. Mommy, what sound does a butterfly make?

When a child pulls off a butterfly's wings, nothing happens. They aren't interrupted by the cry of a wounded creature. The butterfly, or the butterfly's body, that is, just drops on the grass and lies there quietly wriggling.

The wolf's prey is not the unlucky but the weak. Weakness of any sort, bodily most often, but also weakness of courage. A weakness to resist in proximity to a wolf turns a species into prey. Wolves most often hunt partridges. They run alongside them, nipping at their thighs, tearing at their flanks and belly. They pester the birds till they weaken due to loss of blood or fatigue. Then they bring them to the ground. Tear open their abdominal cavity and devour them alive. Wolves love the taste of flesh from long-hounded game. Seasoned with adrenaline. Meat marinated in fear.

Life with humans is not for wolves.

That first morning, the morning when she found the boy's bed empty, they waited a while still. As they marched from room to room, it was raining so furiously outside they both hoped to find the boy still at home, safe and dry, under the bed, here he is, behind the wardrobe, here he is. Whew, you sure gave us a fright, but thank goodness, here you are. Phew. Pack up, we're leaving now. Going home. But the boy was nowhere to be found. After searching through the cottage, they went out and combed the meadow. The wet grass slashed at Bohumila's ankles, itched at the rash on her calf. Disturbed by their cries, the grazing does curiously raised their heads. Vacantly chewing, mouths full, they perked up their furry ears, took another bite of grass, and lowered their heads. No cause for alarm.

By the time they made their way up to the village, it was almost noon. If there had been a church here, the bell would have been chiming, given it was Sunday. But the village square was silent. Plastic beer cups and empty cigarette packs wallowed along the side of the road, an empty bottle of Pepa's slivovice lay in the corner. The pub door was locked. They tried pounding but got no response. Despite the rain coming down, they could clearly see a reddish patch with chunks of partly digested food by the bus stop.

They hastened down the deserted street, raincoats creaking. There was always someone here, loitering, smoking, drinking. But today everyone was at home, nursing the wounds from their hangovers. Marcela lay on the couch, face in the pillow, breathing weakly and laboriously. Who knew where Milan was, no doubt off with that slut from Hradec, Marcela would think when she awoke. But as of now she didn't know he hadn't made it home. The stupor from the wine, rum, and slivovice sealed out the pain of waking for a while. As long as she slept, she could be happy.

They set out for Sláva's cottage. Neither one said a word. Bohumila walked a short distance ahead of Bohumil, so she could at least be alone for a while. She had been hoping to see him again. She lowered her eyelids, remembering the feeling that night of the cracked tree bark against her hands, so unyieldingly hard. The old pine. In front of their cottage grew two young birches, bark translucent as a sheet of paper, splitting and peeling off without a sound. It had no scent and didn't scratch when she rubbed it in her palm. Only the old trees had the dark, strong bark, sticky with flowing resin. She bit her scraped lower lip.

Suddenly she stumbled and Bohumil caught her by the shoulder. She looked at him in shock. She wanted to keep her eyes closed, she wanted to relive it all again. She had to relive it all again.

They banged on the gate, there was no bell. Chrastík barked hysterically in his cage. Finally they let themselves in, the gate wasn't locked, just fastened with a hook. The dog was taken aback at first, but then he recognized her and began squealing and prancing about in delight. She walked up and rested the palm of her hand on the mesh. Chrastík whimpered and licked at her hand. Bohumil walked up the few front steps and banged on the door.

"Sláva?" No reply. "Sláva, are you there?" Bohumila remained silent. What is that look he's giving me?

"Slávaaa," he tried again.

Not a sound, just the rain scratching against the metal roof.

They walked away disappointed. Chrastík curled himself into a ball as she shut the gate behind them.

She wondered where Sláva was. Where could he be?

"Why don't we try Marcela's? She babysat the boy, he knows her, maybe he went to see her," Bohumil said.

It was, to say the least, unrealistic to think the boy would have gone off to the village in the middle of the night and slept at Marcela's. She did babysit him, yes, but only once and at their cottage. They went to Hradec for dinner that night. Bohumila put red lipstick on, but wiped it off before she even made it to the car. A touch of red remained at the right corner of her mouth, like a fleck of raspberry. As Bohumil drove, he wondered what had happened. Why did she initially want to look pretty for him and then change her mind? It was all he could do not to snatch the fleck on the tip of his tongue and gobble it up. Devour it. But that was before dinner, where she didn't say a word, then got drunk and adamantly refused to sit in the front seat on the way back. I won't even sit next to you. I don't even want to do that, she said.

They rang the chipped buzzer at the apartment building, hearing it ring through the door and out an open window. They rang for a while. No one came to answer. Bohumil gave the door a kick. It was like everyone had evaporated in the rain. His whole T-shirt was drenched and the cold was creeping into his bones. How could it cool down so fast? How could things fuck up so fast?

Inside on the couch, Marcela sucked her drool, shifting her right leg in a dream, but nothing could wake her out of sleep into the overcast morning. Her head was too soaked through with drink for the sounds of daytime to penetrate, the only sound beneath the surface was the black liquid murmur of night, spilling over from one moment to the next. She slept deeply and quietly, left leg hanging off the couch, it must have been uncomfortable.

Wolf Game I

One boy is the wolf, lurking in the bushes, behind the fence, in the ditch, etc.; a second is the shepherd, and a third one the dog. The other children, the boys and girls, are the sheep, squatting on their haunches plucking grass as if they were grazing. The shepherd sings:

> I'm grazing sheep by myself
> In the meadow of the wolf
> While the wolf has gone away
> Gone to Bydžov for the day
> He'll eat four ewes alive
> And a ram, that makes five
> A white shaggy-furred male
> Golden-horned and stub-tailed.

Meanwhile the wolf creeps up and pounces toward the sheep, who flee in all directions; any sheep he catches, he takes back to his hiding place. The game repeats as long as there is still a sheep grazing. In the meantime, however, the shepherd and his dog defend their sheep, so the wolf boy has to be stronger than them. Once all the sheep have been captured, the wolf catches the dog, too, and finally the shepherd himself.

She pounded again a third time. She was about to turn around and get back in the car. But then she heard the sound of footsteps and a key turn in the lock. A man opened the door. He sized her up with an irritated look and pointed to the buzzer behind the mailbox.

Fine, don't shit yourself.

"I want to report that my son is missing," she blurted out. She startled at her own words. My. Son. Gone. Missing. She leaned against the doorframe, catching her breath. He shot her a weary look. Sunday, half an hour before quitting time, and here was this hysterical woman, staggering in the doorway.

He sat her down across from him, clicked the mouse twice, and quietly sighed.

"All right then, ID."

"Mine?"

"Correct." This was going to be long, very long.

"My son hasn't been home all day," she spouted. "You need to send out an APB and put him in the database of wanted persons." Now she was jabbering at breakneck speed. "Maybe someone will recognize him. Maybe he's at somebody's house and just got delayed, but he needs to know we're worried and he needs to come back home."

He corrected her. Either someone is missing or they're wanted. Her boy was not wanted.

"If a person is missing," he explained, "an announcement is issued that they've gone missing. That means their whereabouts are unknown and they aren't suspected of having committed a criminal offense." He took a breath and articulated in trained fashion: "If a person is wanted, that means they're suspected or accused of having committed a criminal offense and their whereabouts are unknown. In addition, a person may be wanted because they escaped from a facility for institutional treatment or education, or because they have been verifiably diagnosed with a highly infectious illness."

"Are you kidding me?"

"No."

"All right then," she sighed. "Put him in the database of missing persons."

"Yes."

"My son is gone."

"You already said that."

"So you're not kidding?"

"No."

"Are you going to do something about it, then?"

"We'll write up a report."

He glanced at the clock on the computer, fifteen minutes till the end of his shift. She sat facing him, perched upright in the well-mannered way of someone being interrogated. She was pretty enough, despite how haggard she looked, the circles under her eyes.

"What was the missing person wearing when last seen?"

"What was he wearing?" And there she goes, bawling again.

He eyed her up and down. A looker no doubt, but weepy. He couldn't stand that. Forgets her brat at the playground and next thing you know she comes in here, spraying snot all over the place, can't understand a word she says, not to mention it's Sunday. Does she have a photo? Of course not. Of course she forgot. Though wait a sec, she might have one on her phone, don't they all? Pictures of their little sweetheart stuffing their face with birthday cake, but then when their sweetie goes astray they drown themselves in tears. She could probably find it, but not right now. Nobody's going to go looking for anyone anyhow, he knows how it goes. It always ends the same way, the kid'll come running back home as soon as he gets hungry. Or cold, that always drives them back into their mommy's arms. Hunger and cold.

"Tattoos?" he asked, continuing the questionnaire.

"He's twelve." She was trying to be patient. But she saw him hesitate. Twelve. He's twelve years old! "No, no tattoos."

He gave a satisfied nod.

"I need as detailed a description of the person as possible, including their clothing," he said, going back to the beginning.

What was she supposed to say? How did she know what he was wearing? Had he changed into his pajamas before he went to bed? Or did he stay in his sweatpants? How could she not know these things? How could she have left him there all by himself? She didn't know what he was wearing, or if he'd eaten dinner, wait no, he ate, the two of them had eaten together before she left. But why did that even matter? Were there so many boys out there roaming the woods that they had to stop and check to see if their sweatpants were green or blue? Because he had to be in the woods. It was the only possibility. The boy was in the woods.

"Scars from any surgical procedures?"

"Just adenoids."

He looked at her. She looked back.

Was there any bigger idiot in Hradec?

"That doesn't leave scars."

He quietly clicked the mouse.

"Motive for leaving, possible direction of departure or flight from home?" Silence. He moved his eyes from the screen to her.

She'd started bawling again. Why me?

Had he left? wondered Bohumila. Why would he want to do that? Could he really just leave on his own like that? It had never crossed her mind that he might just pick up and go because he was tired of being with them.

He rocked wearily in his chair. She no longer struck him as that good-looking anymore. He waited patiently for her to finish bawling, but what if she never finished? He was already in overtime now. Iveta was going to be pissed, he knew she sure as hell wouldn't warm up his food.

It was the same thing over and over. They look the wrong way at their spoiled little baby bird and next thing you know the rascal's hiding behind a different tree. Let the parents sweat it out awhile, then peep like mad till they come runnin, all emotional, and take out all the bugs they caught, hand the kid the fattest worm, and everyone is happy again, all crammed together in their stinky little nest. Thank goodness he didn't have children. He hoped Iveta didn't want them either, but he was afraid to ask.

"What sort of items did the person have in their possession? ID, passport, cash, credit card, mobile phone, et cetera," he read off.

"None of that, I don't think," said Bohumila, shaking her head. "He left his phone at home."

For the first time he looked at her with sympathy. That didn't bode well, with the phone, but he didn't want to scare her. These kids today don't get out of bed without their phones. His niece was totally obsessed. He'd call her in for supper, she'd take pictures of the food, take a selfie with the food, take a selfie without the food. The fact the boy had left his phone at home was not good news.

"Does he have any close friends he might be staying with?"

"Friends? No, not really." Having it all summed up like this was insane. She didn't understand how she could have left him at home unsupervised. Except that they were supposed to be teaching him independence, the psychologists had said so. They were supposed to be leaving him at home alone. It was their mistake. It was his mistake!

"Did he take, I mean, does he take any medicine?"

"No, nothing." She hesitated. "Actually he does take some enhancers."

"Enhancers?"

"They're kind of like vitamins. He has cognitive impairment."

He stared at her. Well, now, hold on. She should have said from the start that we were looking for a retard. Dammit, tonight was meatloaf. When you reheat it, it gets all dried out.

They finished filling out the questionnaire. He read it back to her.

"Is there anything you want to add?"

She sat across from him fidgeting. That village. That strange village, those strange people. I dreamed—we actually both did—that there was a large animal in the woods,

177

and not just in the woods, but also near the cottage. The village, the animal, they definitely did something to him.

She couldn't bring herself to say it out loud. None of it made sense in this context. What strange people? Locals. What animal? She hadn't seen it. And the fairy tale? So kids read fairy tales, so what?

She was bawling, he was hungry.

"When do you make it public?" She snotted into a handkerchief.

"Twenty-four hours from the time of disappearance." She stared at him blankly.

Did she also forget how to count? "Tomorrow morning," he sighed, and accompanied her out.

Yes, I have your number, of course we'll call if anything happens, no, don't worry, he'll turn up, yes, stay home, in case he comes back. Not in case, for when he comes back. Oof.

He sat down in front of the computer and typed:

Hradec police are searching for a missing 12-year-old boy. He stared at the cursor, thinking. *Slightly defective*, he backspaced. *Slightly disabled*, he backspaced. *Jesus man we're looking for a retard and meanwhile at home my meatloaf's getting cold*, he backspaced. He glanced down at the report and wrote the rest of the sentence in her precise words. He didn't want any trouble: *Hradec police are searching for a missing 12-year-old boy with cognitive impairment. The missing person disappeared from home on Saturday night. He forgot his mobile phone and the family hasn't had any news from him since.* They would paste in a photo on Monday, he wasn't going to hassle with it now.

That should do the trick. He finished typing, stretched, then changed his mind and corrected *from him* to *of him*. There were other people who might let them know besides the boy. He clicked on the printer icon and the machine whirred to life behind him. He scratched under his uniform jacket. He had no idea why they made the uniforms out of nylon, or whatever that material was. It itched under his arms and one time he got a rash of red bumps on his back. Iveta rubbed Fenistil on it for three days before it stopped itching.

As he rose to go to the printer, the telephone rang. He glanced at his watch, no, no more, it was already long past time to clock out. He could feel his stomach running on empty, he needed to send down at least a sausage, or a shot. He hadn't expected to be stuck here so late. Urbanová had some rice cakes or something on her desk. He'd been hungrily eyeing them for an hour now. He picked one up, sniffed it. Nothing about it in any way suggested it was edible.

He walked over to the printer, tucked the document tidily in a transparent folder, and deposited it in the tray for whoever came in tomorrow. The telephone kept ringing. He peered out the window. Pouring rain. He decided to wait until home to change clothes, his T-shirt and jacket were going to get totally soaked anyway. He lived in the apartment building twenty minutes' walk from the station and hadn't brought an umbrella with him. In the morning it had looked like it would only be showers.

The telephone kept ringing.

He opened his briefcase and tossed in his wallet, swollen as a wet diaper. On Friday he'd picked up his meal vouchers.

He reached for the phone on his way to the door. Listened awhile, then sighed. The boys from Podlesí were at it again. He told them the same thing he did every time: "Gentlemen, cut that shit out. I keep telling you. Every single summer." He nodded. "Fine, but this is the last time and I mean it," he told the caller. "And sort it out ASAP."

He hung up the phone and cursed. "Every summer, every friggin summer." He went back to the computer. Clicked twice. Are you sure you want to delete this file? You bet I am. He deleted the file. That meatloaf is going to be dry as a bone, I'll buy some mustard on the way, slap some of that on. Boys, cut that shit out, he thought, but his eyes were smiling.

He took out the missing persons report and switched on the shredder.

Pepa pulled the long rubber glove up to his armpit. Prepared the vaseline. Loaded the sperm from the liquid nitrogen tank into the big gun. Slipped it under his T-shirt to warm it up. Dug his hand into the cow and spread its legs. Only feces came out at first. But the rectum had to be emptied in order to reach the cervix. There it was. He inserted the gun and squeezed, counting to five. Then carefully slid it out. A fly crawled across his sweaty forehead, but he paid it no mind. He would repeat the process once again that evening. Now he needed a smoke. He peeled off the glove and flicked it into the air like from a slingshot. The thumb caught on the dirty metal railing and flapped in time to the melancholy mooing of the inseminated cows.

 He walked out in front of the cowshed and stood next to Jarda. Pulled a pack of cigarettes from his pocket, lit up, reached for the window frame, grabbed a bottle of beer. Took a long drink, then belched and scratched at his crotch.

Jarda leaned against the flaking wall. Watching the puddle in front of him fill, the dust turning to mud.

"I hope you were gentle, Pepik?" He turned around to look at the cow, restlessly shaking its chain.

"Like it was one of my own." Pepa breathed out a puff of smoke and greedily sucked in again.

A fine sprinkle of rain fell on their hands, even though they were under the roof. The water dampened the cigarette but didn't extinguish it. Pepa shifted his weight in the mud, wiping a cowpat off his boot. Thought about all the things he had to get done before winter. He liked winter. The cows had a different smell.

"So we're on for tomorrow, yeah?" Jarda confirmed.

Pepa nodded. It would be late, day three since the disappearance, the two of them in the cottage were going out of their minds. Everything was delayed, it wasn't good, not at all. It wasn't supposed to happen this way.

"I'll call them all together after lunch in front of the pub. I figure right after one, that should give us enough light."

"Mmkay. But it's pissing rain and tomorrow it's supposed to be be the same."

"Maybe not so much in the woods. Plus supposedly he's got a camera with a rain cover, plus he can get some of it on his phone, that'll work."

"I still don't see it happening, they're shittin themselves up to their ears. It's gonna be pretty tough with them, especially her. It was a mistake to wait this long. We should've done it before the ball."

"Well, nothin we can do now. If it sucks, it sucks, I guess."

"What about Hradec, what if the cops come snoopin around? They were definitely out there, I saw the patrol car."

"Hradec is taken care of," Jarda said assuredly. Organizing was something he enjoyed.

"At least that." Pepa finished his beer and carried the bottle inside to the crate. The whole way huffing and puffing something about uniforms.

Jarda wasn't listening. He was thinking about Bohumila. He watched the thick curtain of rain, smiling to himself. They'll be in the woods together. She'll be trembling with fear. Maybe they can snuggle. There was an order, a balance, in a woman's fear of a man. When a woman says she's done, she's always still good for two more.

Pepa stood beside him again, lit another smoke. His face was ashen, he'd doubled his dose in the past few months. He didn't need to eat that much, but he couldn't do without smoking. Sometimes in the morning, eyes still sticky with sleep, he'd fumble around the pillow. There was always a pack there somewhere, a lighter. Someday you're going to fall asleep and roast to death, they warned him at the pub when he boasted that he even smoked in his sleep. Someday I'm going to fall asleep and roast to death, he thought.

He sucked in through his nose and landed a gob of spit in the puddle in front of him. Moving slowly, he headed back into the cowshed. He had been here all weekend again, the pregnant heifer wasn't his favorite. He never would have said so out loud, but he truly loved the animals, even if sometimes he beat them. By nature he was soft as cottage cheese, he'd never liked violence.

Jarda walked with him partway. He didn't open until five today. He had to stop round and see everyone, agree on the details. Sláva was feeling lousy. Yesterday they had found him nearly unconscious in the garden. Wailing, gripping his stomach, coughing up blood. He begged Jarda to keep it to himself, but naturally Jarda told everyone. Down at the pub that night, he did an imitation of Sláva spewing up blood and wiping his hand in the grass. Then Chrastík rolling around in it. It left long dark streaks on his fur.

"Who's gonna run it after he's gone?" asked Pepa.

"Whoever wants to, I guess. Not me, that's for sure, though I could if I had to. His cottage is nice, should be easy to sell. It'll help the club out a lot."

"We'll see, maybe he'll make it."

"He won't make it. Not him."

Pepa cleaned the udders, hooked up the milking machine, and turned it on. Inside the cowshed it was dark and damp. Two hungry cats slipped past, there was always a little spilled milk to lap up. He kicked the railing to shoo them away. He couldn't stand cats. The cow stirred, looked back at him. Pepa gave her a flick in the eye, What're you lookin at, cow, just keep that milk comin. He was feeling kinda sad today, friggin rain, friggin fall.

Jarda made his way back from the cowshed. He walked slowly, despite the rain, but pulled his hood over his head. Did he have everything he needed for tomorrow? The bonnet was in the closet, he still had to ready the basket, it was probably out in the barn. Or was it the shed?

It had been raining only two days, but Bledá was choked with water. It would burst at any moment. He knew about the hollows left behind from the rotted-out trees, which had eaten away at the dam. If the pond overflowed, the whole shape of the landscape would change.

There was no way for the water to run off through the pond's outlet. The dam would burst tomorrow. It would flood the meadow, undermining the soil and compromising the structure of the two older cottages. The current would sweep away the bridge. But you could still easily hop across the stream.

The wolfsong is the sound of the rending you will suffer, in itself a murdering. Again so much about sounds and tones, eyes and velvety black noses. I'm tired and don't want to be alone anymore. Sláva laid his head in his hands like a toddler in its crib. He went on reading. [. . .] *He strips off his trousers and she can see how hairy his legs are. His genitals, huge. Ah! Huge. The last thing the old lady saw in all this world was a young man, eyes like cinders, naked as a stone, approaching her bed. The wolf is carnivore incarnate. When he had finished with her, he licked his chops and quickly dressed himself again, until he was just as he had been when he came through her door. He burned the inedible hair in the fireplace and wrapped the bones up in a napkin that he hid away under the bed in the wooden chest in which he found a clean pair of sheets. These he carefully put on the bed instead of the tell-tale stained ones he stowed away in the laundry basket. He plumped up the pillows and shook out the patchwork quilt, he picked up the Bible from the floor, closed it and laid it on the table. All was as it had been before except that grandmother was gone. The sticks twitched in the grate, the clock ticked and the young man sat patiently, deceitfully beside the bed in granny's nightcap. Rat-a-tap-tap. Who's there, he quavers in granny's antique falsetto. Only your granddaughter.* [. . .] *What shall I do with my shawl? Throw it on the fire, dear one. You won't need it again. She bundled up her shawl and threw it on the blaze, which instantly consumed it. Then she drew her blouse over* her head; her small breasts gleamed as if the snow had invaded the room. What shall I do with my blouse? Into the fire with it, too, my pet. The thin muslin went flaring up the chimney like a magic bird and now off came her skirt, her woollen stockings, her shoes, and on to the fire they went, too, and were gone for good. The firelight shone through the edges of her skin; now she was clothed only in her untouched integument of flesh. This dazzling, naked she combed out her hair with her fingers; her hair looked white as the snow outside. Then went directly to the man with red eyes in whose unkempt mane the lice moved; she stood up on tiptoe and unbuttoned the collar of his shirt. What big arms you have. All the better to hug you with. Every wolf in the world now howled a prothalamion outside the window as she freely gave the kiss she owed him. What big teeth you have! She saw how his jaw began to slaver and the room was full of the clamour of the forest's Liebestod but the wise child never flinched, even when he answered: All the better to eat you with. The girl burst out laughing.

Getting ready to go see him, she showered and put on clean underwear. Brushed out her hair. There was more hair left in the comb than usual, she hadn't noticed the small bald spots taking hold on her scalp. She lowered her eyelids a moment, then rubbed her fingers together, her palms had begun to sweat.

She ran into Sláva on her way back from the police. She stopped the car, got out, she was shaking but didn't cry.

No, he shook his head. No one had seen a thing, no one knew a thing. He didn't give her a hug, but the tone of his voice was calm and gentle. He would definitely turn up, he had just run off somewhere. Like a goat chasing the scent of fresh-mown clover.

I'll be there, she told him. I'll stop by after one more round through the village again. She didn't tell him she needed another fear to help overcome the fear.

Sláva left the gate open and put Chrastík in the garden behind the cottage, with the flower beds and the little henhouse fenced in with mesh. The hens didn't even raise their heads from the worms in the dirt, by now they were used to the dog. It wasn't until he was inside the cottage that Sláva remembered he could lock up the hens. He started out the door again but then suddenly stopped, looking down. He had already washed his shoes, guess he wouldn't be going back out after all. Circles of sweat stained his otherwise clean collared shirt. The evenings were dominated by humidity, leaving not even a crack to take a breath and get relief. For weeks now the temperature hadn't dropped below twenty degrees, the sultry nights had turned his face flush red, he had a constant fever, and his mouth was dry all the time. The last two days had been cooler, but that hadn't helped. His hair was matted to his forehead with sweat. He had thick hair for his age, hard as splinters.

He paced the cottage nervously, keeping an eye out. What am I getting so stressed for? It's no big deal. She isn't going to say anything, she isn't going to ask anything, since she doesn't know a thing. He'd been with her, that's it. That she remembered. She had to remember. Today he felt better, almost good, adrenaline gurgling through his veins, the nervousness and anticipation took his attention away from the pain. His gaze kept swerving to the bed: He had smoothed the bedspread several times, stowed the sheet with the telltale stains away in the laundry basket. He plumped up the pillows and shook out the patchwork quilt, he picked up the Bible from the floor, closed it and laid it on the table.

Rat-a-tap-tap.

He took a deep breath and went to the door.

She had stopped at the bottom of the steps. A blue vein pulsed on her neck. The moment he saw her, it started pulsing faster. He greeted her with a smile. Her eyes were grown over with yellow grass, she'd been withering up so many months.

He stepped back from the door and she entered.

The cottage had a musty reek, the toilet ran. The calming sound of water accompanied her into the sitting room. She tripped a bit, he'd recently dug up the entire floor and changed the pipes because they kept getting clogged. Part of it was smoothed down again, the tiles were all that was missing, but there was a gaping hole at the threshold to the kitchen, with only a board laid over it. It sagged and made a faint crack underneath her weight.

So this is how you live, she thought, swallowing in shock. From the small dark entryway she stepped into a large room with two low windows. In the past this was how cottages had been built, constant dark and damp inside and little room for air and light. To the right of the old kitchen counter (he still cooked on a tin stove!) sat the bed, next to it an antique secretary desk with a small shelf of books. Their spines had contorted in the damp like arthritic fingers. Running her hands over them, Bohumila held back an achoo as she felt the mold spores whirl. She sounded out the titles: *Gamekeeping with Camera and Rifle*; *Deer Species in Our Hunting Grounds*; *Into the Fields, Rifle in Hand*; *The Steppe Wolf*; *Estimating Age in Mouflon Sheep*. She had to smile a little. She had seen a little mouflon in the forest once. It looked like a giant sheep. He didn't react to her smile.

There was still another row of books on the shelf, but then he called her to the table. She hadn't seen the collection of old fairy tales about wolves, a CD with a date on the cover.

The table was massive, with tiny cracks between the boards. Doesn't the rice fall through when you eat? He just shrugged.

In the middle of the table stood a tea rose in a vase. He

nodded to it. She smiled. Was the rose for her? Was he going to say anything? The flower smelled sweet.

She sat down in a chair, folded her hands in her lap. He sat down across from her. No, I don't know where your boy is. He will definitely turn up. Definitely.

He poured them both some red wine, each in a different type of glass. He offered her the nicer one, engraved with two roses. A bit too many roses, she thought, taking a sip.

She spoke, he listened. Boy. Gone. Missing. Will turn up. Definitely.

He was starting to get impatient.

He filled her mouth with wine, it was strong, almost crunchy. He waited until she was sufficiently drunk. Then took her by the hand. At last. She felt the relief. She was afraid of him. He terrified her. With those old eyes and old hands. A hot spring fed his veins. It cracked his skin, corroding it with dark age spots. His palms were rough, she clearly felt the hardened calluses. She ran her palm over his. Bumping over a blister, sinking into the pitted scars. You must be a hundred! You'll die before I do and won't remember a thing. And the reason I'm here today is for memory. That's why I'm moving so slow. Depositing everything in a reservoir of heightened excitement. I plan to return many times to this old cottage, these old hands. When I chase them both to bed at night, I'll close my eyes over a glass of wine and relive it all again.

He wanted to kiss her but first asked permission. It was different from in the woods. He hadn't had a woman in the cottage in such a long time. And he liked this one. She talks a lot. She talks too much. But he still knew how to shut a girl's mouth. Yes, you may, she leaned toward him. One empty bottle of wine spun on the table but didn't fall off. The second, almost finished, sat perched on the peeling slab of wood. The chairs were incredibly uncomfortable. She got up and sat on him. He purred. They awkwardly got to their feet. She stood up on tiptoe and unbuttoned the collar of his shirt. What big arms you have. All the better to hug you with. They head into bed. The chair they have been sitting on wobbles and overturns. He strips off his trousers and she can see how hairy his legs are. His genitals, huge. Ah! Huge. The bedsprings squeak annoyingly beneath their weight. The bed is not uncomfortable, just too soft and too accustomed to a single body in the middle. It can hardly chew on two. Bohumila is bogged down in a little valley, she feels like she's imprisoned, she can barely move. He is heavy on top of her. He bears down on her belly. Touches her with his hands.

Her body is stiff as a chilled hog, she growls. He wants to kiss other parts of her too. She refuses to submit.

What big teeth you have! She saw how his jaw began to slaver and the room was full of the clamour of the forest's Liebestod.

She refuses to submit. She can't, she shakes her head.

What big teeth you have!

All the better to eat you with.

This is my love. I'm sick and don't want to be alone anymore.

In the garden out back, Chrastík began to bark furiously, scratching the door and squealing in an unpleasant falsetto. Something was going on in the henhouse. But he couldn't get over the fence, no matter how he jumped and scratched. No one was coming. He barks like mad, slobbering from his jaws, adrenaline biting beneath his skin, he whimpers and turns in circles. He trots from the gate to the henhouse and back, returning to the house, circling it ever more frantically, sprinting to the corner of the garden, back and forth. His chops are soaking wet, his front paws scraped bloody.

After she left, he carefully made the bed and stowed the sheet with the telltale stains away in the laundry basket. He plumped up the pillows and shook out the patchwork quilt, he picked up the Bible from the floor, closed it and laid it on the table. All was as it had been before.

It was like the path to the cottage had never been there at all. The flooded stream ran down into the ravine, taking with it clumps of grass, pine cones, mycelium, colorful leaves. Anyone waiting below would have caught the whole autumn basket. Bohumila in her rubber boots slipped down to the very bottom of her bottoms. This was the third day of rain. And the third day the boy wasn't home. The sky had burst out in tears, making a veil of water so no one could see its bloated and aged face. But it couldn't cover its eyes. Imprinted on those drenched pupils were his image, his gestures, the sound of his voice, his laughter and shouts echoing through the ravine and frightening the jays in search of plunder. She heard him all the time. There were times she let out a sigh of relief, thinking he was back now, he was here. She stood on the doorstep, smiling faintly. Spread her arms wide, awaiting the impact of a warm child's body. But between her arms was nothing but emptiness and cold, the mist swishing in her armpits. Not even a doe capered in the meadow, bending the blades of grass. There was nothing but silence and rain, her sad personal symphony. Drops of water from the gutter drilled into the mournful silence at a precise staccato, a dead mouse floated in the rusty rainwater basin. She couldn't even look at it, she refused. The basin overflowed and all the grass beneath it was worn away by water. All the dipping, splashing, dripping was nothing but a meaningless fireworks of sounds to her. Without a child's voice around.

Bledá Lake had burst. The brooks had turned to streams. The water brought with it ruin, the recently sown seeds all dead and washed out of the soil. Lettuce leaves spun in puddles. Nothing remained around the cottage but cold heavy mud, blazing a path into the ravine. To a place deeper than it had ever dared before. But now she sensed it had to. It was coming for her son.

"Bohu?" Bohumil called to her from the cottage.

"Coming." She slowly made her way back. In the entryway, she took off her raincoat, kicked off her boots.

He sat on a chair in the kitchen, arms resting on the table, elbows wrapped in his palms like a first grader at his desk. He was pale, unshaven, nothing but skin and bones. His cheekbones strained at the skin, there was no fat to get in the way.

"Where were you?" He felt a need to be near her.

"Outside. You almost can't even get up there anymore, though, the water is everywhere. The village is completely cut off, Bledá burst its banks, the bus isn't running, you can't even get through by car. We're totally on our own."

He looked at her without a word. "Did you run into anyone?"

"No." She averted her eyes. "No one."

"Everyone disappeared. They've got it all worked out."

"You don't know that for a fact."

"Oh but I do. Pure evil like this is smart. Precise, well-planned, cool, purposeful. That's how their evil is."

Clearly he had been drinking. He couldn't see that she had too. Her lips were red with wine.

"Now you're overestimating them."

"All of them except one."

She swallowed.

He reached for the bottle and poured himself a drink. Hands trembling, he blotted a spill of whiskey on the table with his finger. She watched as the wet stain spread into the tabletop seams, seeping under the bottle.

"Liquid evil. It's liquid. Like that," he said, pointing to the stain. "Nothing is an obstacle for them. They saturate everything, soak it up into themselves, and then destroy it—dismantle it, dissolve it. That's what's happening here. Sour, liquid evil, corroding us so slowly we don't even notice it."

Bohumila settled onto the chair facing him, leaving her hands to rest on her thighs. Why hoist them up on the table, displaying her bulging knuckles, gnawed fingernails, torn hangnails. Better to knead them in her lap and keep her mouth shut. What could she say to him? She knew these musings all too well, in all their variations. They never led anywhere. Though actually, she realized, they did. Again and again, they led him to run his mouth around in circles.

"Look, our boy is lost. Whatever you're saying, it probably has nothing to do with that," she said.

Bohumil's head sank still lower. "I don't know if I agree. Have you noticed the way they're behaving? Like they're following a manual. They're practically indistinguishable. Do they act emotionally, the way you'd expect from folks who shovel dirt? No, they don't. They act rationally, and that's what terrifies me. Because that's how everyone acts, because all of a sudden everyone switched on their brains and they're being absolutely and entirely rational, like they're following some kind of manual. Doesn't that terrify you?"

"Actually, what terrifies me is you."

"What?"

"Once again, it's all about you. It isn't their intellect, it's yours, all gassed up on how great it is here."

"As usual, you're not being fair. I'm talking about them, our friendly fellow villagers—"

She interrupted: "You're talking about yourself. Once again, all you're talking about is yourself and you don't even realize it."

"As a matter of fact, I know that I'm not."

"I."

"*I* is the subject of the sentence, that's correct."

"So the subject is you. Once again, only you."

"Right, that's what I'm saying." He was feeling the urge to provoke her.

"Sure, who else but you."

"Bohu, this is elementary school material, maybe seventh grade. You actually agree with me, you just aren't able to see it." That ought to get her. Now she would start pounding the table. Yelling at him. It had to work. He needed something to start happening.

"We definitely don't agree. And for a long time now, have you seriously not noticed?" she asked calmly.

"I have," he said softly.

"So what're you going to do about it?"

"I'm going out to look for the boy."

"We have to go look for him," she nodded.

"I know," he replied.

"At least you know something."

He lifted his head with a quizzical look. "You think I wanted this? Jesus, I didn't want it any more than you did. For God's sake, look around, you think I would choose this"—he waved his hands around the room—"voluntarily? Look around, you call this living? Don't you see, you didn't give me any other option? I had to do this, drag you out here, get you away from that jerk and give it another try together, just give it a try, there was no other option."

He wanted her to agree with him. She didn't say a word.

"You didn't give me any other option, you can't deny that."

She kept her mouth shut. She knew sooner or later it had to come up, he had never criticized her until now, never raised his voice even, it was practically impossible to argue with him. This whole thing was nothing but a feeble attempt to provoke an argument, clearly he was out of his depth.

"So you do deny it, if you're not talking. Hm. All of a sudden. All of a sudden you don't want to talk to me, is that it? Not in the mood to argue?"

She wanted to laugh, it was all so off the mark, so irrelevant. As if the life they'd had before Podlesí was an entirely different life, a life in which what mattered was entirely different: a toaster, a new rug for the entryway, when are you finally going to fix that door on the kitchen cabinet, it's falling off again. This argument had nothing to do with their past life and Bohumila knew it. It was about them right here right now, it was about guilt, and most of all, it was about who lost the boy. Because a boy doesn't just disappear, someone has to forget him, misplace him somewhere. And she'd already said her piece as far as that was concerned. She wasn't interested in past actions, the only one that mattered to her was this one, this dumbass, who'd dragged the whole family out here. Out here to this cottage, where they lived with these people, these animals. And the two of them both knew who did it, who waved the ad around, who brought the suitcases up from the cellar. For years she hadn't even had a key! She might have even felt sorry for him, he knew, surely he had to know, that it was his fault, and these silly diatribes, digging up the ancient past, all the petty details and hard-won injuries were just ridiculous. Suddenly she was one hundred percent certain that Bohumil was mixed up in matters that were none of his business, creating an aura of superiority around himself with all of his moralizing and intellectualizing, which maybe at first had impressed her a bit, but now? Thanks to you we lost our son, you piece of shit!

Day three. The moment of bluntness, the fleeting reconciliation of yesterday, is gone. Bohumil sits on the floor of the rusty bathtub, places the showerhead on his back, spraying alternating salvos of warm and cold. He stares fixedly at the tile. Reaches for the toothbrush on the sink and uses the pointy end to chisel it out. The tile thuds loudly into the tub, a bit of masonry crumbles loose.

"You okay?" comes a voice from outside.

Am I? he sighs.

He looks between his dirty legs. He grumbles finally like an old animal, yes, even though he's not okay and fears he never will be again. He keeps chipping away at the wall, he needs to find him, seize him by the throat, yank out the hairs on his neck. He looks around. Spider? Oh, spider! Where are you, you little bastard?!

Regret lashes his back with watery straps. Thick welts form on his skin that sting when he sits, stands, lies down. His strength is giving out, he doesn't know what to do. It frightens him that for a while he thought the boy was gone. That that small sigh of relief that stole into his mouth might have finished off the boy, done him in. I never should have wished for my child not to exist, not even for a moment. But I did. Even back in the early days. As he dragged his little legs up the stairs and Nováková stopped at the banister and nodded her head in sympathy. When I rode the tram with him from one end of the line to the other, because what else could I do with him all day long? He realized what bothered him wasn't the boy's screaming, or even so much the child himself, but the outside world, which never accepted the boy, and therefore him either. Because he would always be the dad of a handicapped boy. Never again just a dad. There would always be his son, who was strange, different, a deviant retard. When they shouted insults at him in school, Bohumil felt the boy's pain—he didn't know how to defend himself, didn't know how to fight back. But it often upset Bohumil purely for his own sake. Because it also fucking happened to me, he thought, hunching his back. I'm the deviant one.

"We have to," he said, hair still wet, back at the table again, "we have to get out there and look for him again. We can't just sit here waiting like this. I'm going out of my mind. I'm seriously losing my mind." He bobbed his head nervously. "There's something going on with my brain, I can't control it anymore, it's changing me."

He rose from his seat.

"For fuck's sake, what's the matter with us? He can't not be here. How can he not be here?" He was panting loudly. "We have to go and look for him, maybe he's somewhere out in the woods, wounded, wet, hungry, and we're sitting here calmly at home, waiting. I know we've already looked everywhere. My vocal cords are totally fried from screaming all over the fields. But now," he said, swallowing, "I'm honestly terrified." He sat back down on the chair. Beginnings and endings can happen anywhere, he just hadn't expected that it would end here.

She had been watching him. Three days, three days of desperate, caustic fear, he couldn't even keep water down anymore. For three days he didn't eat. He was starving but couldn't feel it. So feel it awhile, the fear, thought Bohumila, looking at him. Let it nibble away at you, bite into you, slash you like rusty scissors. You're the one who brought us here, now reap what you sowed. Not even a houseleek could grow in this place, and you wanted me to make a new start, a new beginning here.

"I'm scared to death we won't find him," he said, bursting into tears. He hadn't cried in years. Not in front of her at least. She had completely forgotten what he looked like when he cried. He used to cry all the time! Hang his head between his knees and moan like an old bitch in heat. Now he just softly whimpered. It was all so well-mannered, the elbows on the table, the quiet laments. If only she could still touch him, hug him, console him, warm herself against the body of another, lose herself in an embrace, because that was the only safe place for her to lose herself. But it hadn't been for a very long time now. No touches in ages! She couldn't. I won't even attempt to reach out my hand. I won't even try, thought Bohumila, standing up from the table.

The first night the boy wasn't home she locked herself in the bathroom. She found Bohumil's razor, but it was totally useless. She glanced around. The bottom of the shower curtain hung down into the tub of water swimming with potato peels. How many times had she told him: Pour it down the toilet, rinse out the tub, and carry it back to the kitchen. She fished around in the cold water, found the potato scraper right away. Washed it off, it was new and fairly sharp. She sat down on the edge of the bathtub and rested her right hand comfortably on her knee. She needed to peel the green off the scar. She needed it to stop rotting. She scraped at the scar with the scraper. Screamed into a towel in pain. After the first wave of pain came another tsunami, no smaller, no less beautiful. She stuffed the towel in her mouth. The pain anchored her, even now, on day three. She had been ripping her hangnails bloody, attempting to peel the nail down to the flesh, digging her finger into the wounds. She had probably even pulled out those hairs on the top of her head. She needed to feel something. For some time now, she'd been wanting to tell him they couldn't live without joy, but it was never the right time to have that conversation.

"We'll just go out and look for him, everywhere," Bohumil repeated. "In the woods, the fields. The stream, the lake."

She shuddered. Whoa there, not one more word. She begged him not to speak, not to name, not to give voice to her greatest anxiety. Because then it would come alive and grow, and it was menacingly hungry. Feeding on the image of a bloated child's body, cheeks pale, eyes nibbled away by fish, by large voracious catfish embedded in the slimy muck, ungluing themselves only for the sake of fresh young flesh. She dreamed every night now, in her fitful sleep, of wrapping her arms around a cold, wet child. His body in the dream was like a squishy bar of modeling clay. She begged him, don't feed my worst fantasies, don't say *stream*, don't say *lake*. Yesterday they had finally gotten up the courage to look, tramping through the mud, searching on the surface. On returning home her disappointment had given way to a sort of relief, the boy was not in the water.

"Let's head out now," he said. "What are we waiting for? Fuck the police. I can't stand just sitting here hoping the boy will somehow miraculously turn up." He glanced at her. His eyes wide, unblinking.

"Head out where?"

"Into the woods."

Wolf Game II

In some places they play the wolf game with no shepherd or sheepdog. As they graze, the lambs sing:

> Tearing grass up blade by blade
> Here amid the greening glade
> If a wolf should happen by
> I can only hope to die
> But no wolf scares me anyhow
> No matter what I'll milk my cows
> Come on, wolfie, come on!

At which point the wolf jumps out and the sheep make a run for it, throwing the torn-up grass behind them, shouting: "Here's your grass, wolfie!" Whichever lamb the wolf snatches, he takes away and then goes back to lie in wait, until he catches them all.

She is drinking black coffee. Her tongue smarts, she burned it on the first sip. The coffee is so hot it hurts. As a little girl she thought she would never drink coffee.

Children don't drink black things, her grandma used to tell her.

It was early in the morning. The boy and Bohumil were still asleep. She knew it would be dawn before she fell asleep. Her sleep was disturbed by insomnia, the rhythm of her breathing, her restless legs, walking non-stop almost all night long. Not running but walking. The quiet rustle of the blanket at every step, she couldn't stand it. Even just lying there next to him took a sizable dose of self-restraint. Lying next to her own husband was so abhorrent to her, she fell asleep before he came to bed so, engulfed in slumber, she could forget who it was lying beside her. When she slid out of bed in the morning, she didn't even look his way.

Bohumila drinks coffee beside the open window. She watches the sky, a bit overcast. After the terrible heat waves, rain finally seemed to be on the way. They said it was going to rain, it was supposed to start sometime after the ball.

She walked out on the porch with her mug and surveyed the small patch of herbs and salad greens that she had attempted to plant in recent weeks. She wished she knew the tricks employed by more experienced growers. What do you do to ensure a succulent crop? She was salivating for luscious apples and butter pears so soft they melted in the sun. She wanted juice running down her hands when she sank her teeth into them. That was the harvest she wanted. All those sweet tastes and perfumes and the summer sunshine caught in the skin of apples, pears, and plums that would never be worm-eaten.

She looked around, a quiet surrounded the house. An unpleasant calm. She remembered mornings in southern Europe. The clusters outside the cafés, saucers awaiting thick-walled cups, warmed on rumbling machines.

Doughnuts filled with such obscene amounts of cream that it overflowed in your mouth—the only way to eat them was with bad-mannered debauchery. She missed the voices. The sounds. They didn't have even a small chapel here, no bell chiming as you sank a spoonful of soup into your mouth. She sighed. Loudly. There's no life here. The only thing to harvest in my little patch is mold. The basil leaves have rust spots. And she had tried so hard. She even studied the gardening book she had found out in the pantry. While weeding she had identified a long-rooted dandelion, couch grass, field thistle, and bishop's weed. She weeded regularly, to keep carbon dioxide from suffocating the plants, to keep the pests from spreading fatal diseases to the tomatoes and zucchini. She pulled up cat's-foot, dead nettles, nettles, gallant soldier, and speedwell and left them out in the sun for two days to dry. Then stewed the whole thing in a bucket of water and watered the beds with it.

She sighed. There's no life here. My field is nothing but gangrene and mold and rancorous scabs. Even my scars are opening up. She took off her bandage a few days ago. The stitches had been absorbed, but the wound still hadn't healed. The edges weren't just pink, but she also saw sprigs of gray in them, even ocher. The scar was coming undone in the opposite direction, the edges of the wound turning away from each other like bashful lovers.

She stretched and yawned. Tomorrow was the ball. She would wear the red dress, even if she was working the tap all night. Maybe he would come see her. She knew he had been watching her. Thinking of her. Observing her. Heading her off. Closing in. And she was letting him. It's about time something happened. The deathly silence of this summer is killing me. My world is bilberries, mushrooms, shopping at Bubble's, and the bench in front of the cottage where I sit and stare at the sun coming up. I'll bring the boy home. We can live together, alone, watching goblins and dwarves at night and saying sweet words to each other, because she had taught them to him, he knew how to say *love, heart, kiss, honey.* That last one's sweet, he told her.

Inside the cottage, one man's body was waking up, one boy's. The beds creaked, she heard someone hawking up phlegm and a trickle of urine. A fart. Again he didn't flush.

She lowered her eyelids once more, before the cottage swallowed her up. Just a little while longer.

Only now did she notice the leaves in the garden were raked up and piled in a heap beneath the tree. He wasn't supposed to do that. She wanted the leaves to rot naturally. She forgot to tell him.

Ding. Dong. It takes work to get a bell swinging. The two stand facing each other, alternating tugs on the rope, woven of bast and frayed in spots. The bell is so heavy they have to jump onto the rope and pull down with all their weight. Once, no, twice. Then the bell starts to chime. The tone isn't uniform: The first bang of the clapper is a major chord, the second one darker, in a minor key. As the pullers slow their pace, the bell slows too. But that's all right. They've been ringing a long time, everyone has heard it. The bell dies away like a symphony, first the violins going quiet, the bass still resounding, now the flutist running their fingers down the flute, into the deep dark tones, then falling silent entirely. It's the same with the bell. Now it's ringing only once instead of twice. Gearing up for the final thunderclap, now only drum and double bass, then double bass. The ting of cymbals, which only the first rows clearly hear. Then silence.

They let go the ropes. The inhabitants of Podlesí have more important work to do now.

The leaves, yesterday heaped beneath the tree, have been blown all over the garden. During the night the wind joined forces with the rain, holding hands together like little children on a walk. The trees howled, soaked branches crashing to the ground. Meanwhile the rain smothered the smaller trees entirely, pounding their fragile roots bare, till the soaked earth gave up the fight and finally let them go. They swam in gullies of mud, as if their life's calling was to end up on this dead man's float of shattered existence. Sawfly-infested plums tumbled into puddles. Powdery mildew, coating leaves with a white crust of fungus, ran rampant. Not to mention the codling moth. The first generation of caterpillar-infested fruits had fallen off, and now, in early autumn, the next generation was turning ripe, the path to the orchard was strewn with discolored rotten apples. Somewhere here there was joy sprouting from the pain and destruction. Transmitted like rabies from animal to human, like apple scab from tree to tree.

The third day the rain quieted down.

Bohumil is brewing coffee. From inside the cottage he doesn't hear the bell. A thundering sound catches his ear, reminding him of a bell, but he just lifts his eyes and pours the water over the coffee. He knows the village has no church, no chapel, no bell. Nor does Bohumila, warming her hands by the fire, hear the ringing. The wood, damp with moisture from outside, crackles and hisses. Yesterday evening was the first time they built a fire, and they have anxiously kept it alive ever since, as if they wanted to stand the test, not fail, at least in this.

They finish their coffee, get dressed. Bohumila slips into a blue raincoat, pulls on her rubber boots, still slightly damp, she should have left them to dry by the fire. She reaches for the flashlight, but he's already grabbed it. It's silly taking a candle, but so what, she thinks. The city still lived in her. They had only one flashlight, so they would go together. She nods to him, here, take my father's hunting knife, but he shakes his head no.

It was drizzling outside. There was no clear division between the gray sky and the mist drowning the cottage, gray-white from the waist up, white-gray from the waist down. The one anchoring ray of light, dividing the world into two parts, came from the conical lamp above the cottage front door. At last it was working again. It shone through the drops like a fire to warm your fingers by, when the cold turns your knuckles the color of Antarctic ice. Even this light was dimming now, though, blinking on and off. The bulb couldn't withstand such a sudden change in temperature and soon burst amid the afternoon gloom.

A person can still call out, though, even if they can't see. Through the mist and the rain. They tried to scramble up into the meadow, but their feet kept sinking lower and lower into the mud, as if someone were tugging on them. The cottage was sucking them back in. Their flashlight's beam flailed wildly as they thrashed their arms to balance out the wobbling of their legs. A bright line cut across the mud-choked hillside.

Is that our flashlight doing that? they wondered, looking up at the path.

As they made their way back home, Bohumila trembled with cold, her hands covered in slimy muck.

That isn't our flashlight, Bohumil thought.

A whole swarm of them flashed on the path to the cottage.

"What is that?" whispered Bohumila.

Bohumil shook his head and held a finger to his lips.

Bohumila stood still as they watched the light together. It was moving closer. They instinctively stepped back into the cottage, as if they had never intended to leave. They quietly shut the door and stopped, looking at the handle. They glanced at each other, then back at the handle. Lock it? Bohumil hesitated. If he locked it he was assigning the people with flashlights the role of hunters.

"Lock it," said Bohumila.

Bohumil didn't object.

She stood in the entryway, raincoat dripping, clumps of dirt falling off her boots, the shadows from the fire in the room next door dancing a war dance on the walls.

"What is it? Jesus, what is it?" Bohumila asked.

Bohumil said nothing.

"What do they want from us?"

"I don't know, maybe nothing. What are we hiding for, anyway? Maybe they're just stopping by."

"'Just'—what do you mean 'just'?"

"Jesus, I don't know," said Bohumil. "What makes you keep thinking I understand anything here? It just doesn't make sense to me to hide behind the door like this. Let's try and talk to them like normal human beings."

"But I don't want to talk to them," said Bohumila.

"Oh and you think I do? You think I invited them?"

Bohumila said nothing.

"I didn't," said Bohumil.

Bohumila looks like she's thinking it over, but she's really just keeping her mouth shut. Her head is empty, swept clean. She's starting to feel very afraid. She can't stand hiding. Even as a child, hide-and-seek was too much for her. She went along with it, crawling under the table like all the other kids, but the next thing she knew her heart started pounding and her breath began to race. She always crawled out from her hiding place before they could find her, calling out with relief, here I am, here I am, see me?

"So we're gonna just stand here like two dimwits? For fuck's sake, will you say something?" Bohumila went off.

He took a look at her. "Did you ever stop to think I might be just as scared as you are? Maybe even more?"

The lights on the path were closing in. Turning from fireflies into red pinwheels, and now into lightsabers swaying to the imperial strides of their owners. Voices rang out in the mist. The whispers changed to conversation. Based on the number of flashlights and intermingled voices, they estimated the number of people at greater than five.

Bohumila and Bohumil stood behind the door. It was solid, made of wood. How solid, wondered Bohumila, just how solid is this door? The two of them stood in silence. Where else could they run to when they had run here?

Tap.

Tap-tap.

The thump of a log in the fireplace, the ticking of the clock.

Rat-a-tap-tap.

"Who's there?" warbled Bohumila in a high-pitched old woman's voice.

Bang. Something fell in the bedroom.

She screamed.

The cat ran in from the room next door, she was probably hiding in there from the rain, probably looking for something to eat, when was the last time they'd fed her? She strutted proudly past. "Slut!" she meowed, though Bohumila probably just imagined it.

"Hello, is anyone home?"

She didn't imagine that.

The footsteps stopped on the other side of the door. For a moment it was quiet, then they heard a deep breath and the raising of a fist, someone pounding on the door.

"Are you home? We can see the light."

They looked at each other. Bohumil reached for the handle, but she grabbed his hand, holding on to it in the most peculiar way.

You will not open the door, shaking her head side to side. "Please don't open the door," whispered Bohumila.

"So what'm I supposed to do? If they want, they can just pry it open."

"As long as you don't open it, we still have a chance."

"No, nothing is wrong, stop overreacting. We're just freaked out. What could they do to us anyway?" he asked unconvincingly. Overcoming fear by making light of the situation, an old trick of his, she knew it well.

"We came to help you look for the boy," said Sláva on the other side of the door.

Bohumila backed away from the door and shook her head again. Please, no, don't open it.

Bohumil nodded meaningfully, attempted a smile. The only thing separating them was a slab of old wood. It was safer to play their game, better to pretend they weren't afraid. He turned to Bohumila: "There, you see, they came to help."

And he opened the door.

Almost everyone was there. Pepa, Jarda, Milan, even Granny Maruška in a ridiculous purple raincoat. For God's sake, what did they drag her out here for in this terrible weather? The only one missing was Marcela.

Sláva began to speak, not even looking at Bohumila. Really, thought Bohumila, you won't even look at me?

They almost all had hoods on. The shine of the flashlights in the mist altered the proportions of their noses and mouths, contorting the look on their faces into a sneering grin. They looked like white-eyed monsters.

Bohumil's heart thundered loudly in his chest, pounding so hard it felt like it was making his raincoat shake. He was pinned to the wall with fear. This is not good, not good at all. Bohumila reached for his hand, seeing and feeling the same thing, but neither of them registered the contact of their skin.

"Like I said, we came to help," Sláva repeated. He was fully decked out in hunting gear, rifle over his shoulder. But who would pay any attention to that now, the important thing was they were here and they wanted to help. Maybe, just maybe, Bohumil had judged them unfairly. He took a deep breath. He wasn't about to let himself break down in tears like a little girl. Sláva did most of the talking, but Pepa kept stepping in to explain, bouncing with energy. His whole face was red, you could see it even in the mist.

"We'll form a line and sweep the woods," said Sláva.

"Great. Excellent," said Bohumil.

Yes, absolutely, said everyone, talking over each other. They would form a line and comb through every single bush in the woods, they were going to find the boy, because there was no way they wouldn't find him. No way.

Bohumil let go of Bohumila and offered his hand to Sláva.

"Thank you," he said, trembling.

He hugged Pepa lightly around the shoulders, nodded thanks to Milan, then to Jarda, who in turn gave Bohumila a solid hug, not entirely with her consent.

We definitely judged them unfairly, said Bohumil to himself. They just want to help. Good thing it's pouring,

I feel like I'm going to cry again. His chin began to tremble. It's pissing rain and I'm sobbing like a little boy. He spat. A streak of foamy saliva ran down his chin, hugging the rain like a long-lost brother.

Sláva watchfully took in the scene. You idiot, he thought. You slobbering fool.

"Thank you," whispered Bohumil in an almost girlish voice.

"No sweat." Pepa grinned. He was elated, bouncing like a baby goat.

"It'll probably all turn out fine," said Bohumil. "This way, with more of us, we stand a better chance."

"Don't fret, I'm sure he'll turn up," said Pepa almost cheerfully.

"Me, fret? He hasn't been home in three days. You think I'm fretting because I'm worried?" Bohumila blew up. Her husband's calming hand on her shoulder was nowhere to be found.

"Oh, no, I get it, I just think it'll turn out all right."

"Hm," said Bohumila. She nodded: "It better turn out all right. That's the only way it can turn out. We have to find him."

"We will," Pepa reassured her.

The cluster was getting impatient.

"So what are we waiting for, then? Are you ready?" Sláva gave a cursory glance to the couple's equipment. No metal objects, let alone a firearm, just one stupid flashlight, which he was leaving behind. That was good. Jarda had slipped their cellphones out of their pockets when they hugged. Just to be safe. The signal kept dropping out anyway.

Forget good, it was great!

There were stairs chopped into the dirt on the slope in front of the cottage. But after yesterday's rain, they had merged into a stream of mud, there was nowhere to get traction. They helped one another, grappling their way up together. Bohumila wanted to go last, but Jarda stood behind her. I want a little touch too, he almost whispered in her ear. Just a touch, he thought, smiling faintly.

They walked across the meadow, the weather fickle as May. Just a while ago it had been drizzling, but now the mist was rising, and in the distance, beyond the woods, there was even a bit of sunshine. Bohumila didn't see it, though. She was focused on the group in front of her. Fear mixed with revulsion. They were like some deranged amateur theater troupe. Everyone here just a dummy, playing their assigned role. She looked at Sláva, uniform jacket drooping off his shoulders, belt wound tight around his waist, she had seen the new holes when she unzipped his pants. What role are you playing here? Ringleader, seducer. Rapist. Nutjob!

She walked up to Bohumil, intending to tell him calmly, quietly, but emphatically, that they needed to make a run for it. They needed to make a run for it now. Because no way could this turn out well. The whole thing is fishy, Bohumil, for Christ's sake, she wanted to tell him, just look at them. Look around. This whole thing is fishy as a carp on Christmas Day, as Pepa would have said. Their helping like this all of a sudden didn't make any sense.

But then Sláva piped up.

"We'll form a line. You two go a little ways ahead of us, since you know which way you've gone before and which way you haven't. We've got lights and we'll just keep on calling. We'll comb the whole forest. We got this," he concluded, trying to sound convincing.

She hesitated. Standing still, she didn't want to go. But then she went. No use stopping before the woods, they had to go in.

"It'll be better if we split up," Sláva called out.

Bohumil stopped in his tracks. "What for? We're forming a line, aren't we? Didn't you say so yourself? We'll just fan out side by side."

"It'll be better this way, seriously, trust me," said Sláva. He tried to think of an argument and couldn't come up with one, so instead he just kept talking. "Jarda, you go with Bohumila. She doesn't have a light. The two of you walk over there, more to the right. Bohumila isn't familiar with the area. She might get lost and then we would have to search for her too." Excellent. Now the trick was not to start coughing, not to collapse in pain. It'll work, they can do it. True, it was raining a little again, that wasn't ideal. But it wouldn't be so bad in the woods, they wouldn't get more than a sprinkle in there. Which would make for a better atmosphere too.

He was starting to look forward to it. The early autumn sleet suddenly struck him as appropriate, just the way it should be. He shifted his rifle up on his shoulder, it was weighing down on him, like the rain was making it heavier too. Originally he'd thought to bring his pump-action rifle, but in the end he opted for the caliber with the heavier bullets, even if it did have a shorter range. Ideal for lone hunters. For a driven hunt he didn't need an over-under or a double-barrel shotgun, a 5.56 mm did him just fine. Wonderfully lightweight, only slightly more sensitive to wind and rain. It also did less reliable damage in a hit to the bone or an indirect hit, but for a young mouflon it was fine. He had yet to shoot anything bigger with it, but that was just a start. He liked that the high projectile speed produced shock in smaller game. That way they stopped moving before they died, and afterward it looked like a painting.

"Stop standin around flappin your jaws, soon it's gonna be dark. I don't know what your problem is, Bohu. You take that side with Jarda, like Sláva said. I'll come this way with you," said Pepa, nodding to Sláva, "and Bohumil will go that way."

Sláva kept his mouth shut. Maybe it was a good thing that Pepa was butting in. They were running low on time. It had to get started somehow. He could see the folks in the rear getting impatient, looking at their watches, half of them could already picture themselves in the pub. Now they were cold. They were wet. He had explicitly told them to wear raincoats. And did they? He looked around. A couple morons in back, shivering with cold, had come out in tracksuits anyway. His strength was running low. He felt old and tired.

He was old and tired.

"Fine then," said Bohumila, jarring him out of his thoughts. Why bother to fight anymore? She stood in the mist on the meadow together with half the village, about to step into the woods with them. She was afraid.

"I'll go this way then," she said, pointing in the direction of a large bilberry clump.

"Jeez, you act like I'm plannin to kidnap you," said Jarda, trying to be funny.

Sláva shook his head at him.

Bohumila nodded to Bohumil, but he had already turned his back, stepping into the woods. She glanced over at Sláva. Why in God's name would he not even look at her? Hunter, lover, oldster, you prick.

Jarda wrapped his arm around her elbow. "So you don't fall. The roots today are seriously slippery." He gave her a gentle pat on the back and smiled kindly.

Bohumila knew by now that not all wolves are exactly the same: Some are perfectly charming, not loud, brutal, or angry, but tame, pleasant, and gentle.

Once more she turned to look back, slowing her pace a bit. Once more she hesitated. She didn't want to go into the woods.

"I don't want to go into the woods." She stopped. All of a sudden she couldn't go on. She stood rooted in place.

Pepa took hold of her other arm. "Don't be silly," he said softly.

She couldn't tell if they were steering her or helping her not to fall.

Sláva is getting a bit winded, the figures in front of him disappearing from view. It ends so quickly, it's all over with so fast. Licking his lips, he tasted a Christmas-like bitterness. The tough fish for dinner, the hope of hard gifts under the tree, the sadness of nothing but soft ones—a sweater and socks. It ends so quickly, it's all over with so fast.

I'm starting to get sentimental, he thought. I'm old and sick and don't want to be alone, he kept repeating over and over again. The mantra that justified all his actions. No one wants to be alone, after all. Not even an old man. Not even one who's sick.

The sun, after a broiling summer, was dead tired, unable even to lift its rays, just occasionally sweeping its beams through the clouds. Sláva inserted his hand into one, ostensibly to warm himself. But actually he just wanted to grab summer's skirt. No, actually he just felt sorry for himself. Standing alone at the edge of the woods, he was free at any point to turn around and walk home. Instead he was stepping into the forest. Feverish.

Shaking. He thought of her. Refilling her glass with wine. The bottle spinning on the table. He smiled. She had slipped into his arms as easily as a foot into an oversize shoe. When she left, she gave him a kiss at the gate. Opening his lips with her tongue. Every woman wants to kiss when they drink.

After she left, he slept like a rock through the night. It was late morning, almost noon, when he woke to Chrastík's barking. He walked out into the yard in nothing but his briefs, with a cup of Turkish coffee, still steaming. He scratched contentedly at his hairy belly, stretched, belched. Looked at his watch. Either the rooster hadn't crowed or it hadn't woken him. He went out to the back garden, Chrastík squealing at his feet, otherwise it was quiet. And silence is a harbinger of death.

He found six of them. Throats bitten through. The five remaining hens pecked around the discarded bodies like they were nothing but dummies. A marten had eaten a couple of eggs, begun to devour one of the hens, and then killed the rest. The death of an animal without reason is not something hunters like. They want the joy of the hunt, the suspense of tracking, the euphoria of the kill, sticking a branch into the wound and having a taste. And beware of buckshot, it had cost him two molars already. As he shoveled the bodies into the wheelbarrow, the thunk of each stiff hen filled him with genuine sorrow.

He leaned against a tree for a while. His rifle hung from his shoulder like a gutted animal, it was unusually light and seemed to twitch every now and then, like it was in pain. He felt it up and down, no, it wasn't alive. The fever was playing tricks with his senses, it was just his own shoulders twitching in reaction to the rushes of pain. The intensity of it was turning him into a wild animal, a beast driven by the need to dispense pain, screams, and tears. He felt anger, not regret. He felt neither regret nor sympathy. He didn't see any reason why he should have mercy.

He picked himself up off the ground. He must have lost consciousness for a moment. His pants were wet, had he pissed himself? He hoped not.

She stopped and listened. "I can hardly hear them anymore."

"They're not that far away, they must be calling softly," Pepa reassured her.

"There's no such thing as calling softly," she said, shaking her head. "A few minutes ago I could still hear Bohumil and now I can't. I think we're getting too far away, we'd better go back a bit."

"They might be a little ahead of us."

"Just now you said they weren't that far away."

"Let's just go there," he said, pointing forward.

"Where there?" she said, her voice breaking. She hoped they wouldn't notice.

Jarda noticed. And he liked it. Her chin was quivering like a mill wheel in a mountain creek, he loved it.

"So where are they, if we can't hear them anymore?"

"I dunno, probably at the corral by now."

"What corral?"

"I know you're not dumb, but how do you not know there's a corral in the woods?"

"I haven't gone into the woods," she said.

"Why not?"

"I don't like them."

"Scared, huh?" Pepa laughed.

Jarda spat. Pepa grinned. She was pretty, as long as

she kept her trap shut. She gave him a headache like a bottle full of rum.

Her fear returned her thoughts to where they'd been the last three days. The boy.

"You don't have kids?" she asked out of the blue.

Pepa shook his head.

"No one here has kids actually," she said. "I mean, except for Marcela."

Jarda flashed a smile.

"Right." Pepa winked. "Except for Marcela."

Bohumila clenched her lips so hard it hurt. The fear she was choking down inside was squeezing through the crack between her front teeth. She was afraid she would throw up. She badly wanted not to show anything on the outside, but she was trembling like a leaf. How was this possible? She could have slapped herself she'd been so silly. Silly cow. It was just another fairy tale, that's great you've got someone to watch them, sure, to hell with you all and your fairy tales!

"There, you hear?" he asked again.

Bohumila paid no attention. Her eyes were clouded over, her lips moving as if she were whispering something.

Jarda snorted. Great, just what they needed, she was goin off the deep end. What were they gonna do with her out here in the forest? Hit her upside the head with a stick, wasn't much else you could do with a crazy bitch in the woods.

Bohumila nodded. She heard but didn't understand.

"I said, don't stop here, not yet," said Pepa, waving his hand to indicate she should keep on going, and for God's sake not keep stopping all the time.

Bohumila nodded.

They continued on their way. She was walking free between them now, but the pace they set was too fast. For every step they took, she needed two to keep up. She pattered along through the dead forest landscape, thinking this was really too cruel. The punishment doesn't fit the offense, Bohumila thought.

She kept calling out at the top of her lungs. She could feel the strain on her vocal cords along with the cold. The two men walked in silence.

The canopy overhead fluttered, the smaller trees shyly brushing the top of her head with their branches. Calming her. Deeper into the woods it was getting dark, even though it was only a little after noon.

"You should both be calling," she said.

They nodded but still said nothing.

Bohumila shouted the boy's name. Any minute now the boy would have to emerge. When someone is called so imploringly, they have to come. How long had they been walking now? A long time. She was cold. Her rubber boots must have a hole. She could feel water between her toes and her feet made a squishing sound with every step she took. She was shaking.

Jarda took her arm again, Pepa walking calmly beside them. Smoking. Not calling out. As soon as he finished one cigarette, he lit up the next. Why weren't they calling, dammit, she wanted to ask, but she obediently acquiesced to their mutual silence. It seemed safer. Bohumila turned visibly tame. She could no longer bring herself to urge them anymore, trudging along with her head bowed, watching her waders sink into the wet moss.

"I'm hungry," said Pepa. "Did you marinate it a long time? Just hope it won't be too tough."

"You bet, olive and honey, today's day three, it'll melt in your mouth, don't worry," said Jarda.

Pepa let out a loud belch. "That's from hunger."

"You're just a pig," said Jarda.

Pepa let out a loud laugh.

"Just hope it won't be too sweet."

"What do you mean?"

"You know, with the honey and all."

"Naw, it'll burn off."

They stopped by a few stunted trees at the edge of a small grassy clearing. She looked up.

"Do you guys see something?" She couldn't help the note of hope in her voice. She slipped loose of Jarda's grip and took a few steps. Then broke into a run. Her heart was pounding out of her chest, spitting bits of bitter muscle—anxiety can do that.

A stunted sapling jutted up amid the clearing. On one of its branches a piece of cloth fluttered. Not fluttered. Limply drooped, soaked through, the fabric dripping wet.

Bohumila tore it down, crumpling it in her hands, wheezing. Was it his, the boy's? It had to be. A piece of cloth doesn't sprout on a tree in the middle of the woods. Her hand trembled as she kneaded the fabric in her palm, she never wanted to let it go. What if they took him away from her again? What if they hid him from her again?

"Look, you see?" she said when they finally caught up. They had taken their time.

"It must be his, right?"

They followed her with their eyes like two exhausted wolves. Let her jump up and down, butt her horns against the saplings, at least it would get her blood churning, get her flesh warmed up.

"I can't be sure it's his. But I guess it must be, right?" she said, holding the cloth out to Jarda.

He gave the cloth an obligatory scan. "I would guess not."

"Some kinda trash," said Pepa.

"Some kind of sign," said Jarda.

He was hungry and thirsty and Bohumila in rubber boots and wrapped in a raincoat didn't look at all like the Bohumila wet with beer when she took off her apron behind the tap. He wanted her to look like that.

"What kind of sign?"

"A sign that we oughta stop here."

Pepa fished around in his backpack. The red bonnet looked out of place in the clearing, like an old tire in the woods.

"It's recording," nodded Pepa.

Bohumila glanced over at him, then at Jarda. She turned to look behind her, but there was nothing but trees.

"Is this some kind of joke?"

Jarda handed her the bonnet. "No joke at all," said Pepa.

"Are you serious?" said Bohumila.

Jarda watched, not saying a word.

"Look, just put it on."

"Have you totally lost your minds? Put it on yourselves," she said, flinging the cap to the ground and turning to walk away.

Jarda grabbed her arm from behind, gave it a hard squeeze, and yanked her back into position. It hurt.

So they were steering me, not holding me up, Bohumila thought.

They assured her it would be quick.

She wiped her nose with the side of her hand, leaving a smudge behind. She felt like she couldn't breathe, she had a rattle in her chest, at any moment she felt like she would sneeze a blood clot out her nose, and also out her ears, the pressure was too much to take, she was going to explode and crumble to pieces on the moss and pine needles. Without even realizing it, she burst into tears.

"Put it on." Jarda handed her the cap again. "And hold this in your hand. And stop crying."

A wicker bowl.

Pepa behind him spluttered with laughter.

"Hey, jackass, what's with that? She's supposed to have a basket."

"Fuck off," said Jarda. "I left my mushrooms in it. Now it's all moldy and stinks, at least this thing is clean."

"All right, but what is she gonna do with a bowl?" Pepa burst out laughing again. His crooked teeth shone in the afternoon gloom like a cluster of fireflies someone had squashed against the wall. "I can't wait to be here when Sláva sees this. It'll knock him flat on his ass. Guaranteed."

"When Sláva sees what? What am I supposed to do with this bowl?" said Bohumila, shaking it off. He who laughs won't get hit.

"Stop asking questions." Jarda gave her a shove in the back. "Don't worry, you're gonna have fun."

She heard the sound of a phone clicking open behind her. Jarda lowered the pitch of his voice, dropping by about half a tone. All of a sudden he was pronouncing everything distinctly.

"Which path will you take? The path of pins or the path of needles?"

Moss shinnies up the foot of a tree. Waterlogged leaves carpet the earth. The cloying scent of rotted baby bird carcasses tickles the hairs in her nose, making her want to sneeze. But she doesn't. She can't even swallow, and if breathing wasn't involuntary and she had had to control it, she wouldn't be breathing either. Two strange men stand in front of her. One is forcing a red bonnet and a breadbasket on her, the other heehaws in delight, recording her on his phone. The path of pins, or the path of needles. Say it. The path of pins. Or the path of needles.

What do I say? Bohumila wonders. I've exhausted all my paths and I don't even know how it happened. I have one last chance to choose: between pins and needles. How did Bohumil put it? It hurts either way. Both ways hurt. If she had been able to move the muscles in her face now paralyzed with fear, she would have had to smile. She had one last choice remaining: pins or needles. Talk about nonsense.

"Where is the boy?" She knew they had him.

The two men bent over the phone, playing the video

back. Pepa smiled, it wasn't great, but it wasn't bad either. She looked good in red.

"Huh?"

"Where is the boy?"

"Later. For now just answer the question."

"Where is the boy?" She shifted her weight back and forth from one foot to the other. Her head was throbbing. "What did you do to him?"

Pepa went on recording. The illumination from the phone was so soft she hadn't even narrowed her eyes. That is, until now, as she was struck by a ray of sun, breaking through the wet branches.

"This has got nothing to do with the boy."

"What do you mean? I don't understand, none of this makes any sense. Please, just give him back to me, I'll do whatever you want, we'll leave right now and never say a word about this to anyone," Bohumila pleads. "Just don't hurt him." Her breath is racing.

She has to give an answer, though. They insist.

She stands at the center of the clearing, calms her breath, looks directly into the phone:

"The path of pins."

The two of them stand over the phone, checking the sound. It's hard to understand at times, especially when it's raining. Bohumila's going out of her mind, starting to act irrationally. Unable to shake her curiosity, she wants to bend over the screen with them and see how she did, whether the words are audible, whether or not it looks all right. Have them ask the same questions again. Answer differently, see if anything changes. The path of needles, are you listening? I changed my mind. When she asks what they're recording, the two of them both smile.

"The same as every year."

Jarda gave a chuckling snort like the loud exhale of a cow. He glanced up at her again. She looked good in red.

"The same what as every year?"

He shoves her in the back. More like prods, like she's a toddler learning to walk but keeps falling backward.

"Why do you do it?"

"Do what?"

"This." She throws up her hands.

"And what is this?"

Bohumila waves her hands around, this, here, all this you're doing to me now.

"But we're not doing anything, there's nothing going on. We're just out here trying to help you find your boy, right?"

Jarda steps a little closer. If he had a handkerchief, he would wet it and wipe her mouth. But he doesn't, so he just looks. He can see now that her eyes aren't brown. Not entirely. There's a little green shining through at the edge of the iris.

"So tell me, what are we doing to you?" He smiles. "You begged for a job, you got one. I gave Bohouš rides for gas money plus a little bit extra on top. Pepa gave you a nice slab of meat. You got your sun shining, your flowers blooming. Sure, Bubble treats you like shit, but that's no big deal. So what've we done to you?"

I guess nothing, probably nothing really, Bohumila thought. Maybe I did it to myself.

He waited. Opening and closing his knife, with a little click each time the blade slid out of view. In the end he left the knife open. He stood a few steps away from her. Bohumila didn't stir. Not a single visible movement. He didn't like it. He had to fight back the urge to provoke her. For so many weeks he'd been watching her, imagining her squeal and bray. But she didn't do any of that. She just stood quietly, almost deranged, in the middle of the clearing, holding the wicker bowl. Come on, get on with it, thought Jarda. Have at it, give us one of those hysterical fits that womenfolk are famous for, you've got it in you, I know you do. Her chin quivered like aspic, the tears making little hops from her cheeks down to her neck, where a woman's skin after forty is crumpled like the paper they wrap salami in. Greasy, knobby, with those little globby balls that wrinkle creams leave behind. When you lick it, it tastes bitter. He looked at her again. This was too good for him to let slip through his fingers. He wiped his nose, smelling the metal of the knife blade on his fingers.

Jarda cleared his throat. The sun was so darn low. But no use getting emotional about the end of summer, he thought. It would all soon be behind us, like a cow's warm fart, hanging in the air for a moment, then gone by the time you exhale. Some people think the world is a nice place to live. Every day the light comes again after the night. The irises in early summer grow as tall as palm trees. Just when you start to salivate at the thought of a plate of steaming-hot eggs with golden-brown onions and fresh mushrooms, you stumble across a boletus. Then you rapturously sprinkle the whole thing with caraway and slap it into one big heap, so you can't tell the stalk from the cap. Some people think all you need is light, flowers, a meal from the forest with bread so fresh a minute ago the crust was still browning in the oven, and the world is a nice place to live. Jarda smiled. Some people are just idiots. He figured that out a long time ago. It isn't about balance but domination. Strength. For any man who has strength and isn't too chickenshit to use it once in a while, for him the day is truly bright, the food fresh, the women's breasts firm and the nipples hard, reigning over an areola so tiny it's like a freckle, that's the way he liked it.

City bitch, he said to himself, looking at Bohumila. You think just because you smell nice, have long hair, and wear clean clothes every day you're somethin special? The anger and agitation were building up inside him.

"Do you understand what I said?" he asked her again, taking another step. Bohumila stood frozen like she was made of glass. Jarda had the feeling he could see right through her to the trees and uprooted stumps. It was just an optical illusion caused by the low angle of the sun, dazzling him as it reflected off the water-spotted pine needles. And that goddamned perfume, it was messing with his head, it felt like tiny bristles of rope tickling the inside of his nose. He'd always been the helpful type, ready to crack his knuckles and get down to work. He was aware of his physical strength, lifting kegs onto his shoulders with nothing but a slight exhale, less air than an owl needs to hoot.

Bohumila glanced at him. Dammit, she was nice.

"I don't think I do."

He didn't want to take another step, he didn't want to be that close to her yet, but already he sensed that everything was going to be a bit different today. That depth of yours, in those eyes of yours, that quiet depth of yours, you've been through plenty already, I bet. I'm gonna have a nice little ramble around in there.

He knows Pepa is watching him closely. Running his thumb over his unshaven chin, pacing back and forth, clearly he doesn't like what he sees. He may be dumb, but he isn't so dumb he doesn't realize what's about to go down. He still hadn't said anything, lips clamped so tight not even a fly could get through. He kept leaning forward, more and more, but hadn't said a word so far, not a single peep, that chickenshit farmer, he needs to get rid of him now.

"So you didn't understand?"

"I don't think I want to."

You filthy cow, are you trying to get smart with me? He looks at her, thinking how much the two of them have in common, the two of us here in the woods, because that's all that matters now. Bohumila stares at him. Maybe I'm transparent too, Jarda thinks, smiling faintly at the idea. Or maybe it's inside of me, the stones, slippery stones, sometimes things ground inside of him in a strange way. But you and me is all that's real, just you and me, so he said it out loud: "Just you and me."

"So like are you going to take off your clothes?" She had no idea where she found the courage. A courage springing from total resignation. She felt like a dirty rag that they had dragged back and forth over a floor covered in puke and cigarette butts. Still, she couldn't help wanting to laugh. Here I was complaining about my life, ha-ha, and now look at me. Standing here in the woods with some half-wit pervert. And that guy next to him? He's going to film it. Bohumila was undergoing a personality change. She could feel the flippancy, the urge to entertain, caused by being recorded. In this moment when she should have been paralyzed with fear and succumbed, collapsing, sobbing and begging on the ground, she was seized with an unexpected feeling of relief. Her neck freed up. The presence of the two men no longer frightened her. An entirely new Bohumila stood there. If you look at it realistically, Bohumila thought, all your steps have been leading slowly and surely to this clearing. Your whole life, at least as long as the boy has existed, you've wished deep down in your soul that he would be eaten up by a wolf and at last you could be free. Sure it's stupid, but admit it's a relief, you can do that now. Breathe a sigh of relief that the boy is gone. He can't exist anymore, he doesn't. All the strength you feel right now, that in fact you don't even know or acknowledge, comes from that sigh and only that sigh, which ultimately outweighs the pain. You feel free like never before, and while that silly little man standing across from you goes boo boo boo waiting for you to fall apart, you feel so free and liberated in that clearing in the woods that you could fly. That's what this stupid village was here for. Bohumila trembled. For me to free myself, for me to be able to redefine myself, to scrape up that trampled-down me, which yes, through my own decisions, Bohumila realized, through my decisions alone, had hidden away like a frightened fish deep under the rocks.

She turned to Pepa. He stood quietly, holding the phone loosely in his hand. He looked back and forth between Jarda and her.

"Is there anything else you need to record?"

"Not really."

"So what are we waiting for now?"

"Well," said Pepa, clearing his throat, "we don't actually have to wait. We can go find the others. I can film the rest of it there."

Bohumila turned to Jarda.

"So shall we go?" she asked.

The two of them just stared at her.

"You go first," Jarda finally said, turning to Pepa.

He walked toward Bohumila until he was standing right in front of her. He reeked of booze and smokes, she could see how poorly shaven he was, a thin strip of sparse whiskers still on his chin. You beardless buffoon, what a little path of mouse turds you have laid out on your chin!

"Jarda, don't be stupid," whispered Pepa.

"Stay the fuck out of it," said Jarda, his voice rising a notch.

Pepa stepped up to him from behind and soothingly, the way you would with a little boy who doesn't understand the consequences of his actions, laid a hand on his shoulder. "Don't be stupid, you really don't want to do this. It's got nothing to do with anything and you know it. Let's all go back to the corral, or even just us two, okay? Go find Sláva, okay?"

Jarda turned to look at him, his gaze vacant, like someone who'd been woken from a dream.

"Huh?" he said.

"Jarda," Pepa repeated.

"What is it?"

"I want you to leave her alone. Forget about it."

"So what's your plan?"

"Me? What's my plan? We all have a plan together, don't we? Like every year, Jarda. It'll be nice."

"Get lost."

"You're not listening to me."

"Pepa!"

"This isn't what anyone wanted, Jarda. Not like this. Come on, snap out of it. Listen to me."

"You want *me* to listen to *you*?"

"I'm not giving you orders, I'm just saying leave her alone and let's go find Sláva, then we can all have a drink and laugh about it," said Pepa, as if repeating Sláva's name and the reminder of alcohol might lend his words some weight.

"I don't know what you're babbling about, get your ass out of here. And don't look back."

"Jarda," said Pepa. "Listen to me."

Jarda grabbed Pepa by the jacket and yanked him toward him. "Do you hear what I'm telling you? Bitch, get lost."

She didn't make a run for it when they first started to fight. For a few seconds, it couldn't have been any longer, she didn't react at all. The only sound interrupting the perfect afternoon silence was a smattering of dull blows, huffing and puffing. She was still in a triumphant mood. Viewed through her eyes, the fight transformed into a Chaplinesque shoving match, with a poetically graceful flow to their movements, bordering on tender. Until one man was laid out on the ground and the other man looked over at her, then the atmosphere changed abruptly. Bohumila got scared.

She dashed off into the woods with no clear plan. Only now did she come to her senses. Only now did she see what was really going on around her.

She tried to run fast, but the soggy forest floor's uneven surface knocked her off her rhythm. The darkened space transformed into a maze of roots and branches. Her hands kept catching on the bark of the trees, a fine trickle of blood ran from the base of her right thumb. Never had joy seemed further away. The woodland silence idled on every side of her, filled with utter hostility.

She heard rain, the creaking of rubber boots, her own racing breath.

The main thing was to move quietly!

She stampeded through the woods, though, like a startled zebra, making so much noise even a jay with a fat worm hanging out of its beak decided to fly in the other direction. It would feed its young later, once there was peace and quiet. Bohumila noticed none of this. Her body was moving independently of her mind. But still she made such a racket! The woman rolled through the woods like a steamroller down a stone path, kicking up a ruckus.

She sobbed as she ran. Stuffed her fist in her mouth. The main thing was to be quiet. She bit down on her knuckles. I'm not going to look back, I need to keep running forward, she repeated to herself. She looked back. She didn't see a thing.

And the next thing she knows she's down on the ground. Howling in pain. The jay takes to its heels, flying off to a neighboring forest.

Her foot is caught in a root like a steel trap. When she

lifts it to run, it wrenches her whole body painfully to the ground. The sound of her own cry startles her. Quiet! She wasn't sure what was broken. Absolutely everything hurt, her eyes, even her hair. For a while she couldn't move. She stretched her arm out in front of her. Shaking, but it isn't the arm. Her arm isn't broken. Gingerly she lifted her wedged foot out of the rubber boot. The foot. It's her right foot, the ankle is sprained. She cradled it in her left hand, the ankle was red and swollen into the shape of a baroque vase. The pain exploded into the rest of her body. She sat there resignedly on a clump of pine needles and waited for them to come get her. The other boot remained wedged beneath the root. It would stand there at attention until it slumped under the weight of rain and leaves, serving a grass snake as shelter.

Silence. Nothing but the sound of the rain. The soil, dried out over the course of the summer, thirstily drinks it up. The puddles are filled with pine needles and dirt. The intoxicating aroma of mushrooms filters through the mist. She was alone in the deep forest. Like the boy, she thought. Was he out here somewhere? Had he finally gotten over his fear of entering the woods? They had forbidden the boy from going too far. Stay on the edge, on the surface, don't go in too deep. Deep in the woods it's dark, there's mud, it's cold and reeks of the rotting bodies of past lives.

Bohumila's teeth chatter. She attempts to get to her feet and again bellows in pain. Collapses at the foot of the tree. Gropes around till she finds a stick, jams it in between her teeth and bites down hard. Works her way up the tree trunk, hand over hand, till she's standing. A hunched stance, bent in pain. Spits out the stick into which she uttered her curses and tears. Takes a few short, sharp breaths. Almost all she has left in her is exhales. She braces herself for the first step. Steps forward, whimpering, but keeps going. Hops on her left foot, trying not to put weight on the right. Something cracks from behind a bush, but she is focused on walking. Every step costs her enormous effort. Eight, now nine. She senses a movement beside her. She wanted so badly to be brave when it came, but now she just bursts into tears. She weeps, blurting out a fierce no, no, no in pain at every step, as if that might drive him away.

Wolfie! Oh, wolfie!

She peered around. Wolfie! Oh, wolfie! She needed to see the beast. She was terrified but wanted to see him. It made no sense. She was running away from him but turning to look back. She wants to see him. She's been practicing courage. The courage not to shrink away when he pounces. The courage not to shit her pants. Clinging to branches for support, she continued on through the woods. Finally she came to a stop. She reached into her pocket for her phone. Of course it wasn't there.

Reality is revealed only in extreme experience, will this be my experience? wondered Bohumila. She needed to fix her mind on some general question rather than the situation so clearly threatening her. She is inundated with a nonstop deluge of sounds, the whirling of the wind, the cracking of branches, the soft tramping of hedgehogs, the cries of a bird, and then, right here in the tree she stopped beneath, a woodpecker. *Knock knock knock.*

She will not open the door.

He caught up with her easily, but as he tackles her to the ground, she can feel the exertion in his arms and legs.

First the fight, then the chase, he must be exhausted too. Bohumila's arms have seized up in a strange cramp, he pushes down on her head, part of a root indenting itself into her face like a knife into hardened butter. She doesn't struggle or thrash about, just strains back against him. She feels his fingers sink into her hair, she's unable to focus on anything, now he's whispering into her ear, she doesn't understand a word, but she can hardly ask him to repeat it. She just tenses up again, flexing all her muscles so he'd have to tear them apart if he wanted to get inside her. Her face hardens into a waxen mask, no longer even blinking, the veins in her eyes quietly burst. She doesn't register anything, focusing all her strength on the tension in her body, trusting it now as her only possible means of salvation. Wedged against her left cheek is a piece of root or branch. She is paralyzed with pain and it hasn't even begun yet. It doesn't make sense. What was crystal clear a few minutes ago, that intoxicating moment of freedom and sigh of relief, even that doesn't make sense anymore. It's all collapsing in on itself, she feels totally empty. The solid structure of the outside world is starting to blur, everything reduced to what she perceives through her senses. It's all happening too fast, she needs him to slow down, everything around her to slow down, she needs to be able to take a breath in peace and quiet, to calm down and start thinking logically again. She opens her mouth to ask him to stop, but all that comes out is an unintelligible rasp. When he knocked her down, she cracked a front tooth, she hadn't even noticed. But the rasping isn't from that. It's some freaking act of revenge by nature for this violence, she can sense it rising up against her, rousing itself for whatever it has in store for her. Bohumila knows that the whirling, and the rasping, the only sound she is capable of, are the sounds of the slippery roots excitedly coiled around her, the groans of the ancient tree trunks, coursing with thick, hot sap. And this is me, she thinks to herself, a wreck of personal physical pain. To hell with it all.

Jarda again whispers something to her, Bohumila can't understand, like he's speaking in a foreign tongue. And suddenly he stands up. It isn't happening, he won't do it. She hears him fumbling around behind her, walking away but not leaving. She attempts to turn her head a notch, but a branch digs into her ribs. She can sense him behind her but can't really see, his back is turned to her. From this angle he seems enormous, his gigantic legs arching above her like an ancient bridge.

He was just adjusting his phone on the stump. This is too good, this is too good for it to remain only carved into his memory. Bohumila squeezes her thighs together, finally she can feel her individual limbs again, that brief respite at least helped her think a little bit, she can think of only one thing, squeezing her thighs together. Her hands are firmly wedged in place, or tied, or broken, she can't tell. She isn't able to move them at all, it's almost like they aren't there, she can't feel any of the limbs protruding from her upper body. Which is why she is so fervently fixated on her thighs.

But now he's back.

"I didn't want it to be this way," says Jarda.

At last she understands. She tries to answer, but all that comes out when she opens her mouth is a trickle of blood that runs into the moss.

"I didn't want it to be this way," he says again. "But if this is the only way, then it'll have to do."

"Please don't," whispers Bohumila. She isn't sure if she actually said it, or whether she only meant to. She feels herself shiver. For a moment Jarda doesn't move, just lies motionless on top of her, his heavy body pushing her deeper into the branches. Bohumila feels the physical pain distinctly now, mouth twitching, she can swallow only with difficulty.

Jarda pulls her pants down along with her underwear. She doesn't get it, he says to himself. Why in God's name doesn't anyone understand him? Or take him seriously! Now he's going to be sad during it, on top of everything else!

The phone camera takes in a view of moss, wet leaves, and red pine scales. The ground is covered in a thick layer of rust-colored needles and cones. Two dried-out pine needles, fallen from the tree overhead more than two weeks ago, bite into the crunchy bright green pads of moss. The needles are dark brown, with barely perceptible white scales. A tiny branch a short way away, broken in half, is ebony black, coughed up by Lucifer himself. Reigning over the right-hand corner of the picture is the slimy cap of a bolete mushroom, the underside will need to be removed before it's eaten. The microphone registers a muffled cry or cracking. It's hard to tell the difference. A pine needle drops off the top of the slippery jack, the slime puts a brake on it, but gravity tugs it earthward. It hangs only by a thin, slippery thread. The ant who aggressively stepped into the shot headfirst has lost its opportunity. The phone shifts, taking in a naked behind, the top of a head. And then nothing but sky. The blue beauty of it. A small cloud peaceably drifts out of frame. Another acoustic disturbance, hard to identify. The low-battery warning chimes, a bird flaps its wings exactly twice, then exits the shot, the last image to register before the frame goes black. Then nothing but silence and darkness.

She lay still for a long time, head in the ground, breathing into the moss. Has she been lying there a few minutes, an hour, all day? She has no idea. Carefully, she picks herself up. Leg twitching, whole body gripped with chills. She needs to focus, but there's a rat jumping up and down on a trampoline in her brain, that's how it feels, that's what's going on in her head. She lifts her hands and presses her palms to her temples. Focus, Bohuna, you need to focus, now everything is at stake. If it wasn't before, it really is now. But she can sense how little she understands what's happening around her. Back on her feet now, her crotch is on fire. She pulls up her pants, where is the belt. Focusing on simple tasks, her brain can't handle more right now. She has no idea what to do next, but little by little an odd feeling of closure is growing within her, the culmination of all the nonsense she's seen the past few weeks. She knows she must look pathetic, but honestly, Bohu, she says to herself, is there any other way this whole thing could have ended? She wants to nod furiously yes, yes, this abomination against her will is the moment she needs to start over again. No trauma, fuck your trauma, you pricks, you pricks, a new beginning, she thinks, trying to convince herself. There's no boy, there's not even a Bohumila, there's nothing left of her at all, but deep within her a desire is being born, a need, almost, to create a new, radically new, Bohumila. She doesn't have a clue whether the feeling will last. Whether she'll be able to absorb what happened to her this afternoon. But this is how it feels now. Everything is gone, irretrievably gone, don't nitpick it, Bohu, and the main thing is don't beat yourself up. There was only one way this could go and that was how it went. She painfully gets to her feet and makes an attempt at walking. But then stops in her tracks, looks around. Where, which way, do I go? She has a distinct sense this isn't some silly existential question, these aren't the trembling arms that Bohumil raised in front of him. She stands in the middle of the woods, surrounded by them on every side. All of a sudden there's a terrible stillness around her, and Bohumila doesn't know which way to go. She doesn't have the faintest idea whether to make her way out of the woods, or the other way around, make her way deeper into the woods, find Bohumil, take him by the hand, and tell him she's someone else now.

A shot rings out, she lifts her head. The birds are chirping again, flying over the treetops. And Bohumila can hear them. It suddenly dawns on her the woods have been roaring relentlessly this whole time, she just couldn't hear for a while. A sharp rain began to fall. She lifted her head and opened her mouth. Like she's seen people do in the movies. Then, slowly, hissing in pain, she set out toward where most of the sound was coming from.

Wolf Game III

A shepherdess, a dog, a flock of sheep, and a wolf. The shepherdess circles the flock with her dog, twirling a switch in her hand and singing:

> Our mistress always used to say
> I'd better herd well every day
> But I'm not herding anymore
> That's it for me, I'm out the door
> She eats her fill of porridge sweet
> While whey is all that's left for me

> She drinks her milk out of a glass
> I get a shoe, that's if I ask
> For her a carriage clean and smart
> For me a filthy jouncing cart.

The shepherdess calls into the woods: "Wolfie! Oh, wolfie!"—The wolf comes running: "I'm the wolf. What do you want?"

   Shepherdess: "If you're the wolf, then catch the prettiest lamb."

   Wolf: "I don't want a lamb: I want a lovely little girl!"

The shepherdess runs away, the wolf chasing behind her, and when he catches her, they take each other by the hand and, turning in a circle, sing:

> Our mistress always used to say
> I'd better herd well every day
> But now I don't herd anymore
> I'm with the wolf, I'm out the door.

There was rusty barbed wire growing on the fence around the corral. It was the only human encroachment this far into the woods—the wire, the corral, and inside the corral, hidden behind a bush, a small shack with a metal roof.

The woods surrounding them. In the woods the people.

This isn't Bohumil's first time at the corral. He stumbled across it that first afternoon they were running around the forest looking for the boy. He walked past it, calling out, but everything was quiet. He didn't notice the little shack, it wasn't visible from the fence. To see it, you had to know it was there. Naturally he wanted to take a look inside the corral, and he was about to climb the fence, but then he noticed the barbed wire and wet boards, called out a few more times, and headed back out of the woods. He figured it was probably a forest nursery, a corral is for animal young, not a boy.

Today is his second time at the corral. By now he knows it's going to be important. He regrets that he didn't climb the fence, didn't look in there too. He's at the corral because they're all at the corral. Sláva keeps glancing behind him, waiting, watching. Bohumil stands next to him. The ones who had raincoats have taken them off. The men are dressed in white collared shirts and dark pants. Sláva adjusts his uniform. He's got a little green cap with a feather stuck on his head. Apparently playing at hunter, thought Bohumil.

"Why are we standing here?" he asked Sláva.

"This is where we're going to film the part with the hunter," said Milan.

"I figured." Bohumil nodded. Nobody laughed.

"Do you mind stepping away from the corral?" Sláva said.

"Are you serious?"

Everyone nodded.

"Can't you film it some other time?"

"Like when?"

"We're searching for the boy now."

"Oh, right, sure. Actually no, it's gotta be today," said Milan. A murmur of laughter issued from the ranks.

"Fine then. But after that we need to search. It's going to get dark soon. And where is Bohu, by the way?"

"They'll catch up soon. Step off to the side a bit, all the way down, to the end, we need Sláva in there."

Sláva cuts in front of him and leans against the fence. One of the boards moves a bit, it's actually a big wooden gate. Bohumil feels a draft. This whole thing is ridiculous!

He eyes them up and down. Their black-and-white elegance makes him sick to his stomach. What is this anyway? he thinks. Another village specialty, weird-ass folklore. Sláva's hunting uniform glistens in the rain. Must be some kind of village game. Some ancient custom. Harvest thing.

Oh shit, is this Harvest?

No one even looked at him. They just harangued him to move out of the shot, farther away from Sláva.

Sláva rattles the gate, it's stuck. He doesn't want to open it too soon, they aren't here yet. He looks at his watch. They should've been here by now, dammit, they should've been here ages ago. Sweat drips from his forehead, mixing with the rain. He leans on the gate to conserve his strength. It feels like there's a big sharp rock pressing into him, right in the small of his back. He's still bent forward, but just a little, he hoped just a little, he hoped nobody noticed.

Everybody noticed, that's why they were so patiently and calmly standing out in the rain. He isn't well and he's definitely not gonna make it, said Jarda, but there's no need to say so. They can all see for themselves, it's almost eaten him alive! They're recording an old, dying man. He leans against the gate, breathing heavily. Reaches wearily for his rifle, prepares it for their arrival, wiping the head with the sleeve of his shirt.

The pine needles bustle with activity. The animals pay the humans no mind, so long as they're not an immediate threat. And they aren't, for the moment. An ant scurries by under the needles, bearing a load of food to regurgitate for the queen, hidden deeply away in the maze of the ants' nest. With the anthill still heated from summer, the queen is warm—and well-fed, her shiny black abdomen visibly swollen, storing food for the winter. In the shadowy warmth she lays her eggs, her store of sperm from spring mating will last her her entire life. The males die soon after mating, while the queen lies in a tunnel awaiting her food supply. At the sound of the gunshot none of them start. The queen isn't alarmed at all, although she clearly hears it. Only a cuckoo takes flight with a cry. What in God's name is going on today?

Sláva knelt down facing Bohumil, he wanted to see into his eyes.

"Does it make you feel good that it's all about you now?"

Bohumil tries to shake his head no but can't control his body. The shot went off right next to his ear, it feels like he's dying. He feels around his body, but nothing seems to hurt anywhere. He glances down at his hands: no blood.

"So, does it make you feel good? Taking away an old man's rifle? I hope you don't think by doing that you're going to change anything. And if you think she's going to come swooping in here to lick your wounds, you're mistaken. There'll be none of that," said Sláva.

He turned to look toward the woods. "Nothing's going to lick anything for you." He poked Bohumil in the shoulder. "Can't even lift yourself up, huh? Happened to me once too. Can't even lift your hand, can you?"

He turns slightly away, to the cell phones raised behind him. Leans back in to Bohumil, lowering his voice: "At the tree and in bed. You hear me? She didn't even close her eyes once. Not even while we were doing it. Mouth and eyes wide open. It was nice."

Bohumil sits propped against the fence, holding his shoulder as he watches Sláva. Lips trembling. Shaking. Talk about loud! His ears are still ringing. He isn't sure he understood Sláva correctly. Definitely not. Probably not, he probably just misunderstood. No one stoops down to see how he is, no one cares about him. He guesses he isn't wounded. A few of the phones have been put away, but the rest are still shining.

He sits in the damp grass, observing them. And then

it clicks. Dammit, Bohumil realizes, I must be acting in this thing. I'm acting in it right now, he thinks, and lightly closes his eyes. Something dark enfolds him in its embrace.

Why, good afternoon, young man. The sun has yet to set, I know, I know, but the moment it comes creeping over you and things go dark before your eyes, I'll be right here. I'm just going to spread myself out and have a bit of a stretch here, my whole back is sore. My but we've had some fun together! On the farm, in the cottage. Here in the woods. So much anxiety I caused you, look at the bags beneath your eyes. The skin all gray and black. Young man! Is that still you? You've gone all thin on me, look at that saggy neck, wrinkled as a worm. I would pet you if I could. But we both know I'm not here for snuggles, don't we? Remember the first time we met? You were afraid and tried to run away. But now you understand me, though, you're in no hurry now. Go ahead and close those peepers, why don't you, you're staring a hole right through me. Let's you and me just sit a spell, it won't be long. I've already taken away all you have. What to do with you now? You're like a bloated tick that lets go on its own, a withered rosebud that falls off the bush when someone plucks another rose. You've landed face down in the dirt and scarred your face on the pebbles. We both know you're no dreamboat. All right, well, I'll be going now. You know what they say: Even the night can't take away what doesn't exist. That perpetual regret of yours no longer appeals to me. It isn't sweet enough to attract my interest, or small enough to trample into the moss like a cigarette butt. Regret-nonregret. What comes next will be ordinary and no one's about to record it.

Bohumil looks around, thinking, whatever you do, don't snivel. There's nothing worse than a bleating middle-aged man, you really won't get her back that way. I must have misunderstood him, he reassures himself, I'm feeling dizzy and that terrible knot in my stomach is really just from hunger. All of a sudden he's distinctly aware of his hunger. His stomach is growling. Not growling, screaming. Dammit, I bet everyone here can hear it. They see me, they're watching me, they must be able to hear. Stop recording! I'm seriously starving! Don't you care that I'm lying here hungry? Could someone please give me something to eat? he almost wants to beg. I can't stand it, I just can't stand it, my stomach hurts so bad. At least a piece of bread. Or a bilberry. Can someone hand me one stupid bilberry at least, Bohumil silently pleads. He tries to articulate but can't. Even his mouth is buzzing from the gunshot. But no one is paying attention to him. What are you looking over there for, what are you looking at, dammit? Who are you waiting for? Look here, at me. You did this to me, all this. I'm not saying it was good before, but I've never been so fucked in my life. It's not my fault, none of it is. You did this to me.

If this is the end, though, you can't let me go hungry. You hear? If I don't eat, I'll die. Look at me, thinks Bohumil, I'm actually dying of hunger. I haven't had a thing in my mouth for three days now.

Shitheads. He wanted to tell them all this. He can no longer control the anger building up inside him. But given the state he's in, he can't afford to give it rein. Unable to move, unable to speak, the shot from the rifle blasting over and over again in his head. Throw me a gnawed bone at least, some old meat or sour buttermilk. Whatever flees the farm, flies the coop, whatever you bop on the head behind the hutches, put a bullet in inside the barn, I'll even eat it raw, not even chew, just stuff it in my mouth, cram it whole down my throat, the sooner it lands in my stomach the better. I'll eat till my shirt is drenched in blood, cold and sweetly metallic, and my lips are stuck together. But I don't want that, since then I won't be able to eat. I'll eat myself to death to keep from dying of hunger here. You toss me in the corral like a half-eaten rat some rabid fox spat out of its mouth when it started to gag. I'd like to send you all straight to hell, tear down this stupid corral, grab the boy and Bohumila and scream in your face: You can all go to hell. But I'm so hungry I don't make a peep. And it's all your fault, you shitheads, shithead pieces of shit, that the last thing I think of, I can't not think of it, that the last thing I'll see before I close my eyes, the last thing I'll ever think of in my life is tomato sauce. It wouldn't be so bad if it were the one my mom used to make. But the one that I've got stuck in my head is the sauce from down at the pub, with the rubbery white dumplings that're definitely warmed in a microwave, since the edges are lukewarm and stiff and the middle is hot and runny like butter. And the beef on the plate has a white veil of fat running around the edge, it swelled up in my mouth like an aching foot every single time. The tomato sauce at U Parlamentu. I didn't even like going there, thinks Bohumil, shaking his head. They put cinnamon in theirs. The stuff was inedible.

The preparations at the corral are drawing to a close. Sláva brushes the raindrops from his uniform. Maruška, long flowered scarf wrapped around her shoulders, sits in the fold-up chair they brought for her. Sláva takes it all in, thinking, Maybe, maybe today, could be. It's good. This version is definitely going to work. He looks around at everyone. They're cold but laughing. That silly incident wouldn't change a thing. Just a small glitch in the story. Sláva regards them with a feeling of satisfaction, thinking about the extracts, the long passages of the fairy tales he knows by heart. Then he gazes up into the treetops. Just a few moments ago he had to shield his eyes from the sun, and now it's gloomy and raining again.

He assumes Bohumila is still crying as she walks up to the corral, but it's only rain on her lashes. She blinks hard a few times and wipes her face. Her swollen nose throbs with pain, she feels weak and shaky. The clearing before her is partially hidden in mist, but even so Bohumila is conscious of the fact that it's a space with nowhere to hide. She has no idea, no inkling, whether she's doing the right thing, but she has a sneaking feeling it doesn't depend on her decision, her actions at all, and either way it will all end up exactly the same. She reflects on that for a moment, then tells herself the new Bohumila doesn't run away. As she steps into the clearing, she suddenly realizes that the woods provided refuge. Here, out in the open, Bohumila feels like a girl baring her breasts for the first time in front of a boy. She sees light and hears voices, nervously swallows. They are recording here too. In that case I'd better get out of here, I should turn and get the hell out, Bohu, dammit, get yourself together and run. But instead she keeps walking, stepping out of the half light under the trees, hobbling over to Bohumil, propped against the corral fence like a sack of potatoes. The villagers stand lined up, absorbed in preparations. Noticing her, they fall silent and turn their eyes to Sláva. He stands by a tree, watching her in astonishment. My God, he thinks, look at her. Disgusting, slovenly, covered in dirt. No bonnet, no basket. He knew he should have brought her to the corral himself, it was always all up to him, old, sick, and alone. Sláva looks her up and down: grimy, filthy, covered in blood. He knows it can't go on like this, it wasn't supposed to happen this way, this version is definitely not going to work. Guess not, not today, apparently not. At first he feels pity, then anger, then the anger rises in him like a tide. Where are those bastards? Where are those bunglers that were supposed to bring her here? He peers around but no one else is coming out of the woods. Pepa is off somewhere boozing by now and Jarda probably went back to the pub, Sláva knows he's got meat on the grill and doesn't much trust the cousin he left to keep an eye on it, but dammit he had an assignment here, and as Sláva is thinking all this, the urge for violence is growing and getting stronger within him, and now it grips him in its heavy claws, refusing to let go.

Bohumila meanwhile made her way over to Bohumil. Ignoring everyone around her, as if she were all by herself. What does she see? A corral. Just an ordinary wooden corral enclosed with rusty wire, she thinks. A few young spruce trees at the center. Hey, corral, she wants to shout. You've got my husband propped up against you, I see. He's either wounded or dead or both, as if one ruled out the other. Looks like you roughed him up a bit, his shoulders are going to be all full of splinters. Apparently just shredding his skin wasn't enough. Even in just that short time, the barbed wire had grown into his flesh, as if he'd been there for months. She leans in for a closer look. So frail, bone thin. Weak men dream of hard muscles, battle cries, and grand gestures. And they always imagine themselves a little bit taller than they actually are. Bohumila knew.

Still she snuggles up to him. What else can she do? Bohumil's legs are folded beneath him like two loyal dogs. Not a hint of movement, though. His skin is pale and wet. She lays her head on his chest, she is so tired. Then she lifts her mouth to his ear and whispers everything that he was afraid to ask about all those months. Including the feeling of relief, she has to tell him that, because it's suffocating her. The boy is gone and guess what, Bohu, I'm relieved. His frozen ears are cold on her lips. His unshaven whiskers dig painfully into the wounds on her palms, it stings, but she doesn't stop caressing him. She doesn't notice the villagers now drawing near again, doesn't notice it stopped raining again and the revoltingly hot sun is coming back through the clouds, steam rising from the moss. What have the two of us come to, my dear? she wonders, though she's really asking herself.

She takes Bohumil by the hand and begins whispering to him again. She has a sinking feeling that this is the end, tears stream down her face, she's practically choking on them, but she has to say it, she has to say it out loud, because all this horror has paved the way for a new, free beginning, she's still convinced of that, she's still convincing herself of that, though she suspects this new beginning will be short, extremely short, and it will look a lot like the end. Bohumila whispers into his ear that the boy is gone. She sobs and shakes but keeps repeating, the boy is gone, gone, and despite all the grief and tremendous exhaustion and then the grief again, which keeps returning over and over in great big gigantic waves, I feel, dammit, Bohu, I feel relief. I feel freedom. And she leans back against the fence but doesn't let go of his hand.

Bohumila sits in the same position as Bohumil, legs loosely stretched out in front of her. She touches a finger to her split upper lip while her tongue snoops around her cracked central incisor, lolloping back and forth over the sharp corner, rubbing up against it like a mangy dog. Her socks are wet and dirty, with large holes on the bottoms. She has a sporadic twitch in her ankle, her palms sting, and she can feel the tension in her face.

Her immediate surroundings appear to her misshapen, the colors unstable, distorted. She is seized with a feeling of sheer absolute desperation, total exhaustion. Buffeted by waves of emotion, she can no longer tell what she is feeling now. Most likely sadness. Yes, if she had to be honest, she would have to admit she was sad. I'm sad about the way my life looks, sad I can't undo either my actions or theirs, sad for them that they are who they are, for what they've done to me, for what they dragged me into, I'm sad they hid my son from me. Other than that, really nothing but a growing feeling of calm, because she could sense the animal sitting there among them. Scratching itself behind the ear, now turning its head and licking its genitals.

Sláva quietly observes the pair. Attempting to catch a few words or syllables at least of whatever it is Bohumila is whispering to Bohumil. He takes a few steps closer, "What are you telling him, dammit," he asks, but she can't hear a thing. The roebucks outside the clearing are coughing up a storm. Sláva approaches and tries to lift her up. A sharp pain in her ankle propels her gastric juices up into her throat and an arc of vomit spews from Bohumila's mouth. Her body hasn't yet attained the same state of calm as her mind, adrenaline rushes through her veins, emptying her stomach in case she needs to flee. I'm terrified of him, she thinks. I terrify him, she says to herself, thinking nothing of it. Sláva rubs the vomit into the pine needles with his boot, so it won't be visible in the video. Standing right beside her now, he takes a closer look. Face slashed by branches, hair smeared with dirt. She can barely walk. You look nice, thinks Sláva.

Bohumila knows the others are talking about her. She didn't hear the words *boy, alive, Bohumila, alive, Bohumil, alive*. She heard *dirty, filthy*. It's not gonna work. Part of her just wants to laugh at the whole thing, restored to health, ha. She catches sight of someone with a big red scarf in their hand, decorated with a subtle pattern. She doesn't understand one bit, she can't grasp a thing. She's still not sure if it's a game or whether the whole thing is even real. The only thing she was deeply convinced of was they had no desire to harm her. Or all right, harm, yes, but not more than they had up to now. Or just a tad more than I've been harmed so far, she thinks, finding some relief in that.

"Sorry," she says, gesturing with her head to the vomit. It's hard for her to talk. She tries to swallow but can't. She looks back at Sláva and says again, "Please, I'm sorry." But this time she means something entirely different.

"What did you say?" Sláva asks.

"Please, I'm begging you."

"For what?"

Bohumila hesitates. "The boy." She doesn't know where she found the strength. Apparently she still believes something good can happen. Something good can still happen in my life, Bohumila tells herself.

"Now that's what I call stubbornness," says Sláva. "This isn't about him. It never was, you don't get it at all!" He gives her a light shove, Bohumila plops into the grass like a sack of hay.

Sláva still hasn't let go of the rifle, holding it in his right hand, it's starting to get heavy. He rests the rifle partway on the ground as the people behind him slowly move closer, Maruška walking alongside them, they're leading her toward the corral gate. Twigs crunch under their feet. Sláva still doesn't want, can't bear, to accept that soon she'll no longer be a part of it. He shivers, the cold is getting to him. As Bohumila looks up at him standing over her, he seems gigantic, his head towering over even the treetops.

Then Sláva makes up his mind. Today the whole performance is going to be different. He bends down to Bohumila. "It didn't have to end this way. Look at yourself. Filthy as a pig. Running around the woods in your socks. And your mouth! All sloppy and swollen. Who would want to look at that?" Sláva's main mistake, as far as he's concerned, was trusting anyone other than himself. Especially that wimp. He straightens himself back up, standing directly over her now. Milan has his hand on the corral gate, waiting for the signal. The villagers' phones are recording, no one is smiling.

Bohumila lifts her hand to Sláva like a toddler begging for sweets. He wants her, God, he wants so bad to wrap his arms around her again, feel that closeness again for a while. But he knows a line has been crossed and now the girl must meet the wolf. Still, even though he is feeling weak again, and as thirsty as if he had a belly full of rocks, the thought keeps running through his mind, just take her one more time. Take her while she's here, look how she keeps reaching out for you. He checks behind him, everyone is waiting. It's embarrassing how long it's taking, he stands over her, a thousand words and sentences running through his head, yet he can't bring himself to say any of it. He tries his best to make up his mind, to do something, anything. Dammit, Sláva, do something, you're going to lose everything the way it's going now. You won't have a shred of dignity left, nothing to hang on to, and you'll lose her too, in a single moment of awkward silence, everything nice will slip away. He tries to speak, but his voice refuses to leave his mouth. Then suddenly he realizes it isn't his voice. No, Sláva, it isn't at all about what you say. A sneering grin spreads across his face. It's what I do. How I strike. All the hesitation and rocking at the knees can lead to only one thing now, a nice solid blow. He cracks her in the temple with his rifle butt so hard that Bohumila doesn't even squeal.

The dangerous world of the village had intruded on the dangerous world of the forest. The borders had fallen, human merging with animal, it may have seemed at first sight. The sun shone faintly. Up in the treetop, a bird chirped, melodically, peaceably. The people with cell phones surrounded them, standing too close now. Bohumil feels like he isn't able to breathe properly, like they're taking away the breath meant for his lungs. There's a lot Bohumil can blame the villagers for, but in this case he is wrong. There is plenty of air in the woods, his lungs are squeezing him in an oncoming panic attack.

Peering out through the lattice of his eyelashes, he sees the corral gate opening. Slowly, hesitantly, a heavy, fat paw with pampered fur belonging to a gray wolf emerges from the gate. Sláva tenderly pats the wolf on its shoulder, he doesn't even have to stoop, the animal's so large. The wolf seems not even to notice the touch, stopping for a different reason. He sniffs the air in Bohumil's direction, his steel blue eyes lighting up. Bohumil swallows and gropes around for something to use as a weapon.

His head is pounding so hard he can barely perceive anything, and to the extent the reality before him penetrates his senses, it is distorted, misshapen, as has happened so many times before here in Podlesí. What kind of place is this anyway? he wonders faintly. But increasingly he has begun to entertain the question of what in fact he is doing here, why him of all people. He tells himself, this is happening to me. Then he turns and looks next to him, where Bohumila is lying. This is happening to us, because you too, Bohu, are the catalyst of all this. You too, Bohu, you too. At the tree and in bed, that was you, that's you, Bohu, the catalyst, Bohumil tells himself.

Bohumila doesn't move, opening her eyes partway and swallowing with effort. For a moment or two, he's certain she sees exactly the same thing he does, but then he softly asks, "Do you see this," pointing in front of him, "do you see this right here?" Bohumila turns to him with a baffled look. She feels like nothing out of the ordinary is going on, a family of mice squeaking hysterically in her ears. What she sees is as uneventful as taking one step, then the next. She is too dazed to attach any other meaning to the situation in front of her. It's like walking, totally normal, she repeats to herself. She notices Sláva before she sees the wolf. Just like last time, he's so big, so big. With every step the animal takes, Sláva takes another. The animal is badly trained, instead of walking close to heel, getting out in front. Just like his jaw. Why, Chrastík, you have an overbite! Bohumila wanted to laugh, but even despite her misunderstanding of the situation, she can sense it's not one to laugh at. There's nothing to laugh at here, and there never has been, Bohu. So stop simpering like a cow, like a cow, Bohumila.

Sláva is saying something into the one small handheld camera, something from the fairy tales in his pamphlets. Bohumil's and Bohumila's cognitive abilities are now at a level well below those of an eel, which knows to slip beneath a rock in the face of danger. The two of them don't even move. Just then someone violently picks her up, Bohumila gasps. They have to hold her up to keep her from collapsing back into the grass. If this is what I think it is, Bohumila says to herself, peering in front of her, the wolf is going to swallow me whole, he won't even bother to chew. I've got to get out of his belly unwounded. Just like the grandmother did. She glances toward Maruška, huddled in her flowered scarf. The wolf is now almost upon her, if she were to reach out her hand, she would feel his damp, wet snout. Bohumila reaches out her hand, attempting to prevent the girl from meeting the wolf.

The corral gate lets out a groan. How many times has it been opened and closed today? One can get overexerted doing that sort of work. The rusty hinges squeal like a piglet. The bilberry bushes in the corral are incredibly soft, the bodies sink down into them like eiderdowns. There is a smell of mushrooms and wet leaves, germinated trees, periwinkle and dog's mercury. Come spring, the bees will gorge on their sweet pollen while the queen ant makes her way to the anthill's surface to warm her frost-stiffened wings. She will narrow her eyes against the sun, stretching deliciously.

The car comes to a stop at the lights, standing stolidly at the crossing gate like a rain-soaked toadstool, shining redly into the distance. The three people inside sit silently. They aren't even watching for the train. When they pulled up, the gate was already down, rocking gently in the wind—the train will come soon enough. There it is. Huffing and puffing like an old person climbing the stairs. A mottled locomotive. The red paint is flaking, in spots peeled off completely. The blue of the steel, cold and hard, stands out more than the paint. The driver of the car didn't notice the conductor, using the time to study the map spread out on his lap. Long after the train had passed, the gate still hadn't lifted. But none of them are restless, they aren't in a rush. When it finally opens, the driver just lightly taps the wheel and glances back in the direction the train came from. Sort of a habit of his.

It started to rain again. The driver turned on the wipers. Crossing the tracks had lifted everyone's mood a bit, but not enough that anyone felt the need to comment.

"Ten," says the girl in the back. She's nine years old, her name is Věra, but at her request everyone addresses her as Vera, hard *e*. Vera likes trains. She sits buckled into the back seat in a T-shirt with long sleeves, her Brooklyn Team hoodie lumped on the seat beside her. They've had the heat on the whole way, and the stuffy air is starting to give her a headache. The car needs airing out.

"Eleven," says the woman in the front passenger seat, opening the window. "Counting the locomotive."

The first day of fall breathes into the car. They all attribute the kiss it plants in their hair to a breeze.

The girl shares her mother's features. A strong, almost masculine jaw and eyes a faded blue, as if worn out by someone else. The woman is of medium build, her slack, unexercised belly bulging under her T-shirt when seated, rolls of fat hanging over either side of her belt. When she gets to her feet, the situation is markedly improved. But the woman knows gravity helps only in so many areas. The rest she buttressed securely. The underwire in her bra is digging into her, she scratches gently at the underside of her breast.

They pass a series of harvested fields, the road is unmaintained and dotted with potholes, their gaping mouths filled with rainwater. Vera is too big to want to jump in puddles anymore. Her father curses mildly behind the wheel, unable to see how deep the potholes are, what if a wheel gets stuck. Plus he isn't exactly sure where they are. He must have taken a wrong turn, his phone signal keeps dropping, and he's not very good at finding his way around a map.

Suddenly a fat cat appears on the roadway, fixing the oncoming vehicle with a hostile glare. There's no need to yank the wheel, it isn't that dramatic, but the driver has to swerve, tipping the three of them left in sync. The cat remains standing in place, in the rearview mirror the driver sees it sit back down and lick itself. A sign flashes by: U Fandy. The driver eases his foot off the gas, he's getting hungry, he could use a bite to eat. Plus then they can ask where they are and how to get out of there. He hasn't seen any road signs for a while now, is this a village? His fellow passengers agree, clamoring for a pee and a Kofola.

The driver starts to back up, but they're too far past the pub now, it's dangerous to back up in traffic. Although... it's been ages since he saw another car. When was the last time any of you saw a car, he asks, but the woman and the daughter are already deep in discussion about the neon sign in the window of the convenience store across from the pub. The letter C in CHIPS isn't lit up, leading Vera to wonder out loud what other body parts they might sell. The driver isn't amused, but the mother laughs at the childish joke.

They stop and get out of the car. U Fandy appears to be fairly nondescript as far as pubs go, no posters or placards touting the daily menu, homecooked meals, tasty beer. The obligatory signs tempting children with Mrož, Míša, Twister, and Calippo frozen desserts are similarly nowhere in sight. The place is a bit dead.

As the three of them set out toward the pub, the bell jingles on the convenience store's glass door. Stepping out of the shop with the boy, Marcela freezes for a second but doesn't let on that anything's wrong. Without so much as a glance their way, she and the boy walk off toward the apartment buildings. The man calls out to ask if the pub is serving lunch. She doesn't even turn. He repeats his question, his voice now slightly closer. The pain in the ass must have taken a few steps toward her. Marcela finally stops and looks back at him indignantly. Leave me alone, she says to herself. Just leave me alone, all of you.

The boy stands, eyeing Vera with intrigue. She's nice-looking, long hair. Just a thin strand poking out from the hood of the sweatshirt she threw on in haste. She smiles at him. That girl, that nice-looking girl, standing there just a few steps away. He smiles back. Runs the palm of his left hand over his face, it feels like some threads broke in the corners of his mouth. Did he have his mouth sewn shut? He hadn't smiled in ages. How long had it been since the last time he smiled?

The girl's parents reach the pub, the father pulls the door open, that skinny lady was right, they cook here, looks like they even have a grill. As the aroma of grilled meat licks at the inside of his lips, so much saliva pours into his mouth he has to swallow twice. The woman, behind his back, hesitates. Yes, the lights are on, it's warm inside, it smells delicious, still something keeps her from stepping inside. The foreign environment so far from Prague makes her uncomfortable.

She turns back to Vera, walking behind them, hop, she leaps a puddle. She may be too big to jump in puddles anymore, but she isn't too big to take delight in leaping, skipping around, and balancing on the edges of them. Her mom is calling, one more skip and a hop. She turns to look back outside the pub, the boy is still standing there. She raises her hand slightly and waves. The boy stands quietly, watching her.

A savory warmth fills the pub, accompanied by the crackle of logs and roasted piglet skin. And the sound of cracking fingers, the woods were very cold, everyone is soaking wet, their cheeks are still tingling. After all, they haven't been sitting here that long, the last two stragglers only got back from the woods a couple of minutes ago. They waited for Sláva but in vain. Still in the woods, they think to themselves, exchanging knowing smirks. Everyone is hungry and thirsty, there will be time enough to talk later, once their grumbling bellies are sated, their parched lips refreshed, and their brains pleasantly dulled with the intake of alcohol. It isn't going to take long, they're drinking beers and shots.

Jarda carves the meat into thin slices. They did a truly excellent job of marinating it, the juices are dripping all over the grill. He always prepared a batch of homemade horseradish for grilling. Even grated a little bit of apple into it, the sweetness complementing the taste of the meat. The main thing was not to overdo it, he couldn't stand all that cooking and roasting with pineapple and peaches.

Three strangers step into the pub. The man, evidently the father of the family, hollers out a greeting, doing his best to act jovial, since everyone from the city knows that's the way they do things out here in the countryside. No one answers, but he also kind of expected that, they're all one big family here, it's only natural for him to be treated as an intruder. A role he humbly accepts. Before they sit down, he stops by the grill to comment admiringly on the preparation and appearance of the meat. It's a bit unsettling being met with silence for a second time, but he doesn't let it show.

The three of them settle in at the table in the corner. Jarda studies them at length, looks over at Milan, then back at them. With a single look, a single nod, they say everything that's needed. Transcribed into words, it might look like: *This could work.* Maybe an exclamation point, not a period, hard to say, they don't look at each other again. Game restart, Jarda smiles. New game, Milan smokes happily. A better way to transcribe it, actually, might be: *This'll work!* Sláva can't hack it anymore, but I can handle it. This'll work, says Jarda to himself.

Very slowly, as if he were weighing every step, he walks over to the new arrivals' table.

"What'll it be?"

"Nonalcoholic beer, please," says the man.

"Sorry."

"Hm." The man gives it some thought. "Tonic? I'm driving," he explains. He knows the polite thing is to order beer in a pub like this, but he really is the driver. He runs his gaze over the car keys, placed on the table next to his wallet.

Jarda shakes his head.

"Matonka?" He hopefully raises his eyebrows.

"Water."

"All right then, water."

"For you?"

The woman hesitates, ill at ease, fidgeting in her seat. They should have kept driving. She doesn't like it here. It feels like everyone's watching her, and on top of that her underwire is digging in again, but she's reluctant to scratch. Not here.

"Water?"

"Water it is."

"Kofola for me." Vera smiles.

Jarda sets three bottles of water down on the table.

"But I wanted . . . ," the girl starts to say, then quickly closes her mouth. Her mother's look speaks volumes. Though it was more the sharp kick under the table, noticed by everyone comfortably settled in around the pig.

They exchanged smiles: This'll definitely work, the girl is perfect. The alcohol is now coursing pleasantly through their veins, their stomachs ruminating the piglet meat, the place is so warm their raincoats, hung by the entrance, are practically steaming.

"We'll take three orders of piglet," the man says, smiling. All of a sudden the locals are smiling too. The father feels much better now that the atmosphere has relaxed.

Jarda deftly slices the meat onto small paper plates, the bread is out on the table. Taking two plates in his right hand, him being a right-hander it doesn't even shake, he uses his left hand to pick up the third. He senses that he slightly overloaded it, the one on that side weighs about the same as the two in his right. But so what, at least let em eat their fill first.

He sets the plate with the biggest piece of meat in front of the child. A girl, a sprightly little thing, pretty, though she jerks her head like a two-year-old brat. She stares in shock at the mountain of flesh.

The man ignores this act of ill will, glossing over it. There's still a chance they can enjoy their meal, he still might be able to crack the locals' tough exterior. The villagers are smiling so hard their eyes are like slits.

"It's really nice around here," he says, nodding his head, but the smile in his eyes is directed at the meat. "Beautiful countryside," he adds, but after that he really has to take a bite, before the saliva comes shooting out of his mouth.

Fuck your countryside, Jarda nods back.

The girl peers curiously around the room, she isn't that hungry, her grandma gave her a big chocolate bar for the road. She only realized she had eaten it all when she looked down and noticed her chocolate-smudged fingers rooting around in the empty wrapper. She takes a drink of water, lifts her gaze to the wild boar on the wall, then the TV. A woman stands on-screen in a red bonnet, holding a wicker breadbasket, filthy and crying and looking right at her. She's saying something, but the sound on the TV is off. Oo, a fairy tale. Vera settles in comfortably against the back of her chair.

The night watchman was already out in the cowshed waiting for him.

"There's something weird going on," he said, shaking his head and sucking in snot. "I don't get it."

"How long has it been?" Pepa asked.

"Almost three hours. We tried to pull it out, but nothing doing."

He didn't like hearing that. He hadn't even gone to change clothes. If the fetus was in breech position, it was important to act fast, before the calf choked to death on its umbilical cord. He'd been keeping an eye on the heifer for several days, something was off. The moment he approached her, it was clear why they couldn't pull out the calf. There were two hind legs sticking out of the cow, but each one was different. They were obviously from different calves. He immediately shed his jacket and shirt, the vaseline was next to the tub. He smeared his arm in it up to the shoulder, lay down behind the cow and tried to feel his way in. No go. The birth canal was as dry as a stick of kindling. The bright red cervix and the legs trapped inside of it were all that he could see. The cow lay on the straw staring blankly, paying no attention to the goings-on around her. She was getting apathetic. He knelt down behind her and attempted to push the legs back into the uterus. Part of one of the calves was stuck in the birth canal. He had to stuff them back in. He dug in his heels and pushed, sweaty and agitated, fumbling around inside the cow, he could sense the death. He attempted to push back against the cow's contractions, but it was no use. Neither calf budged. Not an inch. He kept feeling around inside, trying to figure out where the head was and where the feet were so he could untangle them from each other and pull them out. But the two calves were wound together in a perfect knot, all he felt was a mass of limbs, nothing for him to take hold of, nothing he could pull.

The cow breathed in and out, eyes half-closed. Her long black lashes hung limp over her eyes, every limb and hair on her had given up on life. She no longer had strength to struggle. She just leaned her head against the metal fence, panting heavily.

Pepa lay down behind the cow, fumbled around awhile, then ordered the watchman: "Hook!"

The watchman handed him a long birth hook. Pepa smeared it with vaseline and carefully slid it into the cow. For a moment or two nothing happened, but then, finally, he pulled out a pair of hind legs. This time the right ones.

"Ropes!" He slid the ropes onto the legs, he and the watchman each grabbed one, and they pulled, again nothing. They tugged again, roaring so loudly that even the exhausted cow lifted its head and rattled its chain. Finally one was out. It slid down next to the cow like an empty shoe bag. He didn't even look at it. Just went on fumbling, grunting, sweat running into his eyes, stinging.

"Head rope!" he shouted after another minute or two. A head snare with an adjustable loop. He carefully threaded it in. Fished around inside the cow a minute or two, then pulled out the end and clenched it firmly in his hand. But he needed another hand.

"Hold that," he told the watchman. The watchman wanted no part of it. He gawked at the first calf, covered in slime and blood, it smelled like it was rotten. He did as he was told and took hold of the end of the rope, allowing Pepa to have another go inside the cow, turn the second calf's forelegs into the right position, slip the legs into the rope, and tug and tug again.

Two young bulls lay on the straw, heads coated in green mucus. They must have been dead a few hours now, possibly since evening. He gave the cow an IV of calcium and phosphorus, antibiotics and vitamins. More to have a clean conscience than anything else. It was a hell of an infection, no way it could survive a uterine torsion like that.

He went out for a smoke in front of the cowshed, splashed off his hands in the tub a bit first, they were covered in feces and birth juices. He balanced the lit cigarette in the corner of his mouth, exhaling puffs of smoke. Mornings it was so cold now, the breath steamed from his mouth. He was in no hurry to get the gun. People don't like the taste of meat with fear. There were more and more of them, butchering cattle right in the meadow instead of at a slaughterhouse. The animals weren't stressed that way and the meat was supposedly tastier. He didn't approve. He felt like the animals should know the end is near, should release all that nasty stuff into their blood and flesh. Because that's what death is like, Pepa thought. Filled with dread, anxiety, sticky sweat, urine, or a trickle of runny shit that you just can't get to stop. He shot the cows, whenever possible, from the side, so they weren't looking him in the eye. Their big cow eyes filled up with water just before they died. Not tears but some sort of bluish liquid that gets released under stress. He didn't care about that. It's just that right before the gunshot, when that whole big eye was flooded with it, he saw himself reflected. A tired, gray-haired man, holding a bolt gun to a temple.

He tossed the butt into the puddle in front of him. A cat meowed sleepily on the windowsill at his back. He went and fetched the keys for the gun closet. Loaded the cartridge into the gun. Stepped over the two dead bulls, knelt down to the cow. She didn't register his presence, lying apathetically on her flank, breathing softly in and out. He leaned away slightly and fired. Nothing changed, the cow made no noise. A small bubble at her rosy nostrils burst.

They lay, all three, side by side. He sat down on the ground with them, resting a hand on the cow. She was still burning with fever. He would sit here till the morning shift came and help load them onto the truck. The boys could use it as fodder, around here there was always an appetite for meat. No one would ask any questions.

He looked up. The dawn light shone through the small dirty window into the cowshed.

He was already craving a beer now, in the hour between the dog and the wolf.

Credits

vii   From the Tristan Tzara poem "Le condamné," in *L'Arbre des voyageurs* (Éditions de la Montagne, 1930). English translation excerpted from "The Condemned," in *Chanson Dada: Tristan Tzara Selected Poems*, trans. Lee Harwood (Black Widow Press, 2005).

58–59   From Angela Carter, "The Werewolf," in *The Bloody Chamber and Other Stories* (Victor Gollancz, 1979).

89   Carter, "The Werewolf."

102–104   From Charles Perrault, "Le petit chaperon rouge," in *Histoires ou contes du temps passé, avec des moralités: Contes de ma mère l'Oye* (Éditions Barbin, 1697), trans. Maria Tatar, in *The Classic Fairy Tales*, ed. Maria Tatar (W. W. Norton & Company, 1999).

151–52   Perrault, "Le petit chaperon rouge," in *Histoires ou contes du temps passé, avec des moralités: Contes* de ma mère l'Oye (Éditions Barbin, 1697), trans. Robert Darnton, in *The Great Cat Massacre: And Other Episodes in French Cultural History* (Basic Books, 1984).

171–72   Karel Jaromír Erben, "Hra na vlka I," in *Prostonárodní české písně a říkadla* [Czech Folk Songs and Nursery Rhymes] (Evropský literární klub, 1864). This translation © 2025 Alex Zucker.

185–86   Carter, "The Company of Wolves," in *The Bloody Chamber and Other Stories*.

202   Erben, "Hra na vlka II," in *Prostonárodní české písně a říkadla*. This translation © 2025 Alex Zucker.

242–43   Erben, "Hra na vlka III," in *Prostonárodní české písně a říkadla*. This translation © 2025 Alex Zucker.

Zuzana Říhová studied Czech language and literature and comparative literature at Charles University in Prague. She has been working at the Institute of Czech Literature of the Czech Academy of Sciences since 2007 and was the head of Czech studies at the University of Oxford from 2014 to 2017. Říhová, who has a lifelong interest in Czech avant-garde literature, has published a collection of poetry, *Pustím si tě do domu* (I'll Let You in My House), and a novella, *Evička* (Little Eve), which was named a 2018 Book of the Year by a Czech literary magazine.

Alex Zucker's translations include novels by Magdaléna Platzová, Jáchym Topol, Bianca Bellová, Petra Hůlová, and Tomáš Zmeškal. He has also translated plays, subtitles, young adult and children's books, poems, philosophy, art history, and an opera. He worked with the Authors Guild on its surveys of working conditions for U.S. translators and the Guild's model contract for literary translation, and is a member of the Translators Organizing Committee of the National Writers Union.